SHADOWS
ON THE GRASS

Misha M. Herwin has written short stories, plays and novels, for both children and adults. She has two grown-up children and lives in Staffordshire with her ever-patient husband. When not writing she likes to bake. Muffins are a speciality.

http//mishaherwin.wordpress.com

Also by Misha M. Herwin
House of Shadows
Picking Up the Pieces

Writing as Misha Herwin
Dragonfire
Juggler of Shapes
Master of Trades

SHADOWS
ON THE GRASS

Misha M. Herwin

PENKHULL PRESS

Published by Penkhull Press
Staffordshire

ACKNOWLEDGEMENTS

There are many people I would like to thank for their help with the making of this book.

My excellent editors, Jan Edwards and Peter Coleborn. I could not have done this without you.

Jeanne Wood for her insightful reading of the manuscript; Pauline Woodhouse and Lynn Smith, trusty beat-readers, for their comments; and the members of Renegade Writers and Newcastle Writers for their feedback.

My sister Anuk Naumann for allowing me to use her image for my cover.

Mike Herwin for being there.

And finally, my family for giving me their stories. Although some of the incidents in this book are based on what I have been told, all the characters spring from my imagination.

DEDICATION

For Jeanne

CHAPTER ONE

The bus lumbered to a halt. Mimi furled her umbrella and marched to the head of the queue. Once inside, she annexed the first available seat.

The journey was short, but almost unbearable. Streaks of dirty water slid down the windows and the air was humid from the steam of damp overcoats and the fumes of the engine. The conductress jutted her ticket machine into the faces of the seated passengers. Mimi pressed her knees together to avoid touching the large woman's greasy overcoat that spilled out from the other half of the seat.

In a civilised country there would be a first-class compartment for first class passengers; in a civilised country she could afford to travel by taxi.

The bus slowed. The conductress called out their destination but Mimi was already on her feet. The floor heaved and swung, and holding tightly to the poles at the end of the seats she worked her way to the back of the vehicle. Before she could step down from the bus, however, the conductress's hand was on her elbow and Mimi was being helped onto the pavement.

After the lurch and sway of the bus the ground was unyielding and Mimi had to fight to retain her balance. Her head spun, the edges of buildings blurred, then came sharply into focus as the faintness passed, leaving her with a feeling of unease. It was not possible that she was about to be ill. Here in front of strangers. In an attempt to shake off her fear she scolded herself for her weakness and walked briskly away from the bus stop. The wind caught her, sliding beneath her coat and tugging fiercely at her umbrella.

Jesus kohany, what a climate. November and in this benighted country there was not a flake of snow, no crisp white carpet to cover the dirt and grime of the city, no blue sky to lift the spirits, only an overwhelming greyness that seeped into the very bones.

In Warsaw, back in the days between the wars, winter cold had been invigorating, heralding brightly lit shops, elegantly dressed women, and the promise of Christmas presents under the tree.

Treading carefully, she made her way along Queen's Road until she noticed a display of evening dresses in the window of one of Bristol's most upper-class stores. With a sharp click of the tongue she cast a critical glance over the mannequins, her fingers moving as if feeling the material, assessing its quality, the cut of the cloth. Pursing her lips, she shook her head. In spite of its superficial glamour anyone could see the fabric was coarse stuff, the garments shoddily put together.

It was time to go. It would not do to be late for her birthday tea, but as she moved something inside her shifted. She was aware of a pounding in her head, then her vision clouded and she was back in another time and place.

* * *

Stefanowskis is the finest department store in Warsaw. It is the place where everyone who is anyone comes to buy, and those who cannot afford it come to wonder at what is on display. Today, in the centre of the main hall, a single white dress stands on a marble dais.

"The latest model from Paris," Aunt Celeste says. "You like it, non?" Mimi gazes, enraptured at the waterfall of silk that cascades from the simple beaded bodice. Her aunt slips her arm around Mimi's waist. "You must try it for me, Cherie. Wear it, show it, and all Warsaw will come flocking."

* * *

Like the closing of an album the snapshot disappeared and Mimi was back in a wet November afternoon in a foreign city. Her Aunt Celeste had had an unerring eye for quality and an instinctive feeling for style. There was nothing like it now, not even in the best shops in Bristol. Lips drawn into a thin line and with a faint throbbing in her temple, Mimi turned away from the window.

The doors of Forte's Ice Cream Parlour were etched with elegant plumes of white glass; their brass work, however, was dulled by the prints of damp gloves. Stepping in to the fug of drying coats, shoes and fresh coffee, Mimi wrinkled her nose. Judging by a faint underlying smell of bleach, it was possible that the glass-topped tables had been given a more thorough clean.

There were few customers: a mother watching her children eating ice cream, the boy in his school blazer, the girl in a grey tunic, her hair plaited tightly against her head; a young couple, the man in a suit, the woman with a bright red beret covering blonde hair. In the centre of the long narrow room, a group of women, carrier bags at their feet, poured tea and ate cakes. They talked quickly, quietly, the flow of their conversation interrupted from time to time by a raucous burst of laughter, which betrayed their lack of breeding.

Behind the marble-topped serving counter, a waitress in a black dress gazed absently through rain-smudged windows, but Mimi was becoming accustomed to this lack of respect. When she was young, shop staff knew their place. They bowed and curtseyed to all customers, but especially to her, to the owner's niece. Nowadays, one could drop dead before anyone took any notice. With a snort of disapproval, she tapped the handle of her umbrella against the counter.

"Yes?" The waitress forced her eyes away from the brightly lit windows of the department store on other side of the street.

"A table for two," Mimi rounded the syllables on her tongue.

"Yes, Madam. Upstairs or downstairs?" Mimi hesitated. If she chose the first floor she would deprive Marianna of her grand entrance, but downstairs, where it was easy to catch the eye of the waitress, there would be better service.

"Which do you want?"

I may not be English but I am not yet senile, Mimi thought. "Downstairs," she said firmly. The waitress gave a half-nod and Mimi followed as she wove her way through the tables.

"Not too close to the door. We do not want to be in a draft," she stipulated. The waitress made an abrupt turn to the left and indicating a small table pulled out one of the gold wickerwork chairs.

"Shall I take your coat, Madam?" Mimi shook her head. The woollen dress she had on was serviceable but the coat with its astrakhan collar was quality. On the other hand, it would not do to get too hot because in an hour or so she would have to go back into the interminable rain. A compromise was necessary. She undid the buttons letting the coat fall open, then pulled off her gloves and placed them neatly in her handbag. After a few minutes she looked at her watch. It was ten past three. Mimi took an impatient breath. As usual, Marianna was late, even today when she was hosting Mimi's birthday treat.

It was another five minutes before the door opened and in a swirl of wind and rain her cousin Marianna swept in. Extravagant feathers curled over the brim of her hat and a long velvet cloak swung from her shoulders. A fox fur nestled at her neck and swathes of the same fur encircled her wrists.

"My usual table." Marianna smiled at the waitress. The girl hurried forward but Marianna was already swooping down on Mimi. "Oh there you are, quite hidden in the corner." She spoke in Polish, her voice low and husky, yet carried to every corner of the room. The women with the shopping bags paused in their conversation, heads turned, then quickly averted. The boy with the ice cream held his spoon midway to his mouth.

Conscious of being the centre of everyone's attention Mimi stood up and let herself be kissed.

"What's she talking?" the boy asked.

"She's foreign," his mother said dismissively.

Marianna laughed deep in her throat. "How they would love to know what we are saying, but unless we fracture our tongues on their terrible English we will have to keep them guessing." Sliding her cloak from her shoulders, she sat down. Her perfume was rich in musk and spice. Amber glowed like drops of sunlight around her neck and in the heavy rings on her fingers as she leaned forward and touched Mimi lightly on the arm. "Happy birthday, my darling," she murmured.

"And to you too."

"Not for a week or two. You have the advantage of me there. You will always be the eldest, my dear Mimi. Who would have thought we would both live so long? Still we don't look too bad for our age."

"You've worn well," Mimi said a little grudgingly. There was no denying it, Marianna with her green eyes, high cheekbones and aquiline nose was still a handsome woman. The red hair, too, was somewhat of an advantage because, unlike Mimi's own dark locks, it showed no sign of grey.

I was the prettier one. Mimi patted the back of her hair, tucked carefully under the sleek pair of feathers that made up her hat. *I was smaller, neater, and my skin was whiter.* "Cold cream," Mimi said. "Even in Russia I took care of my complexion."

"Of course you did." There was an edge to her cousin's voice that Mimi did not like but before she could say anything the waitress was at their table with a tray of coffee and cream cakes.

"I ordered your favourites." Marianna nodded at the plate filled with fluted pastry horns and thick rectangular slices topped with white icing.

"Not quite the Café Bristol, but thank you." Comparing their surroundings with the most exclusive coffee house in Warsaw, Mimi looked with disdain at the thick white china. Marianna picked up the coffee pot and poured.

"How ironic it is. That we should end up here together."

"Oh yes," Mimi sighed. "We have come so far and suffered so much." She paused, waiting for sympathy. Marianna, ignoring the invitation to relive past tragedy, cupped her chin in her hand, her eyes dreamy.

"I have always thought that there is some almost mystical connection between us," she mused.

"We are cousins," Mimi said tartly. Marianna could be tiresome with her flights of fancy and it was necessary to keep her in check. Given free rein, her imagination would run away with her.

"Ah Mimi, so down to earth." Marianna picked up her handbag. "And now, to celebrate your birthday, I have something for you."

"A present!" Mimi clasped her hands.

"What else? It is your special day."

"I did not expect anything." *And I have nothing for you.* The small explosion of pleasure at Marianna's announcement soured into irritation as, once again, her wealthy cousin had her at a disadvantage.

"All the better then. It will be a good surprise." Marianna reached into the depths of her bag and took out a small box wrapped in rose-coloured tissue paper tied with gold ribbon. Mimi's breath caught in her throat. By the shape and size of the box it must contain a piece of jewellery. A present from the Princess Marianna, the gems would be of the highest quality, and how Mimi loved those clear-cut statements of wealth and status.

As she held the box in the palm of her hand she was assailed by another memory. Rising like scum on greasy water, the image was of a skeletal woman, a necklace of emeralds around her throat, her skin yellow as sour milk. Hollowed eyes stared from a skull-like face. Heavy bracelets twisted on bone-sharp wrists.

A moment of vertigo swept away her recollection and Mimi was left looking down at the soft pink and rich gold wrappings. Fingers stiff and awkward, she tugged gently at the ribbon, pulling it free of its bow and rolling it up tight before putting it in her bag. Next she unwrapped the paper, smoothed it out on the glass-topped table, folding it into squares, which she added to the ribbon.

The box was of blue leather embossed with gold. Inside, on a bed of white velvet, lay an enamelled flower. It had four petals, two were deep pink and two violet, and each one was dewed with a sprinkle of diamonds.

"You always liked that broach." Marianna smiled.

"Faberge," Mimi sighed. "I can't take it." Her fingers closed around the box.

"Why not? You should have had it years ago and if I choose to give it to you now, where's the harm?"

"It was your mother's."

"My mother was your Aunt Helena. She would hardly object to me giving you a trinket from some long-forgotten admirer. She never wore it. Here let me." Marianna took the broach and, squinting, pinned it on the shoulder of Mimi's coat. "Just what it needed, to lift it." She leaned back in her chair to admire the effect. Mimi stroked the cold petals. "It's hardly a family heirloom," Marianna continued. "And even if it were, who else would I leave it to? You and your family are the closest relatives I have left. Talking of which, how is my goddaughter, my lovely Hannah?"

"Hannah is how she always is. She runs to fat."

"And Gregor and the grandchildren?"

"Piotr is a delight, a little cherub. As for Kasia, she is an awkward, difficult child."

"A woman almost, I think."

"Still a girl," Mimi corrected. "She's so sharp she could cut herself."

"A little like you then," Marianna teased.

Mimi flushed. "More like her great-aunt, you mean. I was the good girl." *I did not drive my mother to madness or live wildly abroad and scandalously at home.*

"Yes, you were always the good girl."

"Don't mock me."

"Heaven forfend," Marianna laughed. "Don't take it so seriously. If I cannot tease my family who can I make fun of?"

"There are the relations in Poland."

Marianna threw up her hands. "Communists!" she cried theatrically. "They live in a different world from us. What possible connection could we have with them?"

"They are our blood and they too have survived."

"Only because they will have compromised their beliefs, their standards, and everything that made them who they were. Still, no doubt locked in behind the Iron Curtain, they had no choice."

"You can always choose to do the right thing."

"Come on Mimi, don't tell me you really believe that?"

"Of course."

Marianna sighed and shook her head. "I'm afraid that as I grow older I am no longer so certain."

Mimi drew in her breath. How typical of Marianna to deny absolutes and reduce everything to a universal greyness. Life was simple. There was right and there was wrong and so it remained regardless of circumstances.

Once her cousin would have been eager to argue the point but today she appeared to have lost any relish for the fray. Which was fortunate because they were supposed to celebrating their joint survival, not engaging in a spurious philosophical debate.

"Do you ever want to go back to see what became of them all?" Marianna said as if she, like Mimi, was determined to avoid confrontation.

I do not, thought Mimi, *want them to see what became of me. All those years ago I had such dreams, and look at me now. I am an old woman in a foreign land, dependent on her daughter and son-in-law.* "The family in Poland does not interest me," she said. Marianna raised an eyebrow. Her smile invited intimacy but Mimi had had enough. "It is time for me to go."

"So soon?"

"I must."

"Then let me call a taxi."

Mimi was tempted. If she did as Marianna suggested she would avoid the rush and hustle of another bus journey and the ever present threat of being crammed into a seat next to some uncouth person. Nor would there be a breath-snatching walk up the steepness of St. Michael's hill. On the other hand she would, once again, be beholden to her cousin. The ever fortunate Marianna who had never, not even in the worst of times, had to scrimp and save, or worry about keeping up appearances.

Mimi glanced out of the window where the rain had settled into a damp dreariness. Unlike the feckless Marianna she had chores that must be done. "I have shopping to do." She stood up slowly, careful to avoid a repetition of the dizziness that had plagued her all afternoon. "Thank you for my present." Mimi touched her broach. "And the tea." She waved a hand over the half-filled cups and empty plates. Then, head held high, back straight, Mimi left the ice cream parlour.

* * *

Watching her leave, oozing martyrdom from every pore, Marianna felt a deep need of a vodka. She opened her bag and took out a monogrammed case and a silver lighter. Letting the tang of tobacco slide over her tongue she watched the smoke wreathe upwards.

* * *

Mimi put up her umbrella and pulled a string bag out of her handbag. Her arms were tired, her legs leaden. In the past there had been a girl to run the errands, now she must go herself. What a way to end her days. Yet she usually enjoyed the challenge. Demeaning though it might be it was also stimulating, this hunt through alien territory, negotiating a language she found difficult and customs she did not understand. It was only today she had to fight an increasing lethargy and intense desire for sleep.

It was almost dark and the queues at the bus stops were growing making it harder to thread her way through the crowds. The lights from shops and offices glittered in the puddles as she hurried down the street to the greengrocers.

Under the harsh neon strip lights, fruit and vegetables were banked up on trestle tables covered in green raffia. Pyramids of red and green apples, white parsnips, reddish-pink turnips, creamy-hearted cauliflowers and shiny wax-skinned lemons and bright-coloured oranges. The red-and-white striped awning sagged with rainwater. The floor was dirty with the passage of many feet but the white tiled walls gleamed, as did the brass till and the weights that stood by the side of the scales. It was cold inside; the door stood open to the night. Soon the shop would be shutting, always the best time to find a bargain.

What was needed was the grit and determination that those tight-faced English women lacked. They had no idea that fruit must be pinched and squeezed to sniff out the fresh from the over ripe, the perfect from the rotten.

For them it had been too easy. They had never known what it was like to go hungry, or worse, to fear that there was no food for their children.

* * *

White light dazzles as another image floods her memory. The

sun beats down on her head. Already, she feels the sweat spring up on her shoulders, is aware of the dampness under her arms. Her hands grip the handle of her basket.

"Please," she prays, "let there be meat today. If only a bone to make stock."

The shopkeeper opens his shutters, the queue shuffles forward. Mimi brings the corner of her basket hard into the side of the woman in front of her and forces her way past. She will do whatever she must to make sure her family does not starve.

* * *

"The apples are good today." The scene shifted. A striped apron, then a red face came into focus. Mimi's hand closed on a Russet.

"These are bruised," she sniffed.

"Never!" The green grocer threw himself into the game. "Firm as my mother's breast." Mimi snorted. The breath came strangely down her nostrils. She tasted metal. Her head spun. "Only one and sixpence a pound."

"You expect me to pay full price for damaged fruit!" she cried.

"It is perfect. I swear."

Mimi's hand delved into the base of the pyramid. "Then what about these?" Triumphantly, she withdrew two apples, their skins wrinkled and their flesh mushy.

"Those are not for you. They are for other customers, for those without your eye," he protested.

"I will have six of those." Mimi pointed to the fruit on the top of the pile. "And I will pay you ten pence."

"For perfect fruit!"

"For yesterday's fruit. In a minute you close. Then it will become yesterday's fruit."

He groaned. "Anything else?"

"Two pounds of King Edwards and five oranges. I will pick them myself." The potatoes were weighed and tipped into Mimi's string bag.

"Is it not too heavy?" he asked, concerned.

The black lines on the tiles wavered. "I am strong enough." She must not admit to weakness, although as she left the shopping hung heavily on her arm, pulling her to the right. Pain pulsed behind her eyes. She tried to blink it away but it was growing stronger, wiping out all conscious thought until there was nothing but darkness.

* * *

A tide of maroon uniforms swept down the hill. Girls talked and laughed, arms linked, satchels swinging from their shoulders, hats pushed to the back of their heads. At bus stops and junctions the flow was checked and diverted until only a small group remained. Straggling behind the others, a dark-haired girl was deep in conversation with her taller, sturdier friend.

"I don't know how to tell him," Annie said. Kate shrugged. Her hair was bobbed so that it swung across her cheeks and the heavy fringe half-covered her eyes.

"Just say it."

"I can't."

"Why not? You don't want to go out with him anymore, so tell him and put yourself out of your misery."

"You're hard, Kate."

"I'm right." She lifted her chin defiantly. Beside her, Annie, her fair hair curling around her flushed face, struggled to explain herself.

"I know I should. I know it's the right thing to do but I don't want to hurt him. After all, it's not his fault if he likes me more than I like him. And it's not as if I want to go out with anyone else, or anything. I don't want to see him anymore. At least, not like that. I wouldn't mind if he was a friend, but somehow boys can't ever just be friends. I don't know why, but they can't."

"Sex," Kate said simply. How could Annie be so naive? It was obvious. Boys only wanted one thing but any talk of sex and her friend went all hot and bothered as if she was some Victorian lady and not an eighteen year old in the middle of the twentieth century, for goodness sake.

Annie turned her face away to hide her blushes and Kate had to grab hold of her arm to stop her walking straight into the old woman who lay spread-eagled on the pavement, her legs shamefully apart, stocking tops tight on mottled flesh, head to one side, eyes vacant, mouth hanging open, a thin trail of vomit down her chin, grunting and snorting like a sick animal. An ambulance stood at the kerb and two men were taking out a stretcher. Annie gasped.

Kate stared. "My God," she said. "It's Gran."

CHAPTER TWO

Hannah walked down St. Michael's Hill towards the Infirmary. The white bulk of the building rose like a cliff above the traffic. Three stories up, a glazed balcony jutted out over a small garden where patients' beds were wheeled out to catch the morning sun, giving the hospital the air of a grand hotel – an impression heightened by Grecian pillars and swirls of stone over doors and windows. Built in the Imperial style, there was no concession to illness or infirmity.

The visitors' entrance was at the top of a steep flight of steps. It was a hard climb for a middle-aged woman carrying slightly too much weight. At the top, pausing to catch her breath, Hannah looked down on the remnants of the morning's mist, a thin grey discharge unravelling into the thick air; it looped and twisted ghostlike around the chimneys of the alms houses across the road.

A premonition of death? Shaking the thought from her head she pushed open the door and was assailed by the familiar mix of antiseptic, hospital polish, starched uniforms and rubberised floors.

"Is she any better today, your mum?" The cleaner raised her mop and plunged it hard onto the metal lip of her bucket. Hannah smiled, warmed by the woman's concern yet at the same time keenly aware how bitterly Mimi would resent such interest.

"I'm going to see her now."

"She's a one." The woman clicked her tongue and Hannah's hands tightened inside her gloves. "They don't give up easy, that sort. My grandma, she had a stroke." She leaned forward confidentially and Hannah, sensing some personal revelation, began to back away. "Never spoke again," the cleaner continued, "but that didn't stop her. A terror she was with her eyes. Gave you a look and you knew what she wanted. Uncanny it was."

The thought of her mother silenced was so ludicrous that a giggle rose in Hannah's throat. Instantly she flushed with shame. What pleasure in life did her mother have other than the indiscriminate exercise of her tongue? What if she caused her daughter pain? Hannah should be able to rise above it. Mimi was old and had lost so much and she deserved her daughter's compassion, her consideration and respect.

Yet how often had Mimi set one member of the family at odds with another? None were immune to her poison. Only the youngest, her beloved grandson Peter, escaped her venomous comments and the snide remarks designed to undermine confidence and upset the balance of a relationship.

God forgive me, but if she could not speak how peaceful it would be, Hannah thought.

"Mrs...?" The ward sister was bearing down on her, the full impact of her authority tempered by hesitation as she struggled to avoid using the name that rattled like pebbles in a tin.

"Dzierzanowska," Hannah supplied wearily. She understood how hard it was for an English tongue to wrap itself around that particular combination of consonants, but at the same time there was a sneaking resentment that people did not bother to attempt it.

The ward sister cleared her throat. Hannah's anxiety rose. She grew a little dizzy and light-headed, as if someone was turning a screw at the top of her head, lifting her feet from the floor, holding her suspended a few inches from the ground.

"The doctor would like to speak to you." Could her desire for release be responsible for a deterioration in her mother's condition? "If you would wait outside his office."

"Is there a problem?"

"I am sure there is nothing to worry about." The sister was brisk, competent, unfeeling. "Doctor won't be long."

I should ask. I should demand to know. I am as intelligent as this woman and as well qualified. I nursed throughout the War but she sees me only as a foreigner with an accent, which singles me out as incompetent and of no account.

She allowed herself to be led to a row of plastic chairs where she sat patiently, hands folded in her lap, until finally a young doctor appeared. Hair rumpled, rubbing his eyes as if he had just woken up, he held open the consulting room door.

"If you would come this way."

"I thought I was going to see Mr Bold."

"I am his registrar. That means..."

"I know what it means." Hannah sat down in the chair opposite the doctor's desk. "Now please, if you could tell me what it is you have to say about my mother." The doctor frowned at his sheaf of papers. "She is *Pani...*" Hannah stopped. "I mean Mrs Bernadinska," she finished hurriedly. "She was brought in a fortnight ago. She had suffered a stroke. I would like to know what the prognosis is."

The doctor lifted the corner of a piece of paper and studied it at some length, taking so much time that Hannah was afraid she had offended him.

"I'm sorry, but I really do need to know."

"Of course you do. You are down as the next of kin. Naturally you want to know when she will get better. We have conducted some tests and I am afraid..."

You are afraid of giving me bad news. And I am afraid that if you tell me she is going to die I will be pleased because a great weight will have been taken from my shoulders. I should not feel like this and yet I cannot help myself. To her astonishment her eyes filled, her nose began to run, and she had to rummage in her handbag for a handkerchief.

"As things stand there is unlikely to be much improvement," the doctor said.

"Is there nothing we can do? I was a nurse. I will do anything that needs to be done."

He watched her carefully, as if assessing how much he should say. "The stroke was massive. The end may come soon, or it may be a few months off. With good nursing she could last for years. However, we are reasonably sure that she will not improve a great deal from how she is today."

"I see." Hannah pushed back her chair.

"Is there is anything else you would like to ask me? Anything about her treatment you would like to discuss?"

She shook her head. "Not at the moment. You must understand that we, as a family, will need to make decisions about how we care for her."

"That was not what I was referring to. I meant that she might be better off in a nursing home. That is an option you and your family should seriously consider."

"We shall think about it." She smiled at him. "And thank you."

* * *

Mimi sat in bed, propped up by a pile of pillows. Her eyes were black as currents in her white face, one side of which was twisted into a parody of a smile. One arm lay limply on the bedclothes, the other beckoned impatiently to a young nurse.

"I am not comfortable. I need to be moved. If I am not moved regularly I will develop bed sores."

Raising her eyes, the nurse came to the side of the bed. Taking Mimi by the shoulders she rearranged her. "There you are Mrs B. Will that do? I only settled you a minute ago." Mimi gave a little groan. The nurse frowned. "Still not comfortable?"

"My water is not fresh. If you could bring me a new jug..." The authoritative tone softened into a sweet-natured appeal. "Thank you, my dear. You are so kind to an old woman." Mimi patted the young woman's hand. Then seeing Hannah standing at the door of the ward her voice broke into a wail. "Hannuisha." The fluent English disappeared. "Where have you been? I have been waiting for so long. *Jesus kohany*, I thought you had forgotten me, that you had abandoned your poor old mother."

"No. You know I would never do that to you." Hannah was spiked by guilt.

Mimi clutched at Hannah's hand. "There are some poor souls like that in here. Their families never visit. They are quite alone. And the nurses, they do not care."

The nurse, who had obviously not understood a word, put a fresh jug of water on the bedside locker. "Been a good girl today, your mum. Eaten all her breakfast. Haven't you Mrs B?"

Mimi shuddered and looked piteously at Hannah. "How can I live among people like this?" Her eyes grew wet. Her voice became a little girl's. "Please, I want to go home."

* * *

A pale sun floated in a watery sky as Hannah walked slowly away from the hospital. On her left cars and buses thundered towards the white walled canyons of the newly built shopping centre. On her right was the row of dusty second-hand shops where she had often browsed in search of a bargain. Once she had found a perfect vase in blue and white, which Gregor had made into the base of a lamp. It stood on the shelves he had put up in the living room.

He was good to her. He would understand. But first she must find the right words.

Rounding the corner she began the steep ascent up St Michael's Hill. To live under the protection of the archangel was something she had never imagined, but Bristol was a city of saints and angels. Devastated by German bombs, the ruins of its churches had stood defiant, blackened and twisted above the rubble. Some had been rebuilt while others were no more than empty shells, their walls cloaked with ivy and bindweed; banks of rosebay willow-herb flourished among the echoing stones. From her windows halfway up the hill she could look out on a townscape of towers and spires.

Her house was tall and thin. A facing of stone hid its true age. Up in the attic the heavy beams ran from the eaves; the floor sloped, and the walls were soft and pliable.

Putting the key in the lock, she allowed the house to gather her in. Daylight filtered through the fanlight, its greenish glow a constant reminder of the emeralds that had bought her this house.

* * *

"Take it," Princess Marianna says, holding out the necklace.

Hannah, heavy with her first child, sinks into a chair in the small damp kitchen that smells of cabbage and blocked drains.

"Now that you are about to be a mother you will need something extra for the little one, or whatever else you might need," the Princess continues. "It is for you to use as you please." In the light of the single bulb that dangles from the ceiling, the jewels glow with sullen fire. "I sewed them into the lining of my dress when I escaped from Warsaw. I would not let the Germans have them."

The emeralds slide through Hannah's fingers like the beads of a rosary.

"I wore the same dress for weeks. How I must have smelled." The Princess laughs.

"I cannot. I am not..." Hannah pauses, searching for the right word.

"Worthy?" Marianna prompts.

Hannah lowers her head.

"Who is?" Marianna spreads out her hands. "I am not. My mother, who had them from her husband, definitely was not. She looked on the Zapolski emeralds as booty. And does it matter? After all, what are they? Bits of green stone. You deserve them as much as anyone."

Instinctively, Hannah shakes her head.

"Oh yes you do." Marianna leans forward and puts her hand over her goddaughter's. Her skin is dry and ridged, like the scales of a snake. "You are a good woman, Hannah. You take care of your family. You put up with Mimi."

Hannah stiffens. No one, not even the Princess, must be allowed to criticise her mother. Marianna releases her grip.

"It is my pleasure to give you something. I want to do this. It would be too cruel of you to refuse me that indulgence."

Under Hannah's ribs, the baby gives a sharp kick, and she presses her hands against her belly to hold down the hot gust of excitement that sweeps over her. The possibilities opened out by the jewels are more than she can ever have imagined. Accepting the emeralds will make her godmother happy and Hannah can use them in a way which will benefit her whole family.

"I will buy a house," she announces. "But Gregor must not know where the money came from."

Marianna nods. "Men are so fragile."

"Not Gregor," Hannah says quickly, refusing to admit to any flaws in her husband. "He is strong. It is just that..."

"He has his pride," the Princess's voice is dry, her tone ironic.

"Yes," Hannah whispers. "He has his pride." And his pride makes him difficult and over sensitive, seeing insult and injury where there is none, needing her to soothe and protect. He would resent the gift, judging it a reflection on his ability to provide for his family. Perhaps it would be better if Hannah refuses the jewels, but even as the thought comes to her, anger white as phosphorus flares in her chest. For once she will have what she wants. Whatever the cost she will have her house, a place where she and her family can be safe.

The Princess rises to her feet. "Levi Goldsmidt will sell them for you. He will get a good price and will not cheat you." She bends her head. Her lips touch Hannah's cheek, and musk and spices perfume the air as Marianna slips the Zapolski emeralds into the pocket of her goddaughter's overall.

* * *

Hannah had told Gregor that she had come into a legacy. Inheritance being more palatable than a gift, which he would see as charity. It was the first lie she had ever told him and what shocked her more than her own guilt was how easily he had believed her. Did he not see how she avoided his eyes as she stammered out her explanation? Or was it that he could not bear to think that his wife was anything more than a rather simple, straightforward woman who might prove irritating at times, but never devious.

And now she had to persuade him that bringing her mother home to die was the right thing to do. Anxiety prowled through her veins. She pressed her wrist into her mouth, holding it with her teeth. The sound rose in her throat but when the cry came, harsh and afraid, it was not hers. Head cocked to one side, she listened. The air vibrated then settled around her. She sensed fear and loneliness and was swept by the need to comfort.

Hannah pushed open the door to the front room. The grey morning pressed against the windows. The room was empty. She hurried up the stairs. On the half-landing she looked into the bathroom. A tap dripped faintly. Tiled walls threw back the sound of her entry. There was no one there.

In the bedroom she shared with Gregor the covers were thrown back on the bed, the curtains half-drawn, her clothes on a chair, a cupboard door ajar. A fine layer of powder covered the polished surface of the dressing table; a pair of stockings lay, knotted together. Later she would tidy up but now she must find who it was that was crying so piteously in her empty house.

Could the crying be malevolent? Gripping the handle of her son's bedroom door, she was overcome by an illogical terror of what might be lurking inside. Fearing unknown horrors, she was reassured by the neatly made bed and the row of teddy bears staring at her with their button eyes. There was nothing out of the ordinary here.

Relieved, but still apprehensive, she went to look in her mother's room. A deeply ingrained taboo against intruding on her parents held her back. Until her illness Mimi had taken care of herself, and Hannah had found it difficult to go through her mother's cupboards to find what she needed for her stay in hospital.

She did not want to enter but she had to know where the crying was coming from. Pristine as always, the room was obviously unoccupied. Rugs covered the floor and the wall at the head of the bed. Above lace-edged pillows piled high hung an icon of the Madonna of Czestochowa. The red velvet curtains were drawn to keep out the light. Whatever pain had caused that cry, it was not here.

Halfway down the stairs she stopped. She stood, her senses stretched as fine as wire, to trap the sound she knew was there but could not quite hear. Her knees folded. She put out her hands and steadied herself against the wall, limp with relief. It was so simple: in her heightened state of emotion she had misread the obvious.

She ran down to the kitchen, where the ginger cat overflowed the wicker chair like a puddle of marmalade. Front paws flopping over the edge, tail dangling down a chair leg, its head rested on the arm, yellow eyes shut, plump body heaving in sleep.

"Puss?" The creature did not stir. "Was that you?" The cat twitched but did not wake.

Hannah opened the door and looked out into the back yard. The air was still. There were no neighbourhood cats stalking along the dividing walls, no children in the street, no distant sirens. Nothing that she could have mistaken for a child in distress. Whatever she had heard she was certain had come from inside the house.

Taking a tea towel from the rail, she set the kettle on the Rayburn. When the tea was brewed she sat at the table, cradling the cup in her hands, but the hot sweet liquid could not drown her overwhelming feeling of sadness.

That sense of melancholy clung to her throughout the day. To rid herself of it she went early to collect Peter from school. She was the first of the mothers to arrive and the juniors were on their last break. Hannah watched from behind high wire netting as they chased and ran; holding her breath as she anticipated the tumble on the tarmac that tore at soft flesh and bruised bare elbows. Gradually the other mothers arrived. They greeted each other, laughing and chatting. Some lit up, leaning on the handles of their prams as they breathed out plumes of smoke. Hannah stood apart, distancing herself from their youth, their broad working class humour and rough manners.

The bell rang and her heart leapt as her son ran towards her; he was so young and so vulnerable. Beautiful too, with sturdy rounded limbs, a shock of fair hair over candid blue eyes fringed with dark lashes. Then a hand was thrust into hers.

"Mummy why are you so sad?" asked her little boy.

CHAPTER THREE

Gregor Dzierzanowski put the key in the door of his wife's house and stepped inside. Grey faced and weary, he paused to hang his hat on the stand catching, as he did so, a whiff of the tobacco odour that clung to his clothes. He turned to frown at the rectangle of light spilling over the black and white tiled floor at the far end of the passage. Hannah was in the kitchen but he knew she would not come out to greet him, because he needed those few moments to shed his working man's skin and become the solemn and dignified man that was her husband.

Before the War he had been a man to be respected; had moved in circles of influence; had been consulted on matters of national importance. In England, he had known it would be different. What he had not expected was a lack of suitable jobs and, when he arrived at the accounts office of the tobacco factory, how he would be treated by his work mates.

Gregor Dzierzanowski. The chief accountant had looked at the name on the top of his file, sucked his breath in between his teeth and shook his head. *Gre–* he had attempted, tapping his pencil on the paper.

Gregor.

Can't have that. We'll never get our tongues round it. Tell you what, we'll call you Greg. Easier all round. I'm Jim McAlester. He held out his hand and Gregor shook it, accepting defeat.

They had robbed him of his name and identity. Careless of his feelings, too lazy even to try, they had transformed him into Greg, the Polish fellow. *Clever, mind you, and not a bad chap for a foreigner.* Reducing his tragic history to *had a bad time in the War, those Poles.*

Hannah was standing by the stove, her hair escaping in wisps around her face, her cheeks red. She was stirring something but her eyes were on the door and as he opened it she came to him. Solemnly, he put his hands on her shoulders. She lifted her face and he bent and kissed her on the mouth. She tasted of soup and smelled of vanilla and cinnamon that may have been some perfume she wore, or the very own scent of her skin.

On the table there were two sets of knives and forks and two table napkins, each in its own silver ring. The plates were warming on the Rayburn. They would eat alone. The noise and chatter of the children could not be allowed to intrude on this time. Gregor sat down and waited for Hannah to serve him. The kitchen was quiet. The house free from the malign presence of his wife's mother. A feeling of peace and relaxation stole over him.

"I went to the hospital today." Hannah's hand shook slightly as she handed him his bowl. Gregor lifted the spoon to his mouth. She laced her fingers, holding them still. "I saw the doctor."

He put down his spoon. He waited.

"He said she can come home." His jaw tightened. It had been too much to hope that they would be granted an extension of this time together, this opportunity to live as a family of four. "She hates it in the hospital," Hannah said miserably.

"*Tak*." Gregor nodded, the single syllable of the Polish word bursting like gunfire into the room and making Hannah wince. "If that is how she feels, then of course she must come back," he said.

"You're not angry? Oh, you're so good." She seized his hand and lifted it to her lips.

"She is your mother. It is our duty." He pulled her close, breathing in the smell of her as he choked back his disappointment. To be alone with her was all he wanted. The one thing that so many men dreaded, avoided as much as possible, he longed for and throughout their marriage had been denied. Mimi had always been there. Right from those very first days, when they had met in the army hospital in Italy, Hannah had never been free of her mother and neither had he. "When?" he said finally.

"Next week. They want her - no..." Hannah corrected herself. "She wants to be home for Christmas."

* * *

Kate stormed in, slamming the front door. The glass shivered as the house recoiled from the wave of anger that swept down the hall.

Hannah slipped the pot of soup back on the hot plate and braced herself. Gregor was immersed in the evening paper. Peter sat opposite his father eating a sandwich. Scarlet jam oozed out from the white bread as he carefully cut each piece into quarters before putting it into his mouth. The cat purred loudly from the wicker chair.

Her daughter exploded like shrapnel into the room. Gregor's head jerked up, his anger rising. Startled, Peter dropped his crust onto the plate, his fingers red. Hannah stepped between the table and her daughter, hoping to shield her son and placate her husband.

"There's soup for tea, shall I pour you some?"

"Soup? Again? You know I hate soup."

Hannah's grip on the table tightened. She could see Gregor half rising in his chair ready to intervene, Peter's eyes lowering, his lips trembling. She clamped her teeth down on the words that rose to her lips. What right had Kate to disturb their peace? *Can you think of no one but yourself?* She wanted to shout, but shouting would only fuel her daughter's anger. There would be an outpouring of hate and bitterness. Peter and Gregor would be hurt and nothing would be achieved. She tried to smile, to soften herself for this selfish child of hers.

"What will you have then?" Hannah feared her daughter would go to her room without eating.

"What's that?" Kate glanced at her brother's plate.

"It's mine." Peter plumped his hands over his last piece of bread.

"Jam sandwiches. I'll make you some, shall I?" Hannah said swiftly. *Please God the sugar in the jam will sweeten her,* she prayed as she wielded her knife. *I want,* the knife, synchronised with her thoughts, moved one way, *to ask her,* the knife swept back, *if she has had a bad day.* She picked up one slice and

— 30 —

pressed it down on another. *But if I do, it will only make her worse.* Handing her daughter the plate she said, "Granny's coming home."

"She's what?"

"Your grandmother Mimi is coming home from hospital," Gregor said.

"I thought she was dying."

"Katarzyna Dzierzanowska, how can you say these things?" Hannah was appalled.

Kate shrugged. "She looked dead enough to me when I saw her in the street."

"She's recovering. If you had been to the hospital you would have seen that for yourself."

"I had too much to do. Homework. Studying. As you keep reminding me, I've got my A Levels this summer." Kate glared at her parents. However much her mother had nagged, she had refused to go the hospital. That sick old woman sprawled on her back on the wet pavement was not her grandmother.

Her grandmother was neat and round and forceful. Sometimes she trembled with energy, sometimes she brooded reptile-like, then spat her venom, terrorising her mother, making her father clench his fists and shake with unexpressed anger. She had finally got the measure of her grandmother. Watching her, working out how she operated, had immunised Kate against the barbed comments and constant comparisons between herself and girls whom Mimi considered better brought up, better mannered, and more successful at school. And now that she had the weapons to defend herself, Mimi had become a sick old woman who would dribble and smell and wet herself. Kate's mouth twisted in disgust.

"We'll all be together for Christmas," Hannah said.

"That's only two weeks away," Kate moaned. "Can't she wait until afterwards? It will be horrible. We'll have to wash her and feed her and things."

"She's not incapable," Hannah said sharply, fearing that indeed she was.

* * *

Peter looked from his mother to his sister. He was glad his

grandmother was coming home. He liked the way she spoke to him, her voice a little whispery as if they were sharing a secret, and the feel of her plump body, her arm curled around him, as he leant back against her and listened to her stories of the Little Eagles, the boys who had held the city of Lvov against the invading Russians.

"I'll help. I'll feed Granny." He picked up a spoon. "Open your mouth. Here we go, wait for the aeroplane." He mimicked the way his mother used to feed him as a toddler. Then the spoon dropped with a clatter to the floor as he was overcome with laughter.

* * *

To allow for Mimi's return the natural order of the house was upset. Furniture was moved and rooms lost their identity. Mimi's bed was brought downstairs. The sofa and chairs were banished to the dining room where they hugged the walls like unwelcome guests. The television skulked in the corner by the window where, in spite of everything Gregor tried, the picture was either grey and ghostly, or haunted by dark smuts dancing across the screen; and no matter how far the table and chairs were pushed to one side, the only way to reach the controls was to climb over the furniture. This delighted Peter, who spent his time balancing on arms, bouncing on cushions and wriggling under chairs as he changed from one channel to another.

In the front room Hannah removed some books from the shelves and replaced them with Mimi's picture of the Madonna of Czestochowa. Beside the icon she put a small night light, a bottle of Lourdes water someone had given her, and a rosary made of olive wood from the Holy Land. The table at the side of the bed was cleared to make space for all the things she needed for nursing her mother.

When it was done she stood back and let the anger and resentment flood through her. It was the best solution but her pretty room had been ruined. Pulling the curtains shut, she went into the kitchen where she sat and stared at the slice of lemon floating in tea that tasted sharp and bitter.

* * *

In the attic bedroom, Kate lifted her head from her books and watched her breath curl into the air. Leaning forward, she blew onto the window and looked out onto the ice-rimmed roofs. Her face was white with cold, her fingers numb. She wore an old jumper over her school uniform and on top of that a dressing gown. Thick woollen socks were pulled up over her knees and still she was frozen. Leaving her pen on the page to keep her place, she shut her history book.

As she went down the stairs the air grew warmer and by the time she reached the kitchen her chilblains had begun to itch. Pushing her hands under her sleeves she shivered at the touch of cold fingers against skin, and backed herself up to thaw her bottom against the Rayburn. Her mother did not look up.

"I've done two hours. My room's freezing. Is there any tea?"

"In the pot." Hannah's voice was flat. She did not offer to get up.

Kate poured herself a cup. "I will probably die of pneumonia." There was no reaction and Kate resorted to an old family joke, the half-serious threat that could never be realised, because to abandon education in the Dzierzanowski family was tantamount to committing the gravest of mortal sins. "On the other hand, I could give it all up and go and work in Woolworths." Still Hannah did not respond. Kate came up to her mother and putting a hand on her shoulder felt her quiver under her touch. "Are you all right, Mum?"

"Yes."

"It's the house," Kate said with sudden insight.

Hannah stared at the rim of her cup. "There's nowhere to sit. Nowhere to be comfortable." She paused, then her voice trembled as it rose. "And where will we put the Christmas tree?"

Kate considered. "In Gran's room," she said finally.

"No one will see it there."

"Mother!" Kate shook her head at her mother's apparent stupidity. Hannah's shoulders slumped. "I'm sorry. I didn't mean..." Kate stopped, then began again. "What I meant was, why don't we put it all upstairs? We can make Gran's old room into the sitting room. For the time being," she added quickly, unwilling to cause more pain.

"I don't know." Hannah said slowly.

"Come on Mum. It's the perfect solution."

"Yes, but..."

"It'll be really good," Kate interrupted. "Proper Christmassy. There's a gas fire and that Victorian grate, and we could put the sofa and chairs around it to make it cosy." The hesitation cleared from her mother's face and she pressed on. "I'll help. If we start now we could get it all done before Dad gets home from work tonight." She seized her mother's hand and pulled her to her feet. "We've got an hour or two. Let's do it."

The dining room curtains were drawn and the blue-grey television screen flickered in the dusky afternoon. Peter lay on his stomach, his chin balanced on the arm of the sofa and watched the children's presenter construct a castle from empty bottles of washing up liquid. A triangular piece of paper glued into a cone was about to be set on top of one of the turrets. Peter watched as the roof wobbled, slipped sideways and began to slide downwards. Would it fall or would they save it? He lifted his thumb to his lips and wriggled deeper into the cushions. Above him a black shape blotted out the picture.

"I can't see."

"Get up then," his sister ordered.

"Won't." He screwed up his face.

"Will." Kate rolled her hand underneath him to tip him onto the floor. Preparing to resist, he curled up tight. "Go upstairs and hold Gran's door open for us."

"Why?" His interest piqued, Peter sat up.

"You'll see. Hurry up. We haven't got all day."

He went, climbing calmly and methodically with one hand on the banisters. It was dark at the top of the stairs and he did not want to go into Gran's room on his own, but Kate had said he must and Kate could be mean and sharp with her fingernails. Putting his thumb in his mouth he peered back down the stairs where his mother and sister were wheeling a chair in to the hall. They turned it on its side and Kate clambered over it and took hold of the arm, but her fingers slipped on the worn moquette so she grasped the hessian underneath. While Hannah pushed Kate pulled and slowly they began to move the chair upwards.

On the half-landing they paused for breath.

Hannah leaned back against the upended chair and pushed the hair from her eyes.

"Nearly there." Kate's cheeks were flushed, her green eyes excited.

"*Jesus kohany*, let me rest a minute," Hannah begged.

"Only one more." Kate was poised cat like on the next step. "Ready?"

"Ready," Hannah agreed.

"Ready," Peter cried. Emboldened by their presence, he ran to the door of his grandmother's room and flung it open, pressing it back as far as it would go and holding it open as they pushed the chair inside.

"Now the sofa," Kate declared.

"You're a slave driver," Hannah moaned.

Peter looked at the chair. "There's no cushion." Kate raised her eyes to the ceiling. "I'll get it," he offered, eager to avoid her wrath and gain her praise.

Back in the dining room the sofa squatted against the wall, heavy and cumbersome. Kate gave it a push and it jerked forward then stuck as a castor caught in a snag in the carpet.

Hannah leaned against its rounded back. "We'll never do it," she sighed.

"We got the chair up, didn't we?" Kate would not be beaten.

"That was smaller," Hannah said.

"Not much. The sofa's not wider or fatter, just longer." Kate slid herself between the sofa and the remaining chair. She pushed. Nothing moved.

"You'll break your back," Hannah said. "Here let me." She bent and smoothed out the wrinkle in the carpet. "Now try."

Kate shoved. The sofa slid forward knocking Hannah off balance and sending her sprawling onto its seat. Kate stifled a giggle. Hannah kicked out, her legs swished backwards and forwards, laughter bubbled from her mouth. Kate bounced down beside her. Screeching with laughter, mother and daughter clutched their sides. Tears rolled down Hannah's face; Kate's nose ran and she wiped it on her sleeve.

The sofa was wedged firmly half in and half out of the

doorway. Aching with laughter, Hannah held it firmly while Kate slid through the narrow gap between it and the door frame. At the bottom of the stairs they leaned against the wall.

"We can't take it up there," Hannah gasped.

"We can." Kate tipped the sofa onto the step and began to push, muscles bunched hard and hot in her back and arms.

"You'll hurt yourself," Hannah worried, but Kate felt strong and invulnerable. Like some female Hercules engaged in an impossible task, she would not give up. Together they heaved and the sofa went up a step; they pushed, it went up another. Step by step it rose above the black and white floor tiles, until at last it reached the plateau of the half-landing. Hannah's heart beat loudly, her breath was hard in her chest.

"You know what," Kate panted, "if I fail my A Levels we can set up in business Hannah Dzierzanowska and Daughter: Removals."

* * *

A crazy idea, a mad scheme, and for one insane moment Hannah could picture it, could see herself and Kate working together. United, bound in a way that they had never been since she had expelled her daughter from the safety of her womb. Even then the tiny crotchety baby had refused comfort, flailing with her fists against the softness of her mother's breast, throwing back her milk in sour smelling posset and screaming and screaming through the long dark hours of the night.

"It's like halfway up the mountain." Kate looked down through the banisters.

"In that case let's get it to the top," Hannah said.

The sofa slid up the final flight of stairs. It lay on its side, its castors in the air, the torn hessian of its underside rudely exposed.

"Now we know how, we can do anything," Kate said as she and Hannah, their shoulders touching, sat on the top step and steadied their breathing.

Later when the room was done, Hannah lit the gas fire. An acrid tang tainted the air. Blue flames licked the honeycomb of burners, then glowed a steady red in the darkness. At the back of the house, away from the road, the room was quiet. Kate was in her attic, Peter in bed, Gregor in the kitchen, reading. She leaned back in her chair. Everything was as it should be. There was somewhere to sit and somewhere to eat. A sense of order had been restored; she had been given back her house.

* * *

Two days later, Peter sat on the window seat in his room and watched the ambulance pull up outside. The door opened and metal steps were let down. The ambulance men climbed inside and appeared a moment later with a bundle on a stretcher.

"That's not Gran, is it?" Peter said. This was not what he had expected. His granny was busy and bustling, not this lump of something under a blanket. Kate pressed her face against the pane and her breath made a wet patch on the glass as the men carried their grandmother into the house.

"She's ill, that's all," she said, giving her brother a quick hug.

The front door opened and something terrible came in. It hung the hallway, drifted like dust up the stairs.

"I want Mummy," Peter wailed.

"You can't. She's busy."

"I want her." Peter slid off the seat. Running to his bed, he rummaged under the pillow and drew out a scrap of blanket, grey and battered with use. Holding it tightly, he pressed it hard against his cheek.

On the other side of the door the house had changed. There were monsters in the corridors and demons on the turn of the stairs. What had been safe was full of danger. Nothing was certain. The very fabric of the house was wavering and to avoid falling into the abyss every footstep had to be watched, every move calculated.

"Mummy," he said again.

The door to the front room opened and shut; there were footsteps and voices in the hall. Then silence.

"Okay." Kate held out her hand. Curling his fingers around hers made him feel stronger, and he tightened his grip as they went downstairs together.

"One, two, three, four." Counting the steps held the fear at bay, but as they came to the half-landing, that mysterious place where the light from upstairs disappeared and the light from downstairs did not quite reach, he closed his eyes. He moved cautiously, his feet feeling for the next step, waiting for the darkness to claim him. His legs felt wobbly and his tummy was full of water.

"There's nothing to be scared of," Kate said, though there were no words to describe what was happening. "It's all right." Startled, he opened his eyes. He saw his feet in their brown checked slippers on the faded blue and red pattern of the stair carpet and the drizzle of light that fell on the hall floor. "See, it's the same as it was," Kate said.

Peter sucked at his thumb. His sister was right. The hall looked as it always did and whatever it was that waited there was not for him.

His grandmother sat up in the makeshift bedroom. Her face was all scrumpled. One side of it looked like Gran, the other like a goblin, or a piece of root he had once found.

"Did the wind change?" he asked. Hannah shot him a look. Kate choked back a giggle but Mimi's mouth curled into a smile and she held out an arm.

"My clever little darling, come and give your granny a kiss." A dribble of spittle leaked from the slack side of her mouth. Kate flinched and moved away. Peter stared at Mimi. His granny was half the same as she had always been. Climbing up on the bed he kissed his grandmother's cheek and reached up to touch the flaccid skin on the other side of her face.

I should have prepared him. The colour rose to Hannah's cheek. She was embarrassed for her mother and cross with herself for not having protected Mimi from the child's curiosity. She started forward to pull him away but Mimi appeared unaffected by her grandson's scrutiny. Eyes half-shut, she leaned against the pillows, her hand stroking the child's hair, and murmured, "My golden boy, my little one."

* * *

Mimi had sat like that in the old basket-chair in the garden in Lvov; Hannah's brother Jan sprawling over their mother's lap, his thumb in his mouth, his fingers curled in his hair; Hannah watching them from the swing, her hands tight on the ropes. The sun was on Jan's hair, bathing it in light, outlining mother and son in a golden halo: a Madonna and child, luminous with love. While Hannah had sat alone, outside the circle of their intimacy.

* * *

On a dark afternoon two days before Christmas, Princess Marianna came to call. Arms full of presents she swept into the house, filling the hall with her perfume. Kate refused to come down, but Peter raced down the stairs and threw himself at the visitor, burying his face deep in her coat, his hand surreptitiously stroking the fur as he breathed in the feral scent of sable.

Hannah was embraced, warmly kissed on both cheeks, then held at arms' length. As Marianna looked her over, Hannah was the first to drop her glance. She sensed the Princess's concern and her understanding of how difficult it must be to look after Mimi, but she shied away from her sympathy and hurried Marianna into the front room.

The curtains had been drawn and in the gentle light of the bedside lamp Mimi's face was soft and pale. Her dark hair, only faintly streaked with grey, made her look both younger and rather frail. Marianna glanced at the icon above the bed and hurriedly crossed herself.

"I'm not dead yet." Mimi's tone was acid. "She prays for me. She smooths my path to heaven." Mimi jerked her head towards Hannah, who feeling herself diminished, her efforts mocked, flushed with misery and stood awkwardly in the doorway until Peter slipped his hand into hers and she led him into the kitchen to make tea.

"You mustn't mind her," Marianna said later. "She's always had a sharp tongue."

Which she mostly reserves for me. Why is it I can never please her?

"You're a very good daughter to her." Marianna appeared to have read her mind.

"I do what I can." In spite of the reassurance Hannah felt graceless, embarrassed.

Glancing surreptitiously at the kitchen clock she realised that it was nearly time for Gregor to come home and she had not begun to prepare supper. His food would not be ready, his routine upset. He would be irritable and snappy and it would take all her skill and energy to placate him. She could not ask her guest to leave, but why was the Princess so oblivious of the time? Why did she not realise that families must be fed? That there were other things to be done besides chatting and drinking tea?

It was up to Hannah to resolve situation. But how? Could she get up and start peeling potatoes, or should she ask Marianna if she would like to stay for supper, and if she did was there enough food? If her visitor joined them would Gregor be pleased or annoyed? Unable to decide, she twisted her hands in her lap.

Her husband's key was in the lock, his footsteps coming down the hall. Already it was too late.

"Princess!"

"Gregor." Marianna rose to her feet in one flowing movement and opened her arms in a wide embrace. He took her hand and, clicking his heels, raised it to his lips.

"You look well." Her voice was low and husky.

His shoulders straightened, he smiled. Hannah took the teapot from the dresser. "No. Not tea. Vodka," her husband decreed.

"Gregor, I can't impose."

"It is no imposition. How often do we have the pleasure of your company?"

"In that case, how can I resist?"

He brought the bottle from the sideboard in the dining room and set out glasses on a tray.

"*Na zdrowie!*"

He and Marianna drank from the cut-glass tumblers Hannah had found in a junk shop while she, sitting at the edge of their conversation, poured herself a cup of tea and listened out in case Mimi should call.

* * *

Kate, coming down in search of a biscuit, stood in the doorway and watched. Marianna, her elbows on the table, chin cupped in hand, was listening intently to her father. She had never seen him like this, his voice rich, his tone animated. He said something and the Princess laughed, a deep seductive laugh, then shook her head, and her hands, heavy with amber and silver, fluttered like birds as she disputed the point.

"No," he protested. "You mistake my meaning."

"I am only a silly old woman then," she teased, tapping him lightly on the cheek.

Kate glanced across to where Hannah sat and for the first time saw her not as her warm and comforting mother, but as a rather dowdy middle-aged woman, heavy and lumpen, apron stretched over her stomach, eyes half-closed. How could she look so stupid and slow? No wonder her father never treated her like this. She was large and flabby. The Princess, who was as old as her grandmother, had more allure. She could not bear to be in the same room as them.

* * *

"I hate my mother," she said to her cold attic and waited breathlessly for divine retribution. When it did not come she switched on the light and went over to the mirror. She painted her lips a pale pink then, poking out her tongue in concentration, swept a smooth line of black over the edge of her eyelids. Pleased with the effect she went to ring Annie. It was cold in the hall, the tiles throwing off a numbing chill, but the doors to the other rooms were shut and she could be guaranteed some privacy.

"Mothers," she sighed into the receiver.

"Tell me about it," Annie agreed.

Kate sat down on the bottom step. She tore open the wrapper of a Mars bar and settled in for a long talk.

CHAPTER FOUR

The lilac tree in the back garden was heavy with blossom. Hannah leaned across the sink and opened the window to let the heady scent drift into the kitchen. She looked beyond the clutter of dishes piled on the draining board to the bright blue sky, and for a moment she was a child again on a perfect summer morning in Lvov – bees buzzing in the honeysuckle, the sun hot on her back, as she shut her eyes and swung lazily on the swing her father had made for her...

It was the cat threading around her ankles, purring and butting insistently that brought her back to the present.

"Wait, I'll feed you in a minute." She moved her leg to forestall a nip but instead of its usual reminder the cat sunk on its haunches, a warning growl rumbling in its throat, the fur rising on its back as the cry echoed around the room.

The plate slipped from Hannah's fingers splashing her arms with hot soapy water as the baby's cry grew louder, more insistent, then faded into nothing.

"You heard it too." Hannah knelt beside the creature, her hands trembling only slightly less than the cat's ample frame. "It's all right, puss. It's gone now." The cat's tail moved slowly backwards and forwards, its ears straightened and getting up, it leaned trustingly against Hannah's side.

"Are you and I the only ones that hear it?" Hannah got up and opening a tin of cat food scooped succulent lumps of meat and jelly onto a clean plate. "No one else has mentioned it and they complain enough about Mimi."

"*Hannushia!*" A long drawn out wail came from the front room.

"You see," Hannah addressed the cat, "now that is real." Unremitting, insistent, the cry came again. Hannah sighed and wiped her hands on her apron. "I suppose I had better go and see what she wants." The cat chewed noisily. "It's probably nothing but..." The animal turned its yellow eyes on her. "All right, I know you don't like being watched while you eat. I'm going. I'll leave you in peace."

Mimi lay with her mouth open, snoring. Another fruitless summons, another meaningless call. How many times must she come running only to find her mother asleep, or having completely forgotten what she wanted? All seemed well but her arms lying on top of the covers looked cold. Hannah rearranged the blankets, checked that the water glass was full and straightened the icon. Then moved by a sudden impulse, she bent and kissed her mother's forehead, tracing on it the sign of the cross in the same way as she did to her own children before they slept.

* * *

In the slipstream of memory Mimi looks up at drifts of white muslin that hang above her crib. Her sheets are cold and she cries for the comfort of a warm breast. No one comes. Her mother, milk dribbling through her bodice, travels through Austria-Hungary, bullets strapped to her thighs. A terrorist fighting for a free Poland.

Mimi's father huddles beside the stove, his ears closed against his daughter's wails. Hunger gripes her stomach. Knees curled, red-faced and desperate, she starts to scream. A large hand slips beneath her rigid body and she is lifted up. Opening her eyes she sees a round face, forehead creased with anxiety, brown eyes concerned, thick moustaches tickling her cheek as he murmurs her name. "Mimi, come to Uncle Alexei. There, there." He holds her close. She breathes in his scent of cologne and tobacco, nestles against the roughness of his coat, her lips moving until they find his finger. He strokes her head, he hums a lullaby; she sucks and sleeps.

* * *

Cradled in a nest of blankets, Mimi drifted further towards consciousness. Part of her body stretched, luxuriating in the soft warmth of the bed; part lay solid and inert and she struggled to remember why this should be. Then a more pressing need struck. Her bladder was full and taut. She had to get to the commode. Attempting to sit up, to put her feet on the floor, she grasped the side table.

* * *

As her memory slips and slides she pulls herself up onto a different carpet. Her boots sink into the thick pile and she will leave footprints when she moves. Uncle Alexei has his hands around her waist. She knows what is to come and her heart flutters with fear and excitement. He is lifting her up, swinging her high, high above his head. She sees his brown eyes dancing, his moustache, touched with grey, trembling above his laughing mouth.

"See if you can touch it, Mimi," he says, and she stretches out her hand obediently. "Higher, higher," he calls, delighted, and she arches her body and strains towards the shimmering chandelier. Her petticoats rustle; she hears the voices of the shop assistants and grows hot at the thought that they might catch sight of her drawers. She wants to tell him to put her down, to feel the soft solidity of the ground beneath her feet, but this is the game she plays when she comes to see Uncle Alexei, and if she wants her bon-bons, those delicious sugar-coated sweets he carries in his pocket just for her, she must let him toss her into the air and call her his little princess. The ceiling swirls above her, light catches, colours tremble. She feels herself falling, falling.

* * *

The table crashed to the floor and Hannah came running. Mimi lay on the rug, her face contorted, nightdress around her waist, a pool of urine spreading out beneath her.

* * *

Hard hands hold her, lift her, pull at her arms and legs as if she cannot straighten them herself, and when she cries in protest no one listens. Mimi closes her eyes, sticks out her lip, and takes herself back to the nursery where she lays on her narrow white bed under the thick goose-down quilt, while the snow drifts softly onto the roofs of Warsaw.

* * *

Hannah stretched a clean sheet over the bed. She rolled Mimi to one side, slipped a towel under her and began to wash her mother's body. The flesh was mottled, the legs thin, laced with blue veins, the breasts flaccid, the stomach hanging loose over sparse grey hairs and stringy thighs. Less than a year ago she had never seen her mother undressed. Even in the most terrible circumstances Mimi had maintained her modesty. Now her daughter was performing the most intimate tasks for her. Hannah squeezed out the sponge; she took a clean towel and patted Mimi dry, careful of the folds of skin, the crevices where sores might start.

Mimi cried out petulantly. She twisted her head from side to side, groaned, bunched her fist and hit the bed. Hannah worked calmly and skilfully as if the woman on the bed was no longer her mother but a patient to whose needs she must attend.

Mimi opened her eyes and looked at her daughter. "I took care of you in Kazakhstan," she said. "It was hard. We were without your father." The moment of lucidity passed and a meaningless inhuman cry issued from some primeval section of her brain. Only when Hannah placed her hand on her mother's forehead did it cease.

When Mimi was calm again, Hannah drew the blankets around her, straightened the covers and switched on the lamp. The room smelled of Dettol and soap. She would call the doctor but he would simply confirm what she already knew. There had been another stroke. Mimi had moved further into the shadows.

When Gregor came home that evening she did not have to tell him that things had changed.

"She's worse, isn't she," he said. It was a statement, not a question.

Hannah nodded and pouring her husband a cup of tea said quickly, "The doctor said I was taking very good care of her."

"You have always been a good daughter."

Hannah bent her head in acknowledgement then, unable to stop them, the words began tumbling from her mouth. "Nursing is something I am good at and I was thinking that when she dies maybe I could go back. I could take some more exams and perhaps even get to be a theatre sister again and—" She hesitated as she attempted to get her arguments in order.

Gregor gave her his full attention. "There is no need," he said kindly, stretching out his hand to cover hers. "I earn enough. There will be a pay rise for all of us next year. It has been agreed. And we have the house." He finished with that edge that came into his voice when he had to speak of it. His hand was heavy, trapping her fingers. Hannah sat very still, fighting the impulse to free herself from his grasp. "So you see, my darling, there is no need for you to work." He lifted her hand to his lips and kissed it. "Just carry on doing what you are so good at."

"And that is?" Hannah asked submissively, while the demons shrieked inside her head, fighting and clawing to be released.

"I am surprised you have to ask. You look after us all. We come home to find our tea on the table, a warm kitchen and someone to listen to us. What more could we want? What more could you want?"

He was right, Hannah thought. Her family was the most important thing in her life. If any of them were unhappy, or in pain, so was she. She wanted nothing but the best for them.

And what about you? the demon demanded and her stomach lurched as she saw that to give everything to her husband and children was to leave herself bankrupt.

"The children are doing well. Peter is happy and settled at school. Kate will go to university in October. We are so much more fortunate than other immigrant families."

"Yes." Hannah had to agree. "We are."

"So no more silly talk about going out to work. There's a good girl. Yes?"

A half-formed protest rose in her throat but she nodded and glanced quickly at the teapot. He smiled and released her. She picked up the pot and her hand shook as she poured herself a cup.

* * *

Kate sprawled on her bed, the blankets soft beneath her hard breasts. She curled one leg and stretched out the other. Her body felt both languid and alert. She raised her arms and flexed her spine, letting the half-open copy of *Howards End* slide to the floor. There was so much to be experienced, to be lived, but she was trapped in this attic, imprisoned by her parents' expectations. What she longed for was to be rescued like a story-book princess in a tower.

He would be tall and dark, his body hard, and his kisses would burn like fire. There would be a mysterious past, a hidden sorrow, or maybe a talent that elevated him above the common run.

Her eyes strayed to the poster that hung on the slope of the ceiling above her bed. She had seen The Rolling Stones when they came to the Hippodrome; had sat on the edge of her seat and screamed until her throat was raw. The lead singer had the face of the Devil, the body of a snake. If he had touched her she'd have died.

There was a light tap on the door and Peter, his face screwed up in concentration, entered, carrying a glass of lemon and water.

"I brought you this. Mummy said you were working."

"I am. I'm preparing for very important exams. They will affect the whole of my life." She took the glass and sipped the bitter liquid.

"It looks horrid," Peter offered.

"It'll make me slim."

"*Agh!*" The howl reverberated through the house, rising ghostlike to the attic.

"Gran," Peter said.

Kate shrugged. "Why can't she shut up?"

"She's ill," her brother, framed by nature to think the best of everyone, protested.

"Yeah, well." Kate picked up her book. Peter lingered by the door but she ignored him.

* * *

"Mama," Hannah stood in the doorway. "Are you all right?"

Mimi moaned, quieter now, the cries subsiding into whimpers, dying away into sleep. In the kitchen, onions blackened in the pan.

In that mix of dream and memory that was Mimi's reality, the hay wagon sways gently from side to side. The reapers look up and wave at the young ladies. Mimi blushes, then waves back, delighted. On Aunt Irena's estate there is no distinction between Mimi, the poor relation, and Marianna, Princess Helena's daughter. The sun is hot on her face; her sunbonnet lies at her side. Her feet are bare, stockings tucked neatly inside boots. Marianna leans over and taking a straw tickles her toes. The giggles rise from Mimi's feet, scamper up her legs and into her tummy, which bunches and curls as she laughs and laughs.

The image faded and, as the night drew on, laughter darkened into grief.

* * *

Lying next to Hannah, Gregor turned and nuzzled into her soft warmth, his hand cupped her plump breast, his fingers closing around the nipple. She settled into him, her breathing quickened and she gave a murmur of pleasure.

The sound of Mimi's wails slid through their half-open door. Tensing, Hannah moved away from Gregor but he caught hold of her arm.

"Leave her," he whispered.

"I can't." Her feet were on the floor, the night air drying the thin film of moisture on her skin. "I'll be back in a minute." He grunted and turned his back. "I will," she insisted. His shoulders were set against her, but she bent and kissed his ear before hurrying down the moonlit stairs.

Mimi lay on her back, her limbs spread as if she were sunbathing. Hannah felt her forehead and held her wrist. Mimi's skin was warm, the pulse firm and regular. She lifted the feeding cup to her mother's lips but Mimi slept deeply and there was no response. Hannah slipped her hand under the covers. The sheets were dry; tonight there would be no midnight blanket bath, no bundle of washing steaming in the scullery.

Does she do this on purpose? Hannah wondered as she returned to the bedroom to find Gregor asleep. Climbing in next to him she snuggled up against his back, resting her hand on his thigh, her fingers exploring, but he did not wake.

* * *

The smell of sickness lingered in the house. It underpinned the scent of Camay and disinfectant. Fresh air and clean bedding could not dispel it. The cat took to sleeping in the sunlit garden. Kate doused herself in Chantilly.

Because it was May, the month dedicated to the Virgin Mary, Hannah set up an altar in Mimi's room. Her mother might not be aware of what was going on around her but she would still benefit from the family's prayer.

In front of the icon of Our Lady of Czestochowa she put a vase of lilacs and pair of candles and after supper she, Gregor and the children came to say the Rosary.

"Tonight it will be the Sorrowful Mysteries," Hannah said. "The Agony in the Garden, the Scourging at the Pillar, the Crowning with Thorns, the Carrying of the Cross, the Crucifixion, the Death on the Cross and the Descent into Hell."

"Must we?" Kate muttered.

"We must," her father said and Kate wondered, as she increasingly did, what he really believed. Whatever he thought about God and religion, however, he would never go against her mother's wishes.

Joining her parents, she knelt before the icon. The rug pricked her bare knees. Casting a glance at the window she was relieved to find the curtains drawn. She shut her eyes and laced her fingers tightly together, hot with embarrassment. What would the girls at school think if they could see her in the front room praying with her parents and little brother?

Yet some deep seated part of her was drawn to the tragedy of the Crucifixion. The images of the darkened garden, the sweat of blood breaking through skin white with terror; the half-naked man, thorns pressing deep into his forehead, eyes dark with the knowledge of sin, standing patiently under the lash. Then that last journey, under that terrible burden, step by step up the narrow street, while the crowd jeered and jostled for a better view.

How could she resist the feelings of pity and compassion, the programmed guilt at the sight of the broken body hanging from the cross, black against the vivid sky of Calvary? And then the Descent into Hell. Was this the final despair of God made man? She saw the demons, misshapen creatures, some curled like foetuses, others with goblin faces and talons poised to feed on the battered and bleeding figure of the crucified Christ.

Shaken by the strength of the images she had created, she pressed her fingers against her lips and opened her eyes. This was crazy. There was no way she was drowning in religion, like her mother. From under her lashes she scowled at Hannah, who was praying softly, the rapid Polish rising and falling from her lips. Gregor's responses were slower more measured, while Mimi's mouth twisted in what might be an attempt to form the familiar words.

* * *

Peter was enjoying himself. He knelt very straight and concentrated on the words of the prayers. Soon, when he was seven, he could be an altar boy. He would wear a red cassock with a white surplice and if he were lucky, very, very lucky he might even be allowed to swing the thurifer at Benediction, breathe in the incense and pretend he was in heaven.

CHAPTER FIVE

Another letter had come. Marianna stood beside the marble fireplace in her drawing room, her fingers toying with the unopened envelope, tracing, over and over again, the outline of the card inside. Why could the girl not use writing paper like any normal being? Why this insistence on postcards? The only thing in her favour was that she understood the necessity for keeping her correspondence hidden.

The thought that anyone could read her private mail made the Princess shudder. Her guests would delight in picking over any titbits they could glean, searching out the possibilities of ancient scandals, anything to add colour to the drabness of their lives. This was why they came to her At Homes. Why they flocked to her apartment where, in a house reminiscent of Warsaw's Stare Miasto and its squares of painted houses with their narrow windows and doors, she had recreated something of her past.

Her eyes flickered around the room. The walls were hung with rich oriental rugs, and a fine Turkish carpet covered the floor. On one side of the fireplace stood a pair of high backed chairs, on the other, at right angles to each other, two divans were piled high with embroidered cushions, where like a favoured concubine she liked to rest during the day. In front of them she had placed a pair of inlaid tables, on which she kept the book she was currently reading and rested her writing materials, while she allowed her mind to drift. Sometimes, prompted by the photographs of Hannah and her children, her thoughts turned to the present, but more often they lingered in the past.

In one silver framed image from her childhood, her mother, Princess Helena, sat resplendent in evening dress, the Zapolski emeralds around her neck, her wrists and in her hair. Behind her, in his dress uniform, stood her eldest son Henryk, his hand resting lightly on her shoulder. At her side was Valerian, her favourite child, his expression strained as he forced himself to turn his eyes from his mother and look straight at the camera. Marianna, the youngest, leant against her mother's knees, her dress standing out stiffly from its wide sash, her hair tied back with a large bow.

In view of their history these pictures were like something out of myth and legend. A world that no longer existed and in which it was sometimes hard to believe because it was as insubstantial as the reflection of her drawing room in the gilt framed mirror above the mantelpiece. Behind its silvered surface it was exact in every detail and yet somehow different, so that it was possible to imagine that if you glanced quickly, catching it unawares, you would glimpse the life in that other room that was so like your own. It was where the ghosts lived behind the door that opened into the unseen house.

And there they must stay. Marianna's fingers tightened on the envelope. She was tempted to crush the offending missive but if she did, what then? More letters and phone calls? If only she could find a way of putting an end to it all.

In the past it would have been easy. A word in the right ear would be all it took. Even now, though she had no influence, she still had status among her fellow exiles, and she was a rich woman. How ironic that she should owe her present wealth to the father she barely knew, and his regard for the British Empire.

Prince Leon Zapolski had spent time in England, had English friends, and joked that, because it was not run by Jews, the Bank of England was the only place in which one should deposit money, and so some of the profits from his vast Russian estates came to London. Tsarist gold and Maria Theresa dollars lay safe in deposit boxes, while empires fell.

After the Great War her widowed mother took to travelling. Half-mad with grief for her dead sons, she haunted the Cote d'Azur, the Italian lakes. She moved so restlessly from place to place, sometimes spending no more than a few days in a rented villa, a few hours in a fashionable hotel, that Marianna put some of the most valuable family jewels in the Bank's vault for safety.

When the Germans invaded Poland in 1939, and Marianna was forced to flee, she was far from destitute. Clever investments by her friend Levi Goldsmidt enabled her to capitalise on what she already had. She used some of her money to help other refugees and some to buy herself this house.

The Luftwaffe had left Bristol's post-war housing in scant supply. A single woman with no dependants was low on the housing list, but she had gold. The landlord wanted to sell but the ground and top floor flats were occupied, as was the basement, and although it had been Marianna's intention to return the house to a single dwelling, as the years passed, she grew fond of her flat. It was her nest, perched halfway up a tree and provided her with everything she needed. Large enough not to feel cramped, there were no empty spaces or echoing, unused rooms. When one set of tenants left she advertised for another and privately found much amusement in the thought that she had become a landlady in her old age.

In the square outside the house, there was a private garden; a wild and unkempt place fenced by iron railings and a gate, to which only residents had a key. This secret and secluded space inspired the short stories she wrote, strange, magical tales like those for which she had once been famous.

One winter's night, when the curtains were drawn and the room glowed in soft lamplight, she had conjured up a dragon that slept outside her windows. Its sinuous body stretched along the balcony, tail looped around the railings, great black head resting on cruel talons, red, blood-hungry eyes closed against the dark. The creature was her past; it both haunted and protected her, leaving its trail throughout her work.

Today, however, the sun shone on its sleeping place. Pools of light fell on the patterns on the carpet and drifts of summer dust hung in the air. The faint hum of distant traffic purred in the background only to be broken by the sound of the doorbell, harsh and insistent. Marianna put the envelope firmly on the mantelpiece, where it stood white and stark amid a crowd of faded calling cards. She would deal with it later. For the present she must attend to her guests, even though she was not in the mood for entertaining. She felt ill at ease as if something scuttled across her soul, scratching and picking at long buried memories. Drawing back her shoulders, she put it from her mind. People were arriving and it was time to do her duty.

The samovar, surrounded by thin glasses held in silver filigree, steamed gently on a side table. Around it, pale slices of lemon lay on a white dish. On another table were plates heaped with salted biscuits topped with cream cheese and shavings of smoked salmon, thinly cut slices of rye bread, with overlapping layers of sausage, gherkin and tomato. A little distance from the savouries were plates of *mazurkas* and *faworki,* and on a sliver cake stand the Princess Zapolska's famous cheese cake, plump, rum-soaked raisins embedded in a deep layer of baked cream and curd cheese, crowned with whirls of cream and slivers of chocolate.

The doorbell rang again, less stridently this time, as if the guest, having been made to wait, had become uncertain of their welcome. Marianna clicked her tongue impatiently. *Servants these days.* The thought scurried across her mind and she laughed at herself; her low throaty chuckle filled the room. There were no servants, only Basia Helminska, her ground floor tenant, who for a reduction of her rent performed the duties of a concierge. Basia was old, almost as old as she was, had a bad back and could only move slowly; hence the delay between the ringing of the bell and the answering of the door. Something that Boleslaw Grodeszki consistently failed to remember. It would be him; he was always the first to arrive. Marianna drew in her breath, expelling it with a short dismissive sound that was part irritation, part sorrow.

In the mirror her reflection showed a tall woman in black silk, amber in her ears, around her wrists and on her fingers, a flame coloured scarf around her neck. Hastily adjusting her expression, she smiled in welcome as a plump little man came fussily into the room.

"My dear Boleslaw. How delightful."

"Princess." He bent and kissed her hand, his bald head

shining from the exertion of having climbed a flight of stairs.

I had an English lover once, she thought irrelevantly. *A journalist with thick dark hair. In 1939 we lay in bed and listened to the radio, waiting to see if England would honour the promises she had made to come to Poland's aid.*

"Such a magnificent spread." Boleslaw's eager eyes swivelled around the room. "You do us proud."

"Please," Marianna waved her hand, "help yourself."

"No, no. I couldn't possibly, not before the other guests arrive," he stuttered, his lips wet, his hands shaking in anticipation of that moment when he could scoop a prized titbit onto his plate.

He is old and hungry. Like so many of her guests, who could no longer afford the delicacies that reminded them of home, he came as much for the food as for the company.

Professor Nowaczek, grey and spectral, how did he exist between her Tuesdays? Mrs Pawolska, round as a butter tub, would never starve, nor would the Countess Julia. Her son had a job on the docks and her daughter-in-law fed them well. Count Malinowski had his army pension, and so did Major Wojcik and General Gaworski. Generals, majors, colonels. Were all her guests such high ranking officers?

Mimi, who had served in the army and had an unerring instinct for the sham, had turned her nose up at most of them. "Parvenus, jumped up adventurers taking advantage of your ignorance and naiveté. For goodness sake Marianna, why do you take them all at face value? They are here because they want to boast of your acquaintance, not because they are the sort of people you ought to know."

"What sort of people should I know?" Marianna had asked laughing.

"Our own class, of course," Mimi had replied with vinegar in her voice. "It is difficult enough in this God forsaken country without you allowing the hoi polloi in through your doors."

Marianna missed her terribly, her little cousin sitting in a dark cloud of disapproval, deigning to talk only to those visitors she deemed "one of us."

To the General she had been charming. Her face alight, her

hands moving as she talked of times in Africa and Italy, of people they had known and of those they had lost. Her head would lower, her voice drop; the General called her his Lady of Sorrows and those around her had to acknowledge her suffering.

Reminded by Countess Julia of the loss of Mimi's son, something Mimi herself would never mention, Mrs Pawolska would gulp back tears, and taking out a tiny lace-edged handkerchief dab at her eyes, forgiving Mimi for the disdain with which she treated her.

They all knew their place, Marianna thought. Even those who pretended to a higher strata of society were aware of where they really belonged, knowing that if this was indeed the Zapolski Palace, that exquisite honey-coloured house hidden behind high walls, they would never pass through the gates.

Exiled in England, they were busy reinventing their lives. In Warsaw before the War she would have known none of them, but here, drawn by her glamour and the wealth and ease of her house, she was the focus of their expatriate society. For some of them, this was the only place, apart from the public library, where they could get warm in the winter. For many, her At Homes were the high spot of their month. At the Polish delicatessen she had heard Mrs Pawolska confiding, "When I was at the Princess Zapolska's last week, it was very select. Only a few of us were invited."

That fat woman, as Mimi called her, sat on one of the overstuffed chairs, her buttocks spread comfortably, her tiny feet in their fashionable shoes pressed tightly together, as she delicately speared the food piled high on her plate. Beside her, Boleslaw Grodeczki balanced his plate on the back of Mrs Pawolska's chair and kept a constant eye on what she was eating. The moment she had cleared a space he was at the table for more supplies; his apparent concern for his fellow guest enabling him to help himself as often as he wanted.

"Delicious." Plump white fingers lifted cake to lips glistening with butter. "Of course, at home in my grand-mother's house we used lemon not chocolate as a topping."

"These things vary from family to family and from one

region to another," Boleslaw agreed. "In Lvov, for example, we ate our *pirogi* stuffed with cherries. However, the Princess tells me that in Warsaw the filling would be blueberries."

"Mrs Bernadinska would, of course, agree with you. She claims that her version is the more authentic." Mrs Pawolska was eager to claim acquaintance with Mimi.

"Ah, Mrs Bernadinska! How is the dear lady? So sad, so very sad," sighed the General.

"Not expected to live." Mrs Pawolska's bovine eyes filled with easy tears. The General moved hastily away, his hand trembling as he pulled the stopper from his hip flask.

The sun moved over the houses. Silhouettes of stooped figures appeared on the walls and, as the light retreated from the room, the shadow puppets played out their last act.

"Do you know, Slava," Countess Julia leaned closer to her friend, "when Vera's husband died they found it was all in the hands of the Jews. Every last penny."

"Nothing for the family?" Slava said, aghast.

"Nothing. So, what do you think she did then?"

Slava's face creased with the effort of searching her memory.

"She went on the streets." The Countess could not wait to deliver her dramatic pronouncement. Her listener gasped and she hastened to soften the blow. "Metaphorically, of course. She did not stand on the corner. She was kept; a mistress to some industrialist. I think he may even have been a Jew."

Marianna's fingers tightened in disgust on the handle of her glass. *Why do I do this? Why do I give house room to these people? They re-tell old scandals, re-fight old battles. Nothing changes, nothing tempers their prejudices or alters the way they think. I could write their conversations for them, so well do I know what they will say. Yet month after month I open my doors and let them in to my home. It must be something in the blood, some vestige of feudal obligation. Perhaps in a curious way they are necessary to me. My grandfather may have freed his serfs, but still my father's servants kissed his hand, knelt before him and called him master.*

She looked around the room at the frail old men bending gallantly over the fragile old women and listened to the rise and fall of a language which was already becoming archaic.

The court of the Princess Zapolska. She stifled the laughter rising in her throat. *If I were a wicked fairy I would turn them all into toads.* She glanced at the clock on the mantelpiece and her fingers itched to close around the shaft of her pen and note down her latest observations.

Her visitors left as slowly as they had arrived, following an intricate ritual of farewell. The clicking of heels and kissing of hands. Marianna's long fingers brushing gnarled knuckles while she averted her eyes from Boleslaw's bald head, or the dandruff speckled collar of Count Malinowski's coat.

After the men came the women, with their dusty cheeks, spidery hands, little sighs and soft bird-like kisses. Their fragility drained her; even Mrs Pawolska was somehow insubstantial, as if she were a caricature of the solid practical woman who had carved out a life for herself in a foreign country.

I need young people, Marianna thought when the last of them had gone. *I need their energy or I too will slip into this half-life.*

The remains of the sunlight drained from the room. In the dimming light the envelope on the mantelpiece stood out, demanding her attention. If only it were winter. How easy it would be to catch the letter with her sleeve, to sweep her shawl over her shoulder and watch as the paper fluttered into the flames, but the grate was empty; there could be no accident, only the deliberate tearing and scattering of pieces, to be followed by yet another phone call, yet another letter. On the table beside her divan lay an ivory letter-knife. Sliding the point under the flap, she ripped open the envelope, drew out the contents and read,

Dear Princess Zapolska,

Following our telephone communication of last week. I suggest that I come to your flat on Friday next. Hoping this is all right with you,

Yours sincerely,
Nicky Dawes (Miss).

CHAPTER SIX

Trapped under the sloping roof of the attic the early summer heat pressed down on the house. Slippery in its grip, Kate's dress clung to her back, her underwear was damp and there was a line of moisture beneath her breasts.

Through the open window came the soporific hum of city traffic. The muted sound of cars and the distant rumble of buses was broken only by the occasional roar of a motor bike.

Saturday night and she had had enough of studying. Pushing aside her books, Kate stood up, flinching as her skin peeled away from the chair. She stretched, yawned and pulling her dress over her head smelled her own hot smell, salty and sweet. Her underwear fell to the floor, the bra curled like a small white creature, the knickers like fallen petals on the rug.

Stepping over them, she smeared deodorant under her arms, wincing at the astringent sting, then swinging her arms through the heavy air as she waited for it to dry. She liked her body. Her breasts were high and firm, her waist small and her hips narrow. Still naked, she sprayed herself liberally with perfume so that the sweet flowery scent of Chantilly filled the room. Sliding her hands under her hair she held it away from her ears, then experimented with scraping it back so that her eyes narrowed into cat like slits. Pleased with the look, she curled and flicked her tongue over her lips.

What she could do with was a drink, something cool and exotic. The lemon juice on her desk was tepid, the ice long since melted. Kate lifted the glass to the light. The liquid was a clear pale yellow, like watered-down pee. Holding it to her lips, she remembered reading that women used to drink their own urine, to clean the blood and protect the complexion. Wondering what it would taste like, whether she would be able to get over the thought of drinking her own waste, she took a sip. The sharpness rasped her throat, and putting down the glass she folded her arms over her chest to check if her armpits were dry.

There were two chests of drawers in her room. On one stood an icon, a vase of dead flowers, and a pile of school books. From one of its drawers Kate took a clean pair of knickers and a bra. She dangled them, one in each hand, considering whether she could go naked under her dress, then ducked, put her head between her legs, sniffed and pulled a face. Straightening up, she stepped into the knickers. The bra she slipped around her waist, did up the hooks, then slid it the right way round over her rib cage.

Crossing over to the other set of drawers, on which stood a regiment of pots, jars and tubes, wands of mascara, lines of lipsticks, eyeliners, powders and tissues, Kate began her make-up. Green eye shadow gave a heavy brooding look. A thick black line at the base of her lashes elongated her eyes, her mouth faded under pale pink lipstick. Her dark hair swung around her white face, her green eyes glowed, pleasingly feline in the gathering dusk.

Satisfied, she raised her arms and rolled her shoulders, letting the heat caress her body, before taking a lime-green linen shift from its hanger and slipping it over her head.

* * *

Gregor was in the kitchen. The door to the back garden had been left open but there was no movement in the air. The cat lay, huge and orange, on the windowsill basking in the last of the evening sun. A faint moaning came from the front room. This he ignored, indeed he scarcely noticed, for the sound no longer seemed to come from a human throat but rather, if he were honest with himself, it was as if an alien being had invaded his home, making its lair in the front room and staking its claim over his wife. Day and night she was at its beck and call, leaving him without her love or company.

Right now Hannah was upstairs putting Peter to bed. Soon she would come down, make a pot of tea, and they would sit and talk over the events of their week until it was time for bed.

He turned to the newspaper's sports page; his eyes skimmed the photographs, glanced over the text. He could not concentrate, his attention was elsewhere, his ears primed for the sound of her feet on the stairs. The top step creaked. He closed the paper and leaned back in his chair.

The footsteps quickened; there was a clatter of heels on the hall tiles. Disappointed, Gregor braced himself. The door was flung open and Kate appeared in the doorway. Her skimpy dress reached halfway up her thighs, her eyes were bruised, and her mouth looked as if the blood had been drained from it.

"Dad." Her tone was hostile, accusatory. "Where's Mum?"

"Seeing to your brother." His skin crawled with irritation, masking a deeper anger. How could she make such a travesty of herself? How could his lovely intelligent daughter look so common, so like the girls who hung around the factory gates shouting out their comments and screeching with laughter at some obscenity as they waited for their boyfriends? Where was her breeding? Her pride?

"I'm going out," she said, belligerently. Gregor looked at her, appalled. Her dress scarcely covered her body and she was threatening to go out into the street where anyone could see her. "I've done my homework. I've been revising all afternoon. Mum said I could. You ask her," she shot at him.

Gregor swallowed his anger. His shoulders fell in defeat. Had it once been possible to talk to this child of his, or had she always been so ready to take offence? He could not remember. All he had was a memory, as dim as a faded photograph, of a small girl in a flowery dress sitting on his knee in a meadow full of long grass.

"Where are you going?" he asked mildly. Her eyes narrowed. She summed up the situation and her mood changed.

"To the Stations of the Cross," she said, and grinned. He smiled back, delighted by her teasing.

"Really?"

"Really."

"Dressed like that?" Somehow he managed to keep his voice light.

"Youth club." She shrugged.

"Don't be late home. Remember, you have your A Levels in a couple of weeks."

Her face clouded, then she decided to give him credit for his concern. "Okay."

"Don't use that expression."

"Okay, Dad." She blew a cheeky kiss and was gone. The front door slammed, shaking the house and drowning Hannah's soft footsteps.

"Has Kate gone out?" his wife asked, filling the kettle, the cold water drumming against its steel sides.

"She's gone to the youth club," he said, absurdly pleased to be able to tell Hannah something she did not know about their daughter.

"At the church?"

"I suppose so. Where else?"

She smiled. "That's all right then. She can't come to any harm."

He sighed. "That girl is impossible. A Levels coming up and she is gallivanting about."

"Impossible, indeed." Hannah was laughing gently at him. "And you so proud of her."

"She's a clever girl; got a good head on her shoulders. She must not let her academic ability go to waste. A university degree is the way to get on in this country. She must make the most of her chances." He began to fret.

"She will," Hannah soothed. "You worry too much about her. As you said, she is an intelligent girl. She knows what is important in life."

Setting the cups on the table her hand brushed his fingers. He touched her arm and a current of need and desire flowed between them. He slid his arm around her waist and she leaned against him. A fly buzzed; the cat stretched and yawned; and they sat together in the darkening room, letting the peace of the evening settle around them.

* * *

Kate stalked down the hill in her high heels. At the bottom she paused, turning her head one way then another, breathing in the thick smell of petrol fumes, hot pavements and melting tar, as she waited, muscles tensed, for a break in the traffic. Cars flowed past heading for the night clubs, restaurants and bars of Broadmead. Buses trundled towards the other side of the city. Beyond the hospital, the traffic lights changed to red and she dodged through the line of stationary cars. A gang of lads leaned out of a Triumph Vitesse, whistling and calling to her. She thrust out her breasts and tossed back her hair, but when the driver said, "Want a lift?" She shook her head and strolled disdainfully to the other side of the road.

The evening sun slanted across the velvet lawns of the alms houses. Beyond them lay what remained of the oldest part of the city. Ancient half-timbered houses clung crazily to the steep incline of the Christmas Steps creating a dark and narrow alleyway. Overhung by the buildings, the windows of the shops were dimly lit by flickering light bulbs, as if to hide rather than reveal what they had for sale. In spite of her shoes Kate moved silently past shuttered junk shops and second-hand book sellers down towards the pool of darkness at the bottom of the Steps.

The doors of the pub were open and men stood smoking and drinking outside. Two girls, bleached hair backcombed, wearing short leather skirts and ankle chains above white stilettos, teetered around the corner, arms around each other's waists, screeching with laughter as they passed through a barrage of lewd comments and were sucked into to the beer laden atmosphere of The White Hart.

Taking advantage of the banter to hurry past, Kate turned right into a narrow street. Beyond it lay the brightness of the Centre with its clubs and coffee bars. On one side was the church and youth club while in front of her were the bright green lawns and garish flower beds of the municipal gardens, where parked at the kerbside was a pride of gleaming, throbbing bikes; many of their riders lounging nonchalantly beside their machines, helmets slung over leather clad arms, cigarettes dangling from their lips.

She walked across the road towards them, hips swaying, eyes fixed on a point somewhere in front of her, head held high, feigning indifference, while every nerve was conscious of their hot eyes.

"Kate." Dave sat astride his bike, his hands resting lightly on the Triton's handlebars and his voice had the long lazy drawl of the local accent.

"Dave. Hi," she said carelessly, as she considered her options. Should she go for the safety of the youth club with its boring grammar school boys, or this? There was no comparison. The scent of leather, oil and cigarettes drew her. She was not like the usual biker girls and this gave her power. She came closer. She came closer.

"Wanna a ride?"

She shrugged. "Maybe."

"Please yourself."

Do you really mean that? Kate thought. *Do you really want me to please myself?* Hips tilted forwards, she pressed the tops of her legs together, relishing the feel of her skin as she looked at him. Dave leaned back on his saddle and she was aware of his growing interest, but neither of them was prepared to make the first move. Finally, Kate smiled her cat smile.

"Were goin' for a spin," Dave said and Kate did not contradict him. It pleased her, for the moment, to be treated as he would any of his other women. All the more so because it was her decision, not, as he thought, his.

He dismounted and handed her his helmet. She felt the other bikers watching her as she fastened the strap. Then Dave slung his leg over the bike, a booted foot pressed down hard on the kick-start and the engine belched. Kate hitched up her dress, the material tight against the top of her legs as she got on behind him. Her arms snaked around his waist and she leaned into the hardness of his muscled body.

They swept around the Centre, accelerated up Park Street and raced around the Victoria Rooms. Her body fused into his, bending, straightening, moving together. The air was cool on her bare skin, while sweat trickled between her breasts as she pressed herself against him. The bike pulsed beneath her legs; her thighs tight against his. She grew warm and moist, held on the brink of pleasure. Unable to bear any more she closed her eyes. She was riding, riding, faster and faster. She was hot, she was frantic, she was...

The bike stopped. Cheated, she slumped against him and opened her eyes. They had reached the toll booth on the Suspension Bridge. He unzipped a pocket and took out a handful of coins. "We're goin' out in the country," he muttered.

She scowled but with his back to her he could not see the expression on her face. It did not occur to him that she might disagree. His understanding was that, having got onto his bike, she had given herself up to him and must go where he wanted.

Kate looked down at the wedding cake terraces of Clifton, their golden stone touched by the sun; saw the thin grey ribbon of the river below; the tiny cars racing along the Portway. On the other side, woods coated the jagged rock face of the Gorge. She was about to leave the familiar safety of the city and leaning her check against Dave's back she let his scent of roll-ups and leather stifle her doubts as they rode out onto the bridge

What if he came from the rough side of town and had left school at fifteen? Did it matter if they had nothing to talk about? If their families had nothing in common? Her parents would die if they knew where she was, but she wanted more out of life than a few exam results. Riding a powerful bike was almost like flying. Kate threw back her head and breathed in the summer evening. Above her a seagull rode the air currents, then wheeled and flew down river towards the sea.

The road was narrow and hemmed in by tall hedges. It twisted through the bleached countryside to distant villages, where a circle of ancient stones stood in the gathering twilight. Freed from the restraint of city streets, Dave put the bike through its paces, leaning low in the saddle, swerving round corners, riding in the middle of the road. Kate held on to him, her body moving with his, as they became one with the machine.

Branches curved above them, the lane dipped, shut off the light from the setting sun and the pale ghost of a moon appeared above the lattice of leaves. The bike slowed. Kate's muscles strained as her legs clung to the metal sides. Her arms ached. The day's heat rose from the sleeping earth and they turned off the road and bounced and jolted down a narrow track. An owl swooped low and rabbits scurried out of their way. Dave killed the engine and parked the bike at the end of the lane. A tangle of trees surrounded them. Gnarled roots snaked away from their trunks with tall grass growing between them.

Kate's limbs were stiff, her hair knotted, her skin salty. Her heels sunk into the soft ground as Dave took her hand and pulled her into the cover of the wood.

Angrily, she jerked free. He shrugged, took a packet of Woodbines out his pocket and lit one.

"Smoke?" He held out his cigarette and Kate shook her head. However hard she tried she could not bring herself to like the taste of tobacco. "Please yourself." A long stream of smoke writhed up into the branches.

God, she thought, *what the bloody hell am I doing here?* The forbidden words made her feel better. "Bloody hell," she said aloud.

"There's no need for that." She knew she had offended him. In his world, girls like her were not supposed to swear. They lived in posh houses, went to convent schools and spent Sundays in church, all of which made them an unknown entity, and all the more desirable. To have one as a girlfriend enhanced his status in the gang.

Dave dropped his cigarette and ground it out beneath his boot, reached out and seized her arm. She glared at his hand, the fingernails lined with grease, the line of dark hairs running from the wrist to the knuckles. It was disgusting and at the same time strong and powerful. She shivered and he pulled her close, reeling her in like a fish on a line. He was so much taller than her that she barely reached his shoulder. Swinging his arm around her he clamped her to his side. His hand rested on her breast. She smelled his sweat, the sickly sweet reek of tobacco on his breath. He bent his head and his lips, hot and wet, met hers.

She prepared to resist, still angry at the way he had dragged her off into the bushes. Holding herself stiffly she kept her mouth shut. His first kiss was gentle, surprising her. His hands were tender, holding her delicately, as if she might break and she melted towards him, turning her face to his. He kissed her again, his tongue exploring, probing, until her lips parted and she tasted him. Her arms rose around his neck pulling him closer; his kisses grew hotter more urgent, demanding.

She could feel him hard against her. Her legs parted; his breath coming faster now and faster. His hand was under her skirt. His fingers heavy on her thigh, she felt herself open to him.

"Take them off," his voice was hoarse in her ear. She shook her head, but his hand was on the elastic. "Now." He tugged. Her knickers slid down her legs. His fingers dug into her flesh. "Lie down." He pushed her onto a pile of dry leaves. She kicked herself free of her underwear. He lay down beside her. She heard him fumble with his zip. "Give 'im a feel." Her hand came towards him, her fingers grasped, then shrank back.

"No."

"Yes." He thrust at her palm. He was hard and smooth. His finger was inside her; her skirt was around her waist. He loomed above her.

"Open your legs." Eyes closed, he lowered himself onto her, his weight pinning her to the ground. The harsh dryness of the leaves pricked her back.

"No. We mustn't."

"I've got something," his voice slurred, his hand searched his pocket.

"No."

"I won't hurt you."

"I can't," she murmured as her body loosened and her hips rose to meet him.

He was nuzzling her neck. One hand under her dress, pressing her breast, sending shivers of pleasure down between her legs. She wanted him. She needed him. What did it matter if they were not in love? If nothing had been promised? What did anything but this moment matter?

Take me. Don't wait. Don't listen. Give me what I want. Please. She was desperate to absolve herself of responsibility as the fear stormed into her brain. The searing flames of hell. The total despair of utter damnation.

"I can't," she whispered. "Oh God, I can't."

"Bloody hell." She felt him hot and hard rubbing himself against her.

"No." Hands on his chest, she pushed him away. He groaned and something hot and sticky spurted and dribbled down her leg. She smelled chlorine.

"Bitch." He rolled away from her. His back turned, he zipped up his trousers. "Prick teaser." He got up without looking at her and lit another Woodbine. His juice dried on her, tightening against her skin. Swallowing her tears, she sat up and pulled her dress down as far as it would go.

The flame of his cigarette glowed in the growing darkness. "You convent girls, you're all the same." She felt sick. "You're all tarts. Fuckin' tarts."

The ground lurched. The sky spun. She had never heard anyone use that word. Jumping to her feet she swung out at him, her nails catching his face in a long red gash. He lunged at her but she dodged, running round to the other side of the bike, where she stood with one hand on the saddle, ready to leap on behind him in case he tried to make off without her.

"Bitch," he said again, but his voice lacked venom. He dropped the still burning Woodbine. "Keeping yourself are you?" She nodded. He would understand that. Girls like her, they lived by a different set of rules.

All the same, she was filled with a sudden need to explain further. "I wanted to but..." she began. He shrugged her off. His hand strayed to the pocket with the Durex in it.

"Got to get back." He gestured at the bike.

"You're not cross?" she asked, despising herself even as she spoke. After all, why should she care what he thought about her?

He grunted, got on the bike, pressed down hard and the engine roared into life. She leapt on behind him. The leather of the saddle was warm and sticky against her nakedness.

God, my knickers. They lay there somewhere. A little heap of white nylon, damp and slightly stained by her excitement. She put her arms around his waist and the bike roared out of the woods and raced towards the bridge, suspended like a string of lights across an abyss.

Dave dropped her a few minutes from her front door. As she jumped off the Triton and searched in her bag for the key, she realised that he had seen she had no knickers on under her dress. He rested the bike on its stand and came up behind her. His arms around her waist, he kissed the back of her neck. She felt him grow hard against her and smiled. In spite of what she had done she had not lost him. There was still a chance that next time he would take her virginity. Twisting round, she ran her fingers down the scratch on his cheek. He caught her hand and grazed it with his teeth. Her nostrils flared. He saw the glint of her key and let her go.

* * *

Kate lay in bed, unable to sleep. Through the open window she could hear the noise of the city at night. The roar of motor bikes, the distant sound of rock music. Downstairs her grandmother cried out, then moaned softly, mindlessly. The rest of the family slept while her body was hot and restless, her mind a ferment of angry thoughts.

"Your body is a temple of the Lord," Sister Mary Edward had told her Religious Education Class. "You must keep yourselves pure until the day Our Lord lets you know what He requires of you."

"Bloody hell." Kate glared at the icon glimmering in the dusky light. "If that's what we're supposed to do why the hell did He give us sex? And don't tell me," she sat up and addressed the painted Christ, "it was so I could resist temptation." She pummelled the pillow. "Did I ask to be born a Catholic? Did I, hell?"

She lay down again on her back. Shutting her eyes, she recalled the pressure of his body against hers and shifting to her side, she curled and uncurled her legs.

A long, low hopeless moan rose through the house. Kate thrust her hand against her mouth and silently and unexpectedly she began to cry. She cried for her grand-mother, who was downstairs dying and who would never feel the heat of kisses on her lips or the pulse of another body on hers, and she cried for herself. For the hot gusts of shame that wracked her, for the torturing twists of guilt that framed her lips into an act of contrition, even when she was not sorry, and most of all, she wept because she was not free to do what she wanted without the threat of damnation being heaped upon her head.

CHAPTER SEVEN

The afternoon sun hung hot and furious above the street, its heat collecting in the small walled courtyard. The only relief was where the shadow of the house sliced across the stone flags bisecting the area into light and dark. Geraniums wilted in their pots, the ivy clung limply to the wall, and the climbing rose drooped, its leaves white with dust. Hannah opened the kitchen door and stepped out into the back yard. Later, she would water, washing clean her garden, tending and reviving thirsty plants.

Peter lay on his stomach, one hand pushing a bright red car along the flagstones. "Brrmm, brmm, brmm." The noise grew louder, then dimmed, mimicking the ever present sound of the traffic. Hannah sat down on the bench she had placed in front of the kitchen window and watched her son. His face was screwed up in concentration, his forehead puckered, as he accelerated, reversed and leapt over imaginary obstacles. He did not feel the scrape of stone against his skin, or the sun on the back of his neck. Knees and elbows grimed with dirt, he was completely absorbed in his game.

The sunlight caught his hair and she was transported back to another garden, where old trees cast friendly shadows over a wide lawn and the air was fresh and clean.

* * *

On the veranda that surrounds the house Mimi sits in a wicker chair with her son beside her. He leans against the arm of the chair, one hand twisting the lock of blonde hair that falls over his forehead.

"When will Granny come?" Jan asks his mother. Mimi smiles. "When?" he asks again. He does not whine, or demand, that is not in his nature. He simply assumes his mother did not hear him. If this time she does not reply he will not persist.

"Soon," Mimi murmurs.

"Will she bring me a present?"

"Of course. Are you not her favourite grandson? No one, not even Grandma, can resist you, my darling. You are too adorable." She reaches out to brush the hair from his eyes.

"Will she bring Hannah a present too, and Krysia?" Jan is always generous and eager to share his boundless enjoyment of life.

"I should think so. Of course she will."

Hannah, sitting on the swing, is conscious of her mother's glance. In contrast to her brother she feels heavy and plain. She tugs at one of her plaits. It has fallen across her chest and the feel of her plump flesh makes her aware, yet again, how different she is from her brother and sister.

Krysia lies in her pram, a fringed canopy shielding her from the sun. A long, thin dark-haired baby, she sleeps fretfully, her chest heaving, her tiny fists clenching and unclenching, as if to ward off some approaching peril. Her eyes flutter open, her whole body jerks with the shock of waking and she starts to cry. A thin, plaintive undemanding wail that Mimi ignores, but that prompts Hannah to jump off the swing and run to comfort her baby sister.

Taking the handle she bounces the pram up and down. The cries grow softer but do not stop. The shadow of the canopy mottles the baby's face and, for a terrible moment, Hannah thinks Krysia is covered in bruises. Holding her breath she touches the darkened skin; the baby's eyes open, she grabs at the finger and smiles. Hannah's heart bounds as the little fingers curl around hers. She stands in that Polish summer garden melting and overflowing with love.

* * *

Krysia has always been special to her. She came with the snow, slipping into their house like the ice that frosts the windows. In the cold and dark Mimi has gone to her room and shut the door. Jan is upset at first; he cries and screams until the servant girl comes running and tells him he must not make so much noise. She takes him to the kitchen where she feeds him honey cakes and plays with him and soon he stops asking about Mummy.

Hannah refuses to go with them. Knowing that no one will bother with her as long as she makes no fuss, she positions herself by the bedroom door. With her back against the wall, her arms around her knees, she sits and waits. It is very still in the house and she stares hard at the door wishing she could see through it to the room on other side.

Once, when the nurse comes, she catches a glimpse of her mother lying ashen faced on the bed, her eyes closed, her mouth open, gasping like a fish on the fishmonger's slab. Hannah struggles to her feet and runs towards her, but as she appears in the doorway Mimi starts up from her pillow and cries, "Take her away," in a harsh cracked voice.

Terrified, Hannah backs into the corridor, her heart hammering. After a little while the nurse comes to tell her that her mother is resting and Hannah is to be a good girl and go and play like her brother. Hannah shakes her head; if she leaves she is sure something dreadful will happen, but the nurse frowns and like a good little girl she does what she is told.

Snow is falling from the November sky. There are potato dumplings and hot soup in the kitchen, and after supper Daddy comes home. He hears their prayers, reads Jan his favourite story, and tucks the eiderdown around Hannah's ears. She lies for a long time, unable to sleep. Mummy is ill and she must do everything she can to make sure she gets better. She closes her eyes tight, clasps her hands together and prays as hard as she can.

"I'll be good. I'll never be naughty again. I'll say the Rosary every day," she promises Our Lady.

The front door opens and shuts. There are footsteps in the hallway, then her father's voice low and urgent. Unable to bear it any longer Hannah slides her legs out of bed. If Mummy is going to die she must see her and tell her how sorry she is for being a bad girl and such a disappointment to her.

The house is cold and she shivers as she creeps down the corridor, keeping close to the wall in case anyone sees her. She is almost there, she can see a crack of light spilling out from under the bedroom door, hear a muffled groaning, followed by sharp cries. Something terrible is going on, something so awful that no one will tell her what it is, and she presses her hands over her mouth to stop herself from screaming. Then the door opens and her father comes out.

"Hannah what are you doing here?" he asks kindly. Her lips tremble and she begins to cry. "Can't you sleep?"

"No," she sobs.

"There's nothing to worry about, you know." She gulps. "Believe me." She nods. Her father never tells her lies, never pretends things are not how they are. "If you can't sleep, perhaps you'd better wait with me. Come on, we'll go into the sitting room."

He leads her into the warm room and sitting in his chair takes her on his lap and tells her that it will be all right and by morning she will have a little brother or sister. Hannah leans back against him, smells the scent of his pipe tobacco and the soap he uses, and begins to feel safe again. Her eyes close, she drowses; he tightens his arm around her and stares into the coals. Then the nurse comes for him and he puts her down gently and tells her to wait and she sits there in the dark, not daring to put the light on, and the fear knots her stomach again and she has to remind herself that it is only a baby coming. Part of her hopes that it will not be another boy like Jan, who her mother will love more than her, because boys are better than girls and never do anything wrong. And then she claps her hand over her mouth in shame for her mother loves her as much as she deserves and her father loves her even more than that.

The embers glow red in the stove, there is a sudden shriek, followed by a wail. Hannah's insides lurch and her legs go weak. She shuts her eyes.

"Holy Mary, Mother of God, please help. Please," she prays urgently. A hand, heavy and comforting, rests on her shoulder. She looks up into her father's face. He looks tired but he is smiling.

"You have a baby sister," he tells her. "Come and see her."

The baby lies in a wicker basket. She is very white, her eyes are closed and there are blue veins on her eyelids.

Mimi reclines against her pillows, one arm around Jan, who leans against her, his thumb in his mouth, radiant with contentment.

"What do you think of her?" her father asks. Hannah takes another look at the baby. She is thin and still, like a not very pretty doll. Her eyes stray back to the bed. She wants to be there, snug in the circle of her mother's arm, but her father's grip holds her in place. "She has very blue eyes," he says softly.

"She's pretty," Hannah says, eager to please although she is already squirming out of her father's grasp. The baby cries. Mimi gives a little groan; her father releases her and goes to the bedside.

He takes his wife's hand. "My darling, are you all right? Are you in pain?" Mimi bites her lip. "Off you go young man," his father says and Jan scrambles obediently off the bed.

"You can come back later, darling, when Mummy feels a bit better," Mimi whispers.

The baby cries again. Mimi shudders. Their father strokes her hair. Another wail comes from the crib. Hannah is confused. Why is no one doing anything about the baby? She wants to ask if it is all right but her mother has shut her eyes and her father has his arm around Mimi's shoulders and is murmuring something in her ear.

Hannah feels hot and awkward. There is no place for her here, no one wants her, and she is not interested in the baby. Perhaps, if she moves quietly, no one will notice her leave. She begins to tiptoe towards the door. As if she senses her desertion, the baby screws up her eyes, opens her mouth and yells until her face is scarlet and her whole body shakes.

She's going to burst. Hannah glances at her mother, then at her father. The child screams again and again, growing more and more desperate. Hannah wants to put her hands over her ears, to run from the room, to hide from the terrible cries. How can they stand it? How can her parents ignore such grief? Does it hurt so much to be born? Hannah is struck by overwhelming pity for her little sister. How frightening it must have been to have lain curled up in a warm dark place for so long, then to be thrust out to sleep on cold white sheets, alone and forgotten.

Bending over the cradle she strokes the baby's soft cheek with her finger.

"It's all right. I'm here," she whispers. The baby's chest heaves and gasps, but the noise subsides. Hannah hesitates. What more can she do? What is it this little one needs? She examines her sister and it is the tiny fist the baby has thrust into its mouth, as if trying to stop herself crying, that tells Hannah what she must do. Very carefully she slides her arm under the little body and picks her up.

The baby shudders against her; its head wobbles frighteningly and, for a horrible moment, Hannah is afraid that she will drop her newborn sister. She tightens her grip and Krysia grows still and the crying stops.

"Look how good she is with her baby sister," Mimi murmurs. Hannah glows. A pink flush of pleasure spreads from her head to her toes. She kisses the downy top of the baby's head. Krysia smells warm and sweet.

"She's a good girl," her father says affectionately. "They both are."

* * *

I loved you, Krysia. I loved you so much. It was as if you were my baby, not hers. She never cared about you. What was it about both of us she did not like? Jan was her favourite. Her golden boy, she called him.

Her eyes strayed to her son. The game was over. Peter knelt up and rubbed his eyes with the back of his hand leaving a streak of dirt over the bridge of his nose. He saw her looking at him and grinned. Pleased that his mother was there, he was an open, happy child, not like thin, dark, intense and angry Kate, who gave Hannah the impression that she despised her, or at the very least thought her stupid and dull.

I was never like that towards Mimi. Nor was Krysia. We loved her, but she did not love us. Perhaps it was something she could not help. Perhaps she simply could not love us. There was something about us, something that stopped her caring for Krysia and me.

Tears came to her eyes and she got up quickly, impatient with herself. How could she be so self-indulgent? Of course

Mimi loved them. They were her daughters. It was well known that some women cared more for their sons. It was beyond their control. Surely she, of all people, should understand. She only had to look at the difference between her two. Peter was so easy to love. His sister, who would fight off any sign of affection, so difficult. Yet she would give her life for Kate, would kill anyone who threatened her daughter.

When Peter was born, a late and unexpected addition to the family, the eleven-year-old Kate announced that she did not want anything to do with him. Later, she asked which of the two of them Hannah loved most and Hannah had told her the truth, that she loved them both equally. Then Kate, who had hoped for a different answer, stormed off to her attic, slammed the door and stamped around, until Gregor lost his temper and shouted at her to stop.

"How difficult it all is," Hannah sighed. "Love should be easy, not this perpetual state of anguish and doubt, relieved only by sudden unexpected shafts of joy."

The back gate opened.

"Daddy," Peter shouted, flinging himself at his father. Absently, barely registering the child's presence, Gregor rumpled his son's hair while his eyes searched for his wife. She stood by the bench, her hair pulled back from her face, her eyes dark as if she had been crying. Gregor's anger rose. It was that evil old woman again. Even in her dying she had the power to cause such pain. Hannah would say nothing, of course. She did what was necessary and never complained. It was this passivity that he loved in her, her compliance with everyone's wishes, the way in which she was waiting for him to make the first move. Putting Peter from him, he came towards her and her face lit up and she stepped into his arms and rubbed her face against the rough tweed of his jacket.

"Come inside. It's cooler," she said, and with his arm around his wife's shoulders and holding his son's hand, he led his family into the house.

* * *

The doorbell rang. From upstairs came the sound of the television; from the front room, Mimi's groans.

"How are we today?" Sister Williams, the district nurse, leaned over the shrivelled figure in the bed. Like a malicious monkey, Mimi screwed up her face and spat out obscenities. Hannah blanched. Sister Williams shot her an understanding glance. "Don't mind me. They all do it. They're getting rid of all the nasties before they go." Hannah nodded faintly. The nurse went on with her task.

"Comfortable now are we?" Mimi lay doll like against her pillows. "Time for a nice sleep then." Sister Williams gave a final tug at the bedcovers. "My feet," she sighed. "I'm breaking in a new pair of shoes. Should have known better." She looked down at her swollen ankles. "Still, only two more patients to see and my shift is over."

"Would you like a cup of tea?"

"That would be lovely." Sister Williams picked up her case and followed Hannah down the hall to the kitchen. The room was in shadow, the golden evening light framed by the window. The nurse sank gratefully onto a chair.

"Sugar?" Hannah asked.

"Two. Though I shouldn't." Sister Williams looked at the way her stomach rested on her lap. "I need it for the energy, I always say. Life-saving." She took an appreciative sip of hot sweet tea.

"I suppose you must drink an awful lot of it."

"Not really. You'd be surprised how few people offer. In some houses I even have to ask if I can wash my hands after doing some really dirty job. People don't think; they don't think at all."

They take you for granted. They see you as part of the sickness.

Sister Williams put down her cup. "And how are you keeping?"

"My mother seems all right. I don't think there is any pain, though now she can't speak properly it's impossible to know for sure."

"I didn't ask about your mother. She's as well as can be expected. I want to know how you are coping."

Am I coping? Hannah wondered. *I'm still standing. Gregor*

— 78 —

and the children seem to be all right. So I suppose I must be.
She said nothing.

"It's not too much?" The nurse prompted.

"Of course it is." Coming into the room Gregor flicked the light switch. Blinded by the brightness, the two women turned their faces to the sound of his voice.

"Perhaps you should consider a nursing home." Sister Williams leaned towards Hannah. "It's not easy looking after a stroke patient and you look as if you could do with a good night's sleep."

"I tell her. I tell her what she should do, but will she listen?" Gregor spread out his hands in exasperation.

I can't, Hannah thought. *I can't abandon her. Oh why, why can't you understand?* "She's my mother," she said.

"And I am your husband and Kate and Peter are your children," Gregor said in Polish.

Hannah looked at the icon on the wall. Our Lady's face, pierced by a pagan spear had oozed blood. Torn between them all, she too, like the Blessed Virgin, was wounded.

The nurse looked from one to another. "We can provide respite, if you need it."

"No thank you. I am managing," Hannah said stiffly. Gregor shrugged his shoulders and raised his eyes eloquently to the ceiling.

"If you are sure," the nurse persisted. Hannah nodded.

"I am quite sure," she said.

Why won't I take her up on her offer? she thought, as she shut the door on Sister William's ample frame. *A few weeks without Mimi would give us all a break. Kate could finish her exams in peace and Gregor and I could have some time together. But I can't do it. I can't send her away into the care of strangers, to people who do not know her. People who do not speak her language. I know she doesn't talk any more but who knows how much she can understand. I cannot do this to her. She would never forgive me. She is flesh of my flesh, blood of my blood; she is my mother. She expects it and I must take care of her.*

But if I were old and sick, would I want Kate to look after me? No, I would not. I would want my daughter to go out into the world, wild and free, and let others wash and feed me and change my soiled bedding. I could not burden her with this. I could not demand it of any child of mine.

CHAPTER EIGHT

In the garden it was fresh and cool. The roses a bright yellow, the ivy deep green against the wall. Drops of dew slid from the leaves of the geraniums and nestled in the hollows between leaf and stem. The clean early morning smell held out a promise of hope and energy as it kept at bay the cloying heat that lay dormant in the sleeping house.

Already the sun lay siege to the front of the building, beating against the open windows, sliding through a crack in the curtains, and slanting across the bed where Hannah slept beside Gregor. She was on her back, her arms at her sides, her mouth slightly open, lying as she had fallen. Her sleep, snatched from the interruptions of the night, was deep, dreamless and dark, until a sliver of sunlight pressed against her lids. Half conscious, she raised her hand to blot it out, felt the heat on her skin and opened her eyes.

Her body, exhausted, worn almost beyond its limits, longed to slide back into unconsciousness. Sluggish and uncoordinated, it resisted her efforts to heave herself out of bed, her feet searching awkwardly for her slippers, her mouth gaping in huge irrepressible yawns. But she would not give in to it. She craved this time, when the house was silent and her family still slept. For half an hour, possibly more, no one would need to be fed, clothed or washed. No one need be spoken to, chastised or loved. She could sit by herself in the stillness of the garden. Although her limbs were so heavy that she could hardly drag herself from the room, at the same time she felt scarcely anchored to the earth. It was as if she were held by some invisible tether that was slowly working itself loose and, at any moment, she might float away into the ether.

The feel of the banister beneath her hand settled her and by the time she reached the kitchen she felt steadier. She took her cup of tea into the back yard and sat down on the bench. It was still in shadow; later it would catch the full force of the sun. The heat of the day before remained trapped in the brickwork behind her. She leaned against the wall and listened to the purr of the milk float and the clink of bottles as the milkman worked his way along the street. The sweat dried on her skin and she breathed in the summer morning, drawing strength for the rest of the day.

When she came back into the house, her hair smelled of the outdoors. She put on a clean dress; washed and dried in the sun it was crisp and fresh.

In Mimi's room the air was fetid. Twice in the night Hannah had changed the sheets and sponged her mother clean. The basin had been emptied, the flannel and towels removed, but she had not rid the room of the tang of urine, the decay of old flesh. However wide the windows were opened, however much disinfectant was used, these smells could not be washed away. Hannah slipped her hand under the covers. The bed was dry. Mimi rested light as a leaf on clean sheets.

She pulled open the curtains and let in the light. On the bed the old woman stirred. Her eyes opened, her glance was bright and intelligent; her eyes black in her yellow face.

"It's time to go." Her voice startled her daughter. It was so clear and firm.

"Mama, what is it?"

Mimi began to struggle, her stick-like elbow pushing against the pillows. Her muscles corded, her flesh hung loosely. "Get the cases," she ordered.

"What cases? What do you need cases for?"

Mimi's face contorted, grew red with anger. "We'll be late." Her hand grabbed at Hannah's wrist. "It's nearly time." Her good leg flailed uselessly in the bed as she tried to sit up.

"Time for what?" Hannah asked.

Mimi addressed the person she saw standing behind her daughter. "Why won't that girl help me?" she complained. "Useless, useless child. She was never any good," she muttered viciously, her hand clutching the edge of the sheet. "And now she won't help me. Her own mother! Now, when I need her most of all."

"You know that's not true." Hannah defended herself. Strange how the pain still struck. Even though she understood that Mimi no longer knew what she was saying, or even recognised the person to whom she spoke, it still wrenched her heart, reducing her once again to the defenceless child who stood, head bowed, before her mother's furious tirades. Her mother was, Hannah had to keep reminding herself, old and confused, and she had to distance herself from the familiar surge of emotion. "Of course I will help you. Tell me what you want me to do," she said gently.

"It's time to go. We must be ready."

"Where are we going?"

"Away," Mimi hissed, spittle trailing down her chin. "Get away from me." Mimi's hand flapped in front of her face. "And don't forget the cases. Oh why are you so stupid?"

I know that's how she's always seen me, as stupid and clumsy. Her brain is fragmenting. But dear God, it hurts hearing her saying what she thinks of me, out loud. My training as a nurse tells me I should treat her like a wayward child and disregard this outburst, but I can't. Not my own mother.

"I'll get the cases. Don't worry. Rest now," she said. Mimi shut her eyes and they appeared to sink back into her skull, while Hannah tried to make sense of what her mother might want.

If only she could work out which journey Mimi was remembering. There had been so many of them. Was it that terrible journey to Kazakhstan, crammed together like cattle, afraid for their lives? Or the long trek from Persia to Palestine, when at least there had been some hope? Or their final arrival in this cold damp island, which Mimi hated with such passion? The endless grey rain, she said, penetrated her bones, the strange language with its unpronounceable words hurt her ears and shrivelled her soul.

Her soul. Oh how could she be so stupid? Mimi was right, had always been right. Sometimes she could not see the nose in front of her face. What had she been thinking? It was no past journey or distant memory that troubled her mother, but that final one that she must soon take. Did she know how little time there was left? Was she trying to make herself ready?

So often now Mimi was without words. Yet as this morning proved, she was still capable of speech, maybe even of rational thought. Did she choose to remain silent? Or were there simply times when her damaged body would not allow her to speak?

"Mama," Hannah said. There was no reply. Hannah felt a hot spurt of irritation, but her conscience would not let her give up. "Would you like to speak to Father Borek?"

Mimi's eyelids flickered. "That pig." Hannah gasped. To use such language about a priest bordered on blasphemy. Mimi's eyes were wide open, her head half lifted from the pillow. "That fat swine. He cares for nothing but money for his church, for the roof, for the sacristy, for the vestments. Money, always money. I won't give him any. He shan't have any of mine. It is all for you." Mimi pursed her lips, then gave a little sigh, like air escaping from a balloon, and her face collapsed. The moment of lucidity had gone. The connection had been broken, the personality had disappeared.

Hannah could not leave her mother to die without Confession and Mimi must make it now while she was still, at times, capable of thought and speech. If she would not have Father Borek from the Polish church, then perhaps Father O'Brian from St Mary's would be her choice. Whichever priest came to absolve her, Hannah was sure it would be a relief for her mother to rid herself of her sins, whatever they might be. It would ease her mind and make her dying gentler. Mimi's head rolled sideways; she groaned and Hannah realised that whatever she decided she must act soon.

She went into the hall to phone the presbytery. She was the guardian of her mother's conscience. If Mimi could not make her wishes known then she must interpret them. She must be responsible for her, as she was responsible for all her family. She dialled the priest's number. Somewhere in the house a door opened and shut; a faint whimper hung on the air, then faded into nothing.

* * *

The connecting doors of the exam room were open revealing row upon row of desks. Out of the windows, Kate could see the lights of the city sloping down towards the river and, beyond it, the darkness of the countryside. She was alone. In front of her was a blank sheet of paper, blindingly white in the harsh glare of the overhead strip lights. Her pen was glued to her fingers, but she could not write. Her mind teemed with information. 910, a decisive year in European History. 410, the year the Romans left Britain. 1215, Magna Carta signed.

The rest of her class had left hours ago. She tried to stand. The bundle of black material, perched at the high desk at the front of the classroom, unfolded itself. Bat-like sleeves spread wide, Sister Mary Edward's face shrieked at her,

"Go over your work. Go over your work."

Kate's hands were damp, yet she could not prise the pen from her fingers, could not get up from her seat, could not leave the room. Could not breathe. She gulped; she choked. And woke.

Her sheet had twisted around her legs. A history file lay beside the bed, a text book splayed open where she had dropped it. She sat up, her hair damp, her eyes gritty, her mouth foul. She had not eaten for days. Whenever she lifted food to her lips her stomach churned. Her throat was so tight she could barely swallow the unsweetened lemon juice she drank as she revised.

She got out of bed and went downstairs. The hall tiles were cool, the kitchen filled with light, the kettle still hot. She sat, her legs twined around the chair, sipping black tea. The cat, who had not been fed, watched her balefully.

Hannah came in. She picked up the pot that Kate had left resting on the Rayburn and refilled her cup. With her back to her daughter she said, "I've been thinking. It's time your grandmother had the Last Sacraments."

"She's on her way out then?"

Hannah bit her lip. "I think it may be soon."

"Oh." Kate moved her shoulders dismissively, staying hunched over her cup, her face leaning into the steam.

Aren't you sorry? Hannah wanted to ask. *Aren't you*

curious? Afraid even? You, who have never seen death. Looking at her daughter's posture, she said instead, "I'm thinking of asking Father O'Brian from St Mary's to come. Speaking of which, it is Saturday."

"I know. That's why I'm not going to school." Kate was quick with a scathing reply.

"Confession is at ten," Hannah said pointedly. Kate sighed heavily. She put down her cup and looked directly at her mother.

"I suppose you want me in a State of Grace for the old bag's departure."

"I didn't say that," Hannah protested.

"But that's what you meant."

"It would do no harm. It never does any harm to go to Confession regularly."

All that wallowing in guilt and sin. All that sorrow and repentance, Christ's tears and Crown of Thorns. Ugh, Kate thought. "Do you know, when I was little I had to dredge up something to say every Saturday," she said.

Her mother drew in her breath.

With a twinge of guilt Kate considered her options. Being on the right side of God could do no harm. "I might go. I could do with lighting a candle for the exam on Monday."

Hannah smiled. "I'll light one for you too. And say a Memorare. Our Lady will help you. That prayer never fails."

"Mmm," Kate grunted. "Okay then."

* * *

Kate had put on her shortest skirt. It was tight and black. Her white-ribbed top clung to her breasts, and her heels clicked on the pavement as she walked down the hill. If her mother had seen what she looked like, she would have been sent back to change. But if Kate had to go to church then she would do it on her own terms. Besides going to Confession would please Hannah and it might ward off the fates and demons that lay in wait for those that broke the rules. She needed the angels on her side. In spite of all her work and the good grades she had achieved in her mocks, a small core of doubt remained. Even as she walked she chanted, under her breath, significant dates and important quotes from her set texts.

The shops on the Christmas Steps were open. Shadowy customers moved behind thick glass. A group of tourists stood at the corner of the street, heads bent diligently over guide books. Kate turned the corner. With its fluted columns and classical pediment, St Mary's on the Quay looked like a Greek temple transplanted into a Bristol street. Kate clattered up the wide steps. She pulled her mantilla out of her bag and slipped it over her hair.

The green baize-covered door opened with a soft swish. She dipped her fingers in the holy water stoop and made a swift sign of the cross. The lobby was dark and stuffy. There was a smell of people and feet. Beyond it, the church soared, light and airy. Four gold columns twisted around the altar. Plaster saints looked down from their plinths. A row of confessionals stood on one side of the church. Kate looked to see which had the shortest queue, slipped into the nearest pew and knelt down.

The old woman next to her got to her feet. Kate heard the door of the confessional open and close. She sat back on her heels and let her shoes dig into her buttocks.

"Sin is an offence against God, by any thought, word, deed, or omission against the law of God." The words of the catechism burned into her brain. Everything she thought, everything she said and did, was a sin. Even those things she couldn't be bothered to do. They caught you every which way, those nuns and priests. If they had their way, just breathing would break some commandment or other.

Her resentment began to build. Why must she put herself through this humiliation? Why must she reveal her so-called sins to some tired old man? God already knew what she had done and why. But she had half-promised her mother, and there were the exams to consider.

The door of the confessional opened. Kate got up. The box was close and stuffy and smelt of the old woman. She knelt on the hard little stool by the grill.

"Bless me Father, for I have sinned."

"How long is it since your last confession?"

"Three months."

"And?" He prompted wearily.

"I forgot to say my prayers. I was rude to my parents. I was unkind to my little brother." Pathetic, trivial misdemeanours. "Very unkind about my grandmother," she paused for effect, "who is very ill." In spite of herself, she felt a hot flush of shame, as coming to the end of her list she mumbled, "I went in for heavy petting with my boyfriend."

"Is that all you have to tell me, my child?" The priest sounded totally uninterested.

"Yes," Kate snapped. Angry at herself for having been swayed by her mother. Angry, because what she had to say was so unimportant. Angry at her own anger.

"In that case, for your penance say one Our Father and three Hail Marys. *Ego te absolve in nomine Patris et Filius et Spiritus Sanctus...*" The words washed over her. She felt lighter, cleansed.

In a side chapel, the Virgin Mary stood surrounded by flickering candles. Kate took a lighted spill and looked the plaster statue directly in the eye.

"I deserve three As," she said, and the wick caught and the candle flamed into life.

CHAPTER NINE

Marianna chose silk, a simple grey-green dress that fell in folds almost to her feet. She hung rubies and pearls in her ears and an ornate cross on a chain about her neck. Her fingers were laden with rings, huge stones set in gold, rubies like gouts of blood, sapphires dark as despair. She pinned up her hair with silver combs and touched with perfume those points on her neck and wrists where the veins ran blue under the skin.

Drawing back the curtains, she set one chair in a pool of sunlight, the other she pushed back so that whoever sat in it was shaded from the light. She removed her pens and paper from the side table and made sure the samovar was bubbling. She felt curiously defiant, as if she were going to do something she should not and yet, under the bravado, lurked a feeling of unease. She had not slept well. Her night had been haunted by dreams and she had woken tired and irritable. Her face in the mirror reminded her of Baba Yaga, the witch with hooked nose, wrinkled skin and sunken eyes.

"I would like to speak to you on the subject of your life and work," Nicky Dawes had written. "I am a journalist on the *Western Daily Press* and I am researching an article about you."

Marianna swept her hand along the marble mantelpiece. "I do not want anyone writing about my life." She glared at her reflection. "But how do I stop it? If I do not speak to her then she will find other people who will. There are plenty in the Polish community in Bristol who would relish the opportunity. Not that any of them know the truth, so perhaps in the end it will be better to let this woman have my version of events."

The doorbell rang. Marianna repositioned herself on that side of the fireplace where the mirror reflected the half-open door leading to the top of the stairs, so she would not be approached unawares. Old lessons had been learned well. The front door opened. A nasal voice stated, "I have an appointment." The announcement was followed by a shotgun scatter of Polish. She imagined Basia hobbling to the foot of the staircase, pointing an arthritic finger in the general direction of the drawing room, then watching as the visitor went up to the first floor.

The journalist was a young woman in a badly cut brown suit, hair pulled back and piled on top of her head, large pale eyes behind thick brown-rimmed glasses. At the door of the drawing room she lifted her hand, then hesitated, uncertain whether or not she should knock.

"Come in my dear," Marianna lowered her voice, emphasising the husky quality and the Polish sound of her vowels. The journalist glanced uneasily around the room. This was going to be easier than Marianna had expected. Stepping forward, she held out her hand. Before taking it, her visitor surreptitiously rubbed her palms against her skirt.

"Nicky Dawes. Pleased to meet you, Your..." Again the uncertainty, the hesitation. Marianna hid her smile.

"You may call me Princess, although I am not of royal blood." She took the damp little hand and pressed her rings hard against Nicky's fingers.

"But your father was a prince?" Nicky looked confused.

"That means nothing." Marianna waved dismissively. "In Imperial Russia, the sons, daughters, and close relatives of the Czar were Grand Dukes and Duchesses. Princes and Princesses were two a penny. Now please, won't you sit down? Make yourself comfortable." She gestured towards a chair and as Nicky sat the sun caught her glasses, causing her to squint as she burrowed in her bag for a pen. Settling herself in the opposite chair, where her face was in shadow, Marianna smoothed her skirt over her lap. "I am very flattered," she began, "but I do not understand what could possibly interest you in such an old woman as I am. My time is long past; yours is just beginning."

Nicky's fingers continued to scrabble like worms in the bottom of her bag until she pulled out a crumpled tissue followed by a plastic covered notebook.

"I read your *Tales from the Forest*," she said.

"A curious choice."

"Curious?" Nicky's forehead tightened.

"It is not the sort of book I would have thought an English child would know."

"Oh." Nicky's mouth opened. Her teeth were large and slightly prominent. "Oh, I see. I didn't read it when I was little, I mean. A friend of mine at university, well we were talking about what we'd read when we were young and he showed it to me."

"Do you read Polish?"

"No, no." Nicky grew red with embarrassment. "I had a translation. Anything else of yours my friend can help me with. He's Polish, you see, or rather his parents are."

"Forgive me." Marianna inclined her head. "I still don't understand. There are my books but in England they are hardly known, and in Poland they are now forbidden. I am, at most, a very minor literary figure."

"But your life is so interesting."

"Ah." It was what she had suspected and feared. *This woman in the ill-fitting suit wants the old scandals, the old lies.* "How did you come to hear of me?"

"My friend Stefan. The one I told you about. He was brought up on your stories, the children's ones that is. Then someone told him you were here in Bristol."

The Polish community spreads its tentacles deep and wide.

"You are very respected and I'm so grateful you agreed to see me," Nicky gushed.

"You thought I would refuse?"

Nicky shifted awkwardly in her chair. "I don't know, but you took a long time to reply to my letter."

"I am an old woman." Marianna spoke slowly, paused then sighed. "I do very few things quickly. But even so, how could I deny a fellow writer?"

Nicky's eyes glinted behind her glasses.

She suspects irony, Marianna thought. *And the interview is not going as well as she had hoped when I agreed to speak to her. Well, if she thought it would be easy she will soon see how wrong she is.*

Nicky pushed her chair back slightly in an attempt to move it out of the sun. Her feet scuffed against the rich pile of the rug and a fleeting expression of distaste, or was it envy, crossed her face.

She resents me. She sees me as a rich old woman who has never had to work for her living, while she, judging by her accent and her clothes, is the product of an aspiring working class. If I am right she will be the first of her generation to have benefitted from further education and is preparing to claw her way up in the world.

"You must have known all the important people of your day." Nicky flicked through her notebook. Marianna nodded.

"You were born in 1895."

Such a long time ago. Seventy years. Long enough for three generations. Mother, daughter, grand-daughter. Yet I have no progeny myself. I have books not children, and they will not endure. Not even the nonsense this girl will write will last for long.

"Shall we start at the beginning?" Marianna suggested. Nicky nodded, straightened her back, crossed her legs, and took the top off her biro. "The first thing you need to know is that when I was a little girl, Poland did not exist."

"It was divided up between Russia, Prussia and Austria-Hungary," Nicky said, as if answering a question in an examination.

She has done her research. What else does she know, or thinks she knows? Damnation take those Bristol Poles. What have they said to her? What scores do they want to settle? Whose names do they want to blacken? Whose reputation is to be torn to shreds? They are so mean and petty and utterly bourgeois. But why it should matter to me? They can do nothing to hurt me. All those I cared for are dead. The others are mere shadows on the grass. A memory flickered at the corner of her mind. She turned her head to catch it and it was gone.

"Your father was Russian but you identified with Poland and the Polish people. How was that?"

"To be Polish was fashionable in the 1890s. It became very chic in St Petersburg to have Polish blood. My father, seeking a wife, married a Polish girl. I was brought up in Poland. Christened in the Catholic not the Orthodox Church. I had Polish nannies."

"So you had no loyalty to your father's country?"

Marianna frowned. "After the Great War, Imperial Russia no longer existed. It was all swept away with the Romanovs. There was nothing to be loyal to."

"What about the before the War, then?" Nicky's voice was sharp. She was a ferret, with sly eyes and sharp teeth. She would dig and burrow and search until she found what she wanted.

She must be spun stories, told tales. The dragon stirred. Marianna stood up and drew the curtains across the windows, filling the room with a dim golden light. Settling herself back in her chair, her voice low and seductive, promising confidences, she began: "I was born on a cold November night. Snow had been falling for two days covering the city with an icy blanket. Now the final flakes fluttered to the ground, the sky cleared and became brilliant with stars.

"They told me that my mother gave birth with joy and an animal fierceness, glorying in the rise and fall of pain, the final triumphant push of a new child into the world. She bit my cord with her teeth and when they put me into her arms she nuzzled and licked my skin and, holding me to her brimming breast, called me her winter princess. Her little Polish flower."

Nicky gasped at the image.

Marianna hid her smile and continued. "She would not let my nurse take me from her. I slept in a cradle at her side and, night after night, she would walk with me in her arms, telling me about my brave and handsome brothers and the tragic country into which I had been born.

"Story telling is in my blood, you see, and in the blood of my people, for it was with our stories that we kept our nation alive. When I was a small child even our language was proscribed."

"I know," Nicky interrupted. "If you spoke Polish you could be arrested, or even sent to Siberia."

Marianna bowed her head. The girl was irritating but she

would not let Nicky Dawes see how much she annoyed her. To distance herself Marianna slipped into story-telling mode.

"My father," she began, "was a Russian prince. His family was very old and very rich. He was the last surviving son and from *his* father he had inherited vast tracts of land. In Poland there were primeval forests, thick with ancient trees, where bison roamed. In Russia huge empty steppes, mile upon endless mile, stretching out far beyond anything the eye could encompass. In Siberia there were gold mines; in Georgia vineyards and orchards. There were palaces in St Petersburg, in Moscow, in Warsaw, and dachas in the country and summer palaces beside the Black Sea.

"Such riches! Wealth almost beyond imagination. In all his life my father never had to dress or shave himself. If he dropped a handkerchief there was a servant to pick it up. Of course, he did not always choose to live like this, but wherever he went, whatever he did, this background of wealth and opulence was there, keeping us apart from the rest of the world.

"In those superstitious and backward times we were seen as magical beings. Servant girls would sometimes brush my hand or touch my skirt for luck, to bring them a lusty husband, or to ward off the evil spirits that lurked in the forest. Some wore amulets woven from my mother's hair around their wrists. They adored and feared her in equal measure, sensing that undercurrent of violent emotion that ran beneath the milk white surface of her skin. She was so beautiful and so strange. Tall and slender, she had red gold hair that fell to her waist and carried herself like a warrior queen."

* * *

They are travelling to the country estate for the summer. The train draws up at their private station, where the wooden building is hung with flowers and important local dignitaries are waiting on the platform.

Jumping up from her seat Marianna watches the porters unroll the carpet, which is so special that only the Prince and his family are permitted to set foot on it.

Papa and Mama are the first to disembark from the train. The station master bows and everyone else falls to their knees.

Marianna wriggles impatiently. "You must wait. The young princes go next, then you." Her nurse clicks her tongue and Marianna fumes as her hat is set straight on her head. At last it is her turn. She is lifted down and breathes in the scent of sun-warmed wood and pine trees.

Her parents are moving slowly along the line of their dependents, nodding graciously and finding something to say to each person. Her brothers Henryk and Valerian walk behind them. Marianna lets go of her nurse's hand, holds her head high and practises being a princess.

When she reaches the end of the carpet she looks back, hoping to see the servants rushing forward to roll it up and take it away ready for their next visit. Sometimes she wonders why no one else is allowed to step on it. Could it be that it would turn them into toads?

She is still considering this idea when she is lifted into one of the waiting carriages. Her parents and brothers are already driving away.

Marianna sits on the edge of her seat as the long line of carriages enter the forest. The trees are dark on either side of the road. The bells on the harnesses tinkle and the ribbons on the drivers' whips flutter in the breeze. As they drive through a hamlet the peasants gather at the roadside.

"God and His Holy Mother bless you," they call and throw flowers, then kneel as the procession passes and Mama and Papa smile and raise their hands in benediction.

A long drive sweeps round to the front of the dacha; the double doors are thrown open and liveried footmen line the steps.

Like out of a fairy story, Marianna thinks as she walks into the entrance hall. Josef, who has been in charge of the house since Papa was a little boy, kneels at his feet and kisses his hand, but Papa makes him stand up and gives him a hug.

Then everyone else has to be greeted and have their hands kissed, until at long, long last Marianna is allowed to go to her room, take off her travelling clothes, and the holiday can begin.

* * *

"I thought..." Nicky's cough brought Marianna back from the

past. "Your mum ... your mother," she corrected herself quickly, "wasn't..."

"You are right. My mother's family were shop keepers. They owned the largest department store in Warsaw. It was the place everyone wanted to shop."

"So it was sort of romantic? Your mother marrying a prince and that..."

"Oh yes," Marianna sighed, determined to play this to the hilt. "The story goes that my father first saw his wild Polish bride on Good Friday, when she had come to church to view the Easter Grave. This is when a statue of Christ's bruised and battered body is placed, surrounded by flowers and candles, in a side chapel so that the congregation can worship as if He were in His tomb.

"My mother loved the trappings of religion, the gold embroidered vestments, the richly decorated churches, the plaintive hymns, the sensuous Latin chants, but she believed in nothing but herself and her pleasures. In the dimness of the candle-lit church her hair flamed red-gold, her skin was white as alabaster and my father knew he must have her.

"My mother's family were appalled, for they were good patriots, but she paid no heed. Handsome, hawk like, his eyes cruel, he was darkness to her light. He wanted her for his mistress – the social gap was too deep between them for any other arrangement, but she would not give in. It was not ambition that drove her, but a sense that he was her fate, her destiny. She said that he inflamed her in ways no other man would ever do. He did not fear her wildness, her instability; rather, he enjoyed them, played on them, used them to sharpen his own palate, jaded by a surfeit of pleasure.

"For two years they circled each other. She danced and flirted with other men; he embarked on a series of affairs. From time to time he would leave Warsaw and travel to his estates, remaining there for days or weeks, but always returning, drawn by the ever-tightening cord that bound them. Their passion grew, until the Prince proposed marriage and her family finally relented. They were married." Marianna paused.

The journalist's eyes were avid. She licked her tongue over

her lips and scrawled something in her notebook.

"At first they were happy." Marianna resumed. "Their natures called out to each other, complemented each other. Both could be ruthless, self-seeking, pitiless, but she was weaker than he. She was like fire to his ice; she could not temper the inferno in her veins. Her emotions were extreme, plunging from ecstasy to despair and over the years they destroyed her, burning away her mind and consuming her body.

"They had two sons, Henryk, my father's heir, and Valerian, my mother's favourite. I was the last child, born of the ashes of their love. The only daughter. We loved her, my brothers and I. As her children we could not do anything less, for she loved us with the whole intensity of her being, yet she did not curtail us in any way. Within the boundaries of the world in which we lived, we could do as we pleased.

"Perhaps that is why I developed my curiosity about what went on beyond the palace walls, about the lives and feelings of those people who moved so discreetly between the layers of our existence. The housemaids, the cooks and the kitchen boys. The people in the street. My mother, prompted by her family, had a social conscience and gave a great deal of money to the poor, but I rarely saw them, or had any idea of how they lived, not then at any rate."

There was an in-drawing of breath, or was it a hint of disapproval from the aspiring journalist?

"My childhood was a happy one. My mother travelled a great deal and, while I was still young, I came too. I loved being with her. When we were together, without my brothers, I was the centre of her attention. I was played with, listened to, and my feelings and opinions were treated with the greatest respect.

"Every year we went to Paris for new clothes. I had dresses made by Worth and I had to endure hours of standing still while seamstresses knelt at my feet tacking up hems and altering bodices. Then we travelled south to Italy. On one occasion she rented a palazzo on the Grand Canal. I loved its dark rich rooms, the endless lapping of water against the walls, the rose, ochre and russet of the buildings with their green tide marks and leprous stone work. The sea was consuming the city, bite by bite. Death and decay were everywhere.

"My mother grew morbid and we moved on to the harsh white light of the south, to Italy where the air was spiced with citrus and thyme and I ran wild in the orange groves with the servants' children. They taught me to swear and to make the sign against the evil eye so that we would not be harmed by the spirits of the place. But those same gods, that the people feared, invigorated my mother. Sleek and sinuous, she gave herself up to excess.

"There was always a young lover. Handsome officers, counts and princes. The affairs never lasted and she would slink home, dried out and exhausted, to restore herself.

"And what of me, you may ask. I was too young to be my mother's confidant. My brothers were at military academy by now; my father only saw us on family occasions, or on the great feasts of the Church. My mother's lovers treated me like some sort of exotic pet, to be kept happy and contented, for fear that I might whine and complain and so intrude on their romantic idyll. When I grew older and more outspoken I was left behind. I did not mind. By then, I had my own interests and, like most adolescents, I felt superior to my mother's chosen way of life."

And in Warsaw there was my cousin Mimi. We were born in the same month, in the same year. My shadow sister. A pale little ghost.

Should she speak of her? Was she part of the story? Mimi would like to think she had played a part in that world of princes and princesses, to which she had so much wanted to belong. Even as she lay dying, it would please her to be included. Marianna closed her eyes. All this talking was tiring.

Nicky Dawson put down her pen and shook her wrist.

"Will you take tea?" It was time for a diversion and what would be better than a good cup of tea?

"Please."

No doubt Nicky was hoping for something hot, tannin strong and generously laced with sugar, in the British fashion.

Steam drifted from the samovar, merging with the dust mites dancing in the late afternoon sun, and the tea, pale and translucent, came in tiny cups with a disc of lemon floating on the surface. Nicky shifted in her chair. She lifted the cup and took a sip. The colour flooded into her face, her cheeks bulged, and she gulped.

"It will be hot." Marianna's warning came a second too late. It was mean of her, but she could not bring herself to like this woman. Nicky was ugly, her manner abrupt, her accent uncouth. Marianna wished, yet again, that she had not agreed to this interview, and yet how ungracious on her part it would have been to refuse this unprepossessing creature her help. She had dealt with far worse with less reluctance. She needed a drink. Dear God, how she needed a vodka.

But if it was too early for that then maybe a cigarette would calm her irritation and the indefinable sense of unease that that it masked.

She reached over to the box on the side table.

"Do you smoke?"

Nicky shook her head. Marianna's hand trembled slightly as she flicked the lighter. She made herself wait. Watched the yellow-blue flame catch at the tobacco, then, half closing her eyes, she inhaled.

The silence grew awkward. Nicky chewed the end of her pen, probably trying to think of something that would bring Marianna back to her story. There was far more to tell and the Princess had deliberately said nothing, so far, of her racy, rebellious life.

That's what Nicky had come for, Marianna was convinced. Scandal, not some romantic picture of an idyllic childhood – that was what the journalist was after.

"Weren't you lonely?"

Marianna jerked her head in surprise. Was she nodding off? Had she fallen into an old lady's habit of dozing without realising? "I was just wondering, you being the only girl and the youngest..."

The journalist was more perceptive than Marianna had thought. What else would she dig out with her sly eyes and flat teeth? Nicky Dawes would not be deflected by superficial facts. How much to give her? How much to tell? She must proceed carefully. Marianna stubbed out her cigarette; considered lighting another and decided against it.

"Of course I was lonely. At times all children are. Especially girls, I think. I would imagine that you too have sometimes felt distant from other people. Felt that that they did not, maybe could not, understand what you were trying to say. Is that not so?" Her voice was kind, suggesting they had experiences in common, and Nicky was disarmed.

"Is that why you started writing? To make yourself understood, I mean," Nicky asked eagerly.

"The writing." Marianna exhaled, smiling. "Of course, you want to talk about the writing." She folded her hands in her lap, her shoulders relaxed into the back of the chair. "That came later."

"After Poland got its independence you became the voice of the new Poland."

"If you care to call it that."

"So what was it that got you started – writing your books, I mean?"

"I had a living to make."

Shocked, Nicky looked up from her notes.

"After the War it had all gone," Marianna exaggerated.

Nicky frowned, her teeth gnawing at her lower lip.

"The Great War," the Princess explained gently. "Russia became Communist. All the Zapolski estates were broken up. My brothers were dead. My mother," her eyes narrowed, "sick."

Insane, maddened with grief, tipped into delirium by that final, unnecessary death. Dragging me with her. I had to free myself. I had to construct my own life.

"I needed to live. To eat." She laughed quietly. "Money is a great motivator." Pushing her hands against the arms of her chair, Marianna rose to her feet. "I wish you the best of luck with your article." She put out her hand, indicating that the interview was over.

"Can I come again?" Awkwardly, Nicky Dawes shoved her notepad and pen into her bag.

"No." Marianna paused as if she was considering her answer. "I don't think so. I am an old woman and I find this reminiscing exhausts me."

Nicky's mouth dropped open. "But I mean, we've hardly started." She was red with disappointment.

"We began at the beginning," Marianna's tone was mildly reproving.

"I know, but there's so much more. About the rest of your life."

"You could send me a list of questions. That, I am sure, I could manage."

Nicky stood up. "Thanks ever so much for seeing me and for the tea."

She is like a good little girl leaving a party and I have been unkind. "I will answer them in as much detail as I can." Marianna felt obliged to make amends.

"I'd appreciate that. I really would. I'd like to make the best job of it that I can."

"I am sure you will." Marianna's voice was almost kind. Defeated, Nicky turned to go.

I was not too cruel, Marianna thought. *The facts of my life are all there, yet how much of what I told her is true and how much is not, I doubt whether even I know any more. After all, what does it matter? We all do it. We all weave fantasies about ourselves. The truth is too cruel, so it is the only way we can survive.*

Nicky's footsteps clattered down the stairs. The front door opened and closed. Marianna poured herself a large measure of vodka, drank and poured another; sat down and closed her eyes.

* * *

In a decaying palace a princess lies asleep. Dust clouds her chamber. It lies like mist on the backs of chairs, on tables, gathers in downy clumps in corners and crevices, veils the mirrors and powders the thin hands that lie palm upwards on the silken coverlet. Her bones are brittle as sticks. Her hair lies tangled on the pillow. Her face skeletal, her breasts tiny pouches above the lizard ribs. In sleep, the skin is stretched tight, and when she is woken her eyes are deep sockets, shadowed with black.

"Valerian," the voice is cracked, the breath fetid. The young prince leans over the bed. He takes her hand in his.

"I am here, Mama."

"Don't leave me," Helena whispers. Marianna is framed in the doorway. Her eyes meet her brother's. She shakes her head.

"I must go," he speaks to her as much as to the figure on the bed.

"You are needed here," Marianna says. Valerian looks at his sister.

"We must hold back the Bolsheviks."

"But you are on the Prince's staff. You can stay here in Warsaw." *In safety.*

"We need everyone in the field. For God's sake, Marianna, boys of fourteen have enlisted." He lifts the Princess's fingers to his lips. "God keep you, Mama."

"God?" Helena turns her head and spits like a peasant. "If He existed He would not have taken Henryk from me, and now He wants you." She closes her eyes. Her skin is dry as parchment; there is no moisture in her, except for the two slow tears that slide down the hollows of her face.

* * *

Marianna woke abruptly. Head up, neck jolting forward, heart thudding, as she gripped the arms of the chair. The pain was deep, yet dulled by time. The girl she had been, in the course of her life, had suffered greater anguish, more profound losses. Why then had this memory risen to the surface?

Or was this only the beginning? The grazing of the skin, before the knife cut through the flesh to expose what lay beneath. Was this the process that wretched journalist had set in motion? She should have obeyed her intuition and refused to see Nicky Dawes. The past was the past and Marianna had no desire to travel back into that abandoned territory. In November she had thwarted Mimi's efforts to replay past sorrows. Now they were returning to haunt her.

"Damnation," she cursed. "May the devil take you, Miss Dawes, to the lowest pit of hell and drag your memories from you with his red hot pincers." And then, remembering she believed in neither hell, nor its master, she began to laugh.

CHAPTER TEN

"Tell me a story, Mummy." Peter sat mutinously on his bed. The window had been left open all day, the curtains drawn against the sun, and still the room was hot, the air stale and thick with petrol fumes and dust. The little boy's hair flopped damply onto his forehead. In the bathroom, squirming like a fish as she wrapped him in a towel, his skin had been cool, now he was sticky sweet with the smell of hot child.

"I've already told you one."

"Want another." He stuck his thumb in his mouth, glowering.

"Last one then." She sat down on the bed beside him. He snuggled closer, his hot little body welded into hers, his head rammed hard against her chest. "Once upon a time, there was a house full of stories. Every room had a different one..."

* * *

In the kitchen it was cooler. Outside the window, the shadow of the house fell over the sun-heated flags. Gregor was sitting at the table, tea brewing on the stove, when Hannah came in, pushing wisps of hair from her eyes.

"He's asleep."

"At last. Now, perhaps, you will sit down for a minute or two."

She smiled. "I'll be glad to." She poured a cup of tea for each of them, took a sip and half rose from her chair. "I'll take Kate a cup. She must be so hot up there under the roof."

Wanting Hannah to himself, Gregor reached out and touched his wife's hand. "If she needs a drink she'll come down for it. Can you not stay and sit with me for a while."

"You're right," she said.

"Is she working?" he asked, ever the anxious father.

"I told her, tonight she is not to go out." Hannah sighed happily. Kate corralled in her room, Peter asleep in his, Mimi silent, all her family were within her reach. Leaning back in her chair she let the sultry evening flow through her. The lines on her face softened, her lips parted, she began to slide into sleep.

Gregor gave himself up to the pleasure of watching the soft rise and fall of her chest, the little grunts and murmurs she made. A great feeling of protectiveness welled up in him. She mumbled, smiled, then slipped deeper into unconsciousness.

The first cry splintered the gentle quiet. For a moment he could not think where it had come from. Then it came again, longer, lower, deeper and he was seized by an image of a pillow pressed over an insatiable mouth, feathers sinking deep into the cavernous throat. Driven beyond the bounds of his own exacting standards, his code of honour and duty, which demanded he protect Mimi from anything that might threaten her, he cursed. Hannah's eyes fluttered, her breathing quickened.

"Mama," she mumbled.

"Leave her." He was angry.

"No. I'll go." Yawning, she stumbled to her feet.

"Why must you always be rushing off? Why can you never be still?" His voice rose, petulant, whining.

The unfairness of his complaint struck her like a blow. Words boiled in her throat and she swallowed them back. He saw her distress, was glad of her hurt. It was time she knew how he felt. He picked up his paper and opened it with shaking hands.

* * *

Mimi appeared a little feverish, her eyes bright, her face waxen. She had tangled herself up in the sheets and was unable to move. Hannah plumped up the pillows, slid an arm under her mother's shoulders and lifted her. She sponged Mimi's hands and face, moistened her lips and cooled her wrists with eau-de-cologne. The cool sharp smell hung over the bed.

"Hannah." Mimi's voice was clear.

"I'm here." Her mother's fingers closed over hers. Was it a caress? Joy lifted in Hannah's heart.

"She used it on her handkerchiefs." It was Hannah, the spinster aunt, Mimi was talking about. The plain sister who preferred prayers to men. The one who had died unwanted and alone. The one whose name she had been given.

She was swamped by dull misery.

"Hannah." Mimi's voice was fearful now, the grip tighter.

"It's all right," Hannah soothed. "There's nothing to be afraid of, nothing at all."

Mimi began to whimper. She gave a series of short sharp, little sobs. Hannah placed her hand lightly on her mother's forehead, hoping that the touch of another human being would calm her. Gradually, the sobbing subsided, the breathing became quieter, trailing away into a sudden silence. Was this the end? Hannah saw herself closing the staring eyes, spreading the sheet over her mother's body. Then Mimi's mouth gaped, she took in a great gasp of air. Hannah began to shake, as if she had been pushed from a great height. Her legs gave way and she sat down heavily on the bed. Mimi began to snore like any old woman caught by an afternoon nap.

Tears welled hot and salty, but Hannah scrubbed them away with her fist. Her mother still lived. It was not time to grieve. She looked down at Mimi's face. In sleep she was almost her old self.

"Blessed Virgin, please let her sleep a little longer. Let there be a moment of respite. Time to be still." Hannah was so tired. Exhaustion fed on her like some malevolent spirit; it sucked the words from her mouth, the thoughts from her brain, making every action a monumental effort. The weight of her head pressed down on her shoulders. If only she could stay here and sleep but Gregor waited in the kitchen and she must go to him.

* * *

In a fragment of a dream, Mimi's parents stand at the side of the bed and look at her. They hold hands like children, palm to palm, their fingers curled loosely around each other's, their arms swinging slightly. Neither of them is quite sure what to do. Her mother half bends as if she is going to lean over and kiss her child, but her father is already pulling away and she straightens up.

Curled beneath her eiderdown, Mimi listens to her mother's footsteps hurrying away down the corridor. Her father follows, his feet shuffling in broken backed slippers.

* * *

In the hallway, Hannah, worn down by the conflicting needs of her husband and mother, closed her eyes and clenched her fists, as if by tensing muscles she could release enough energy to carry her forward. Her mouth was dry, her eyes raw. She bit down hard on her back teeth.

"You're back." Gregor did not look up from the newspaper. Her tea cup stood on the table where she had left it. Hannah picked it up and swirled the cold tea around, staring at the brown circle it left on the white china. The cup must be emptied, the kettle boiled again, a new pot brewed, and all she could do was tilt the cup up and down and down and up. The liquid moved like the sea in a storm, like the world on its axis.

"Leave it." Gregor took the cup from her hand and put the kettle on the stove.

* * *

Slipping deeper into the past, Mimi sits on a high stool at the kitchen table, her hands spread out in front of her, the nails pink and clean. She wears a black dress with a white pinafore. Her hair is tied back with a ribbon. She is five years old.

Opening the door of the stove is her Aunt Hannah. The stove is black, the coals glow red. Aunt Hannah lifts out a tray of honey cakes. They have been cut into shapes, diamonds, clubs, hearts and spades, and when they are cool they will be iced. The hot cakes smell richly of ginger. Mimi's mouth waters, but she knows better than to ask.

"Go and play. I will hear your lessons later," her aunt says. Mimi scrambles down from the stool. Her plump calves bulge over the top of her boots. She looks at the cakes, then back at her aunt, but Aunt Hannah is impervious to the child's desire. Mimi must not be indulged. It is her duty to the child to see that she is not spoilt. "Off with you." The words are sharp, but the voice is not unkind, merely too busy to pay any attention to a little girl.

Mimi pushes open the kitchen door and peers round it. She

looks down the long corridor that runs the length of the apartment. The brown panelling is almost as high as she is. Above it, on ochre walls, stern faces glower down at her from their gilt frames.

"Go on then." Aunt Hannah is growing impatient. Mimi sidles round the door and stands with her back to it. The empty corridor scares her. Her room is at the furthest end and she wants to be back in the comfort of the kitchen with Aunt Hannah. She twists her fingers in her pinafore, folding and bunching the cotton until she looks down and sees the creases, then stops and tries to smooth out the material. Mimi hates mess and disorder. Her hands rub obsessively up and down and still the pinafore looks crumpled.

Her lips tremble and to stop herself from crying she sticks a thumb in her mouth and sucks vigorously. Curling her finger over her nose, she gives herself up to the comfort of her own taste until, at last, she feels brave enough to venture down the corridor. The hall carpet muffles the sound of her feet. There is no natural light and the gas lamps, which have been left burning low, throw grotesque shadows onto the walls as she creeps past closed doors.

In the drawing room Mimi's father will be sitting by the stove. Fuelled like a furnace it is too hot to touch. The tiles radiate heat, their colours burn almost incandescent and still he hunches in his chair, his old coat over his shoulders, his body, once half-frozen in the Siberian winter, drawing in the heat that cannot thaw his blood.

His hands are cold, the fingers white and lifeless, his feet swollen. But his eyes burn. They glare at her whenever she is brought to see him. Aunt Hannah says the Russians hurt him by shutting him away in a land of ice and snow. There were wolves and cruel men with whips. They kept him imprisoned for ten years before he was allowed to come home.

When her mother returns from the travels, that no one must talk about, she puts her arms around him. He leans his head on her shoulder, strokes his hair and calls him darling. He mumbles and frets about the darkness and the trees, the endless ranks of trees, and her tears fall onto his face.

In another room, her grandmamma lies on a high white bed, her face yellow against the pillows, her grey plait thin on her breast. Opposite the bed hangs a big picture, a painting of Grandmamma's father and her brothers. Great-grandpapa wears a long coat and a sword and has two fierce dogs on the end of a leash. The hounds snap and strain and curl their lips, but he holds them firm. His two sons look on, clutching guns, their curly haired Water Spaniels sitting at their feet.

They are all dead now; the apartment is full of dead people. People Aunt Hannah spends hours praying for. Aunt Hannah, with her dusty black dress and acid breath, has the room next door to Grandmamma's. It is painted white and there is a crucifix on the wall. Mimi saw it once, when the door had been left ajar, and she scurries past now, afraid to look in case she catches another glimpse of that tortured face with the drops of blood falling from the crown of thorns on His brow.

She is almost there. A little bit further and she will be in the safety of her nursery. She doesn't need to hurry any more. Nothing can happen to her now. She slows down, pretending that she walked like this all the way down the hallway, that she wasn't frightened.

To prove how brave she is she looks around and sees that one of the doors has been left open. The room beyond is more beautiful than anything she has ever imagined. Unlike any other in the apartment, it glows with a silken voluptuousness that catches her breath. The walls are covered in delicate green brocade; curtains of the same material, elaborately draped and swagged, hang at the windows, which are screened by blinds made of white lace. Cascades of green silk flow from the ceiling, falling on either side of the curved bed, whose silken coverlet trails onto the thick carpet. A chaise longue upholstered in cream-coloured velvet faces the bed. Beside it, on a small table, is a single perfect lily in an opaque glass vase.

Enchanted, Mimi takes a few tentative steps. She knows she must not, but she cannot help herself. The bed beckons, its filmy curtains whispering in the draught, its silken covers crying out to be touched and stroked. Unable to resist, she stretches out her arms and walks towards it as if in her sleep. Her hot hand rests on the coverlet and she breathes in its silken scent. A white negligee, trimmed with swansdown, has been thrown across the foot of the bed. With one careful finger she touches the soft white fluff. Her fingers close and she presses the silk against her cheek. It smells of her Aunt Celeste. Richer and sweeter than lilies, warmer and spicier than ginger. Mimi sits cross-legged on the floor. Her thumb in her mouth, she shuts her eyes and rocks gently, backwards and forwards.

"*Mon Dieu!*" Celeste's scream slices the air. Witch like, she towers over the terrified child. Mimi clutches the negligee closer, cowering back against the bed as a thin hand, flashing diamonds, swoops down over her head. The edge of a ring catches her cheek. Mimi cries out and tugs the silk over her face, and a hot stream of urine pours over her boots. Scarlet with shame she begins to sob.

Her aunt has her by the shoulders. Bony fingers dig into Mimi's flesh as she is shaken, then held limp; Celeste's face thrust into hers as she screams. "Filthy brat. How dare you come in here and spoil my room, my lovely, lovely room?" The words disintegrate into sobs. Celeste weeps and screams; Mimi howls.

Aunt Hannah comes running from the kitchen.

"Get her out of here." Celeste is almost incoherent. In a moment she will be hysterical.

Hannah seizes the child. Mimi is thrown to the floor, face down into the pool of urine. She wants to crawl away but she cannot move. She wraps her arms over her head, her shoulders quivering. Above her, Celeste shrieks and wails. A servant girl brings a bucket and mop. Hannah loosens her sister-in-law's laces and proffers smelling salts. Celeste sinks onto the chaise. Her chest heaves, as if she is about to vomit. Hannah grabs the back of Mimi's pinafore. Pulling her to her feet, she drags her out of the room.

"How could you do such a thing, you dirty creature? Didn't I train you properly? Now what will they think, Mama, Alexander and Celeste?" she demands, marching her niece down the corridor. In the nursery, as rough hands strip her of her wet clothes, the torrent continues. "Trouble, nothing but trouble. Dirty, filthy child, always making more work, no consideration, nothing but trouble."

Mimi deserves it; she's been bad. She wants to put her hands over her ears to shut out the relentless tirade, but she knows she must stand still and take her punishment.

"What a horrible thing to do. You're not a baby any more. Even animals know better than to foul their own nests."

Mimi's skin is sore; she smells.

"You'll not have clean clothes today. You can put on your nightdress and get into bed. There's no supper. Not for the likes of you."

"I'm sorry," the child says hopelessly.

"Sorry! Being sorry is not enough. You'll go down on your knees, there in front of Our Lady and beg forgiveness for what you have done."

Mimi kneels. The nightdress sticks to her wet skin.

"Holy Mother of God, you who bore Our Saviour in your womb, look down on this miserable child. Bring her out of the darkness of her sinful ways and in your mercy show her the path of repentance. This we ask you, in the name of the Father and of the Son and of the Holy Ghost. Amen."

Mimi's eyes close. Her legs sag and she falls against her aunt. Hannah pokes her viciously. The child gasps on a sob and tightens her hold on the torn negligee.

"Pray." Her aunt's breath scorches her.

Mimi puts her hands together and holds them close to her face, her fingers trailing the silk. Her aunt embarks on the Rosary. Pins and needles stab at the girl's feet. Her knees are numb. She sways in and out of sleep, but every time its comforting darkness claims her, she is jerked back to wakefulness by her vengeful aunt.

At last, even Aunt Hannah has had enough and the child is allowed to get into bed. She curls up in the cold sheets and the smell of her shame revolts her. Pressing the perfumed silk against her nostrils she begins to sob. She is dirty and ashamed. It grows dark. She cries and cries and no one comes.

CHAPTER ELEVEN

Preparing to give her mother a bed bath, Hannah poured hot water from the kettle into a bowl and added cold from a jug. Rolling up her sleeve, she tested the temperature with her elbow before carrying the bowl to Mimi's room. Her mother lay on her back, legs apart, one arm thrown above her head, the other lifeless at her side. Hannah eased her out of her nightdress. Naked, Mimi appeared diminished; her limbs scrawny, her breasts and stomach flaccid. Ashamed to see her like this, Hannah covered her with a towel. She dipped a sponge into the water and squeezed out the excess moisture. Folding back the towel bit by bit, she dabbed gently.

When she was eighteen, she had told her parents that she wanted to go to medical school. At the news that her daughter planned to be a doctor Mimi flung up her hands and said, "Don't be stupid. What you need is a husband, if you ever manage to get one, and a home of your own. A baby or two with the colic, that will soon put you off doctoring."

"It's what I want." Hannah was determined not to give in.

"Rubbish. You say these things to annoy me." Impatiently, Mimi turned to her husband. "Stach, tell her not to be so foolish." Hannah looked at her father.

"My Hannah will do what she chooses," he said placidly, giving her a loving glance. "And none of us will be able to stop her."

Hannah's face softened at the memory. He was right, her beloved father. She had overcome her mother's opposition, gained a place at university and had started her course. It had taken a world war to thwart her ambition. A war and a loving husband. When peace was finally declared she could have returned to finish her studies, as other members of the armed forces given the chance to study at British universities had done, but she did not.

She turned her mother on one side, then the other. After she had dried her she rubbed cream on the pressure points, sprinkled her with talcum powder and gave her a clean nightdress. Hair and teeth brushed, she propped Mimi up against the pillows.

"It's hard work, this dying," Mimi said, unexpectedly. "I did not think it would take this long." Hannah was silent, not knowing how to respond. If she agreed, her mother might be offended. If she did not, Mimi would be angry. "Don't let that fat woman come to my funeral."

Hannah frowned, uncertain to whom her mother referred.

"That parvenu, that Pawloska creature. The one that is always visiting at Marianna's. I don't want her posturing all over the place when they bury me."

She sent cards and little notes wishing you well, Hannah thought. But she said nothing.

"They all like to make out they are somebody, but they are nothing, any of them..." Mimi's voice trailed away. Then she spoke again, more urgently. "Don't go. My daughter doesn't care for me, you know. She leaves me alone for hours." Hannah took her mother's hand and held it. It lay lightly in hers. In November, it had been plump and firm, now the bones were thin and birdlike. "They all leave me. Dimitri, Stach, Jan. Why did they all go?" Mimi's voice cracked with sorrow.

* * *

Hannah's father and her brother.

She shut her eyes and sees the sitting room in their house in Lvov, her father at the piano, her mother sitting upright on the settee, feet pressed tightly together, hands busy with embroidery, her very stance defying the dark forces that gather outside her door. Krysia lies on the rug beside the stove, her face propped in her hands, an unread book open in front of her. Jan paces up and down, his hands skimming over his mother's polished furniture, as if seeking reassurance from solid objects.

Hannah clenched her fists, slamming them hard against her

thighs, fighting the memories that swarmed relentlessly over long erected barriers. She stared hard at the summer light framed in the window, but the images would not fade.

* * *

The lamp-lit room is silent, a restless painful silence full of unspoken thoughts. No one dares voice their fears. To pretend this is an evening like any other might be enough to keep the terror at bay. Stach's finger brushes the keys of the piano, a single note trembles in the air and is drowned by violent beating on the door.

Hannah's glance flies to her father's face. She sees the fear for his family and for himself. Beads of sweat stand on his forehead. He opens his mouth to speak but no words come. Mimi sits motionless, holding back the inevitable moment; beside her, Krysia holds her breath.

"I'll go," Jan's voice cuts through layers of silence.

"No." Stach takes his son by the shoulders and gently moves him aside. His face is quite composed as he leaves the sitting room and goes into the hall. They hear him draw back the bolts and turn the key in the lock. Hear the harsh voices of the Russians.

"NVKD." Two uniformed men push their way into the house. The soldiers are coarse and brutal in contrast to her father, who is so calm and dignified.

"Comrade Bernadinski, you are to come with us."

Mimi groans, limp with shock. Krysia stifles a sob. Jan flushes, his hands balled into fists.

"Don't." Hannah hears her voice but is not conscious of having spoken. She touches her brother and he drops his arm. He is shaking; his eyes wet with tears. Krysia too is crying. Hannah does not cry. She has withdrawn deep inside herself, and from a dark place, somewhere behind her eyes, she sees herself step forward and confront the invaders. "You can't take him. He's not done anything wrong." She is not afraid, for she cannot believe that what is happening is real and not some strange and terrifying dream.

"Hannushia."

"Daddy." She looks up into his deep brown eyes.

— 114 —

He smiles at her and for a moment she thinks that everything is going to be all right. Then he turns and says with authority, "Give me time to say goodbye to my family." The Russians stand back. Her father kneels beside Krysia, who throws her arms around his neck and sobs uncontrollably. He strokes her hair, kisses her forehead and gently puts her from him. He stands up and folds his son in his arms. "Look after them all for me, Janush," he whispers.

"I will," the boy promises, his voice thick.

"And Hannah, study hard, do well." She feels his warmth as he holds her close, the scrape of his chin against her cheek, the whisper of his breath in her ear. She closes her eyes to hold the moment. Then there is nothing.

Krysia's cold hand slips into hers. Jan stands behind her; the three of them moving closer together as their father embraces Mimi.

"That's it." The soldiers pull him away. "You are to come with us."

"I am ready," he says calmly. "Hannah please fetch my coat." She goes into the hall and taking the thick wool coat from its peg, lifts it to her face and breathes in its smell of tobacco and cologne. Returning to the sitting room, she holds out his coat and he slips his arms into the sleeves. Casting a final glance around the room he says, "Don't worry. I will write." Then, without waiting for his captors, he walks to the door. The soldiers stumble into each other in their haste to follow him as he strides out into the night. The road shines like glass in the moonlight.

"Daddy!" Krysia's cry rises from the open door.

Hannah cannot move. She knows what she has to do but her limbs will not work. Icy air seeps into the house and still she stands frozen on the doorstep. Then Mimi lets out a cry and begins to sway. Instantly, Hannah rushes forward to catch her mother.

"Jan, bring the vodka, quickly." Carefully, Hannah lowers her mother onto the sofa. Her arm around her shoulders, Mimi's head against her chest, she holds the glass to her lips. "Mama, drink this. Mama please." Mimi opens her mouth and the liquid trickles down her throat.

"Jan," Mimi whispers.

"Mama, I am here." He kneels beside her.

"Thank God." Mimi closes her eyes. "At least I still have you. The others, Dimitri, Stach gone, both taken from me."

Jan takes her hand. "She's so cold." He looks anxiously at Hannah.

"It's shock. Krysia, run and fetch a blanket. Hurry."

A long shuddering moan escapes Mimi's lips.

"Will Mama be all right?" Krysia chews at her lip.

"Yes," Hannah says shortly, wrapping the blanket around Mimi. "What she needs now is some hot sweet tea." She looks at her brother and sister. Jan is rubbing his mother's hands. Krysia has settled herself at Mimi's feet. Hannah sighs. "I'll make it."

In the kitchen she moves as if she were a hundred years old. Her limbs tremble as she takes the china out of the cupboard, her hands shake when she sets the kettle on the stove, and she has to steady herself against the table before putting the five cups and five saucers on a tray. When she realises what she has done her legs give way; she sinks into a chair and buries her head in her arms.

"Hannah don't cry. Please don't cry." Thin bones dig into her side. Frantic hands stroke her cheeks, lift her head and prise apart her arms. A narrow body slips onto her lap. Krysia's hot face presses against hers. The child's heart is beating furiously. Her eyes dilate with fear. She clings desperately to her big sister and Hannah knows that for Krysia's sake she has to be strong.

"I'm all right." Hannah wipes Krysia's eyes with the back of her hand. "Come on, help me carry this." The tray is heavy and Krysia clasps her arm around Hannah's waist making it difficult to keep it level; the cups rattle and shake, but the child will not let go.

That night she creeps into Hannah's bed and curls up under the eiderdown while her big sister swallows down the tears she dare not shed in front of her.

Neither girl sleeps. In the morning, when Hannah gets out

of bed, the room begins to dissolve around her, the floor waves and sways, her chest is tight and it is hard to breathe. Only Krysia's frightened face prevents her from slipping into unconsciousness.

"I will be all right," Hannah promises, her hands clutching the back of a chair, forcing herself to stay upright.

"Shall I get some tea? Will that help?" Krysia's voice shakes and Hannah somehow manages to nod. When her sister has gone Hannah puts her head between her knees. The blood rushes to her brain, pounding through her skull.

"Mama is up." Krysia is back, carrying a cup and saucer. "I told her you were not well and she says you are to come and eat something." The china trembles in Krysia's hand. Hannah slowly lifts her head. The sisters look at each other, because in times of crisis Mimi's habit is to shut herself away; her closed door making the point that they are all useless and no one can give her the help and support she needs. Krysia's forehead creases into a frown. Watching Hannah drink her tea, she jiggles from foot to foot, desperate that their mother should not be kept waiting. At the same time she sees that her sister needs to take things slowly.

When they enter the kitchen, Mimi is by the stove stirring the thin porridge that is to be their breakfast. "We are very low on oatmeal," she remarks. "I will have to go shopping."

Hannah stares at her mother. The black wool dress that fits perfectly over the rounded figure, the white linen apron, the pearl earrings, all denote a middle-class woman calmly going about her daily tasks.

Rage rises in Hannah's throat like vomit. Mimi does not care. She has never cared. If she had really loved Stach, she would be weeping, lying on her bed, crazy with grief and fear.

I am sick with terror and she stands there as if it's an ordinary day.

"We must eat, whatever happens," Mimi says. "Is your brother out of bed yet?"

"I'll go and see." Hannah is shaking, her whole body juddering, her teeth rattling. What will she do without her father? *What is going to happen to him? Will we ever see him again.?*

Without him she is lost. Clenching fists, she beats them against her temples, over and over again until she grows dizzy with pain.

* * *

"You were gone a long time," Gregor remarked from behind his paper. Hannah looked at the barrier of newsprint between them and suppressed a sigh. Her husband was still angry.

"She was hard to settle."

"Hasn't the doctor given you something for her?"

"Yes, yes." Now she was impatient with him.

"Then why not give her the medicine?" He was making an attempt to sound reasonable but the quiver in his voice betrayed him.

"I will, but it is too early in the evening. If she has it now, she will not sleep later."

"She never does." Gregor sighed and put down the *Evening Post*. "It's you, Hannushia, I worry about. You look so worn and so strained." He stood up and stroked her cheek gently. "It is all too much for you." Her head on his shoulder, her arms holding onto him, she remembered how she had clung to her father, and was overwhelmed with grief. "You see how tired you are."

Suddenly she wanted to push him away. How dare he tell her what she was feeling? No one knew better than her how exhausted she was. What she needed from her husband was help and encouragement. What she got eroded her. His relentless concern made her feel weak and useless.

His lips were on her hair. His breath soft, he murmured, "I only want to look after you. You are everything to me." Holding her tight, he helped her to a chair.

"I'm all right."

I am always all right because I can't be anything else. They all depend on me; they all need me. They have always needed me. Only Jan did not. And my father and the Russians took him.

Her shoulders slumped. Her head fell forwards onto her arms. Gregor's hand lay like a manacle on her neck.

Her brother is slim and fair with a quick joyous walk, which marks him out in a crowd. Even on this dull November afternoon, he moves as if life has cast its riches before him. Hannah, in contrast, is sick with fear, plagued by a constant griping nausea which robs her of energy and appetite and leaves her lying rigid under her covers at night, her dry lips moving in constant prayer for her father, and all those others, who have been taken. Trudging home from her last lecture, books clasped like armour to her chest, she sees Jan coming towards her, smiling and raising his hand in a brief wave, before plunging it back into his pocket. His other arm he holds stiffly across his chest.

"What are you doing here?"

"Walking." He grins.

"I can see that," she snaps. "What have you got under your coat?" Glancing behind her, she lowers her voice. "It's not something forbidden. It's not a gun is it?"

Jan's eyes sparkle. "Not a gun. I promise you."

"Then what?"

"Swear you won't tell."

"Don't be stupid. I'm not going to get you into trouble."

"All right then. Look." With a flamboyant gesture he flashes open his jacket and reveals a loaf of bread tucked under his arm.

"Jan, what are you doing? It will be ruined before you get it home."

"I'm not taking it home."

"What!"

"Shh." Jan links his arm through hers. Drawing her close, he bends his head. "Do you really want to know? It's terribly dangerous," he teases.

Hannah stands still. "Stop playing games and tell me what you are doing," she hisses.

"Keep your voice down."

Fear tightens her throat making it hard to get out the words. "I've got to know. What would we do if something happened to you? What would Mama do? If they arrested you, God help us,

I think she'd go mad."

"Nothing's going to happen to me." He shrugs lightly. "Hannah, we can't stand back and do nothing. Come with me and you'll see."

In the railway yard, standing in the sidings, the trains are waiting. Line after line of cattle trucks, their doors firmly bolted. They have been there for two days. At first they were silent. Resting, as if waiting to resume their journey. Then the voices began. In the beginning they simply called out for attention. Then, when no one came, when no one pulled back the bolts and let them out into the daylight, they became incredulous, then angry and as the hours lengthened and the air grew stale in their cramped and fetid prisons, they cried out, pleading for food and water.

"Polish soldiers," Jan says. "Taken by the Russians. Go and talk to the guard over there so I can get the bread to them."

Hannah cannot feel the ground beneath her feet as she walks the endless distance to the boy with the gun.

"Excuse me." Her mouth is dry as sand. "Hullo there." The guard is a peasant from some distant Russian village, his coat trailing to his ankles, his cap tipped over his ears. She tosses her head and tries to smile, as they do in the films. Her tongue moistening her parched lips.

"I'm Hannah."

"Yuri. That's me." His wide flat face splits into a grin.

"It's a cold night."

"This is nothing. It is much colder in my village. Sometimes the snow comes up to the roof tops," he says proudly. "That's how it is in Russia."

"It snows here, too." Hannah is desperate to keep his attention while behind them Jan tears frantically at the bread and pushes the pieces in through the slats of the trucks. Yuri's face falls.

"Not as much," Hannah assures him quickly. "I'm sure nothing can compare with your village." Her bladder is full and cold sweat is running slowly down between her shoulder blades.

"Home is good." He nods. "Everything is better there."

What do I say next? Hannah's thoughts blur. Her throat

constricts.

"What we love..." she begins. Someone touches her on the back and she spins round, poised to run for her life and catches her face in Jan's coat.

"She's my sister." Jan grins at the guard.

The Russian grins back. "Girls," he says with all the experience of his teenage years.

"They are all the same," Jan agrees. "Come on Hannah. Let's get you home." He takes her by the elbow and steers her towards the street where people go about their business as if nothing has changed.

* * *

Kate ran lightly down the stairs. It was hot, but the well of the house was cool, and the faint film of moisture that covered her skin was not unpleasant. It was like being immersed in a warm bath. Passing the door of her brother's room, she heard his sleepy snuffles and wrinkled her nose in disgust at the thought of his hot, little boy body. Her grandmother was silent. The hall leading to the kitchen full of shadows.

Her mother had her head in her arms, her father was leaning over her, but when he saw his daughter he turned.

"Have you finished your work?" The surprise in his voice irritated her but she bit back a scathing riposte. She wanted a cold drink not a confrontation. "Don't you still have revision to do?" he persisted.

"I'm doing it." She crossed the room and went into the scullery. She dashed lemon juice into a glass and topped it up with water from the tap.

Hannah felt the air move against her arm as her daughter went past. Kate did not look at either of her parents. Balancing her drink in her hand she padded up the stairs.

"What is she doing up there?" Gregor fussed. "She spends hours in her room but does she use the time well? Those exams of hers are so important and she does not ask for help. Remember, when she first started at the grammar school we had to test her on French and spellings, and before that at primary school, it was her tables. Every night there was something. Every night." His mouth set in a thin line, his neck trembled with frustration.

Hannah pressed her palms over her eyes. She too remembered the indignant, impatient child who made it plain that she neither needed nor wanted their help. Sleek and selfish as a cat, Kate demanded only to be allowed to go her own way. Her parent's love and concern counted for nothing. She had so much to give and her daughter wanted none of it.

CHAPTER TWELVE

In the pale-green classroom, rows of girls sat at their desks. Some straight backed, others hunched over their paper, all writing diligently. Sister Mary Stanislaus, her face smooth and unlined under her triangular coif, moved serenely among them.

The hand on the white-faced clock jerked from one minute to the next. Looking up to see how much time there was left, Kate caught the nun's eye and was surprised by a quick upturn of the lips, followed by an almost imperceptible nod of encouragement. Heartened, she returned to the analysis of a Shakespearean sonnet. The pen was hot in her hands and the words flowed easily onto the page.

Beyond the tall windows the sun played on the lawns of the convent garden. The metallic tune of an ice cream van floated in from the street. With muffled footsteps and hushed voices the Lower Sixth hurried past the examination room. Next year it would be their turn to sit at the narrow desks, hands slippery with nerves, hearts beating furiously.

The timer, set for the end of the examination, buzzed. Instantly every girl put down her pen and waited in silence while the nun gathered up each script and placed the pile on the front desk.

"You may speak." Girls, who for three hours had sat in total silence, swivelled round in their chairs. Eager to talk and compare answers.

"What did you do for the context question?"

"I couldn't think of that quote. I just couldn't."

"When I saw the question on *King Lear* I nearly died. I tell you, I thought I was going to pass out."

Kate stood up. She shook out her skirt and pink and white candy stripes swirled around her hips. The air moved over the tops of her stockings, dislodging the petticoat that clung to her thighs. Without saying a word she gathered up her pen, pencil and ruler and walked out of the room. Her classmates watched without comment. Kate, knowing that nothing could be altered, never discussed her answers with anyone.

She sat waiting for her friends to join her on the low wall that surrounded the front of the sixth form annexe. This part of the convent garden, where the huge beech tree drooped its shade over moss-covered stone and the flagged path was always slippery with damp, never saw the sun, and was a place forbidden to the pupils.

Drawing up her legs, linking her hands around her knees, she stared at the street. On the opposite side of the road a woman wheeled a child in a pushchair. An old man in a trilby hat walked a fussy little dog on the end of a short lead. The animal held its tail like a plume and trotted along the pavement on tiny paws.

Kate yawned. The thrill of breaking even the most minor of rules had faded. No one was going to report her to Reverend Mother and even if they did her time at school was almost over, her references for university long since written. There would be no cataclysmic explosion, no expulsion, nothing but a pained lecture on how she had let not only her teachers but, more importantly, herself down by momentarily lapsing from the high standards that they all knew she held.

"Bloody hell, if they only knew." She stretched her back against the pillar at the end of the wall. It was almost hidden by the trunk of the tree beneath which lay a drift of dead leaves. Remembering the lattice of branches above her head, the crackle of dry leaves against her skin, the smell of him, the weight of him on her, Kate began to laugh.

On the other side of the wall a group of girls sauntered towards her.

"What's so funny?" Annie asked. Kate hesitated, uncertain whether to shock or to remain silent. There was pleasure in both, but more, perhaps, in keeping it to herself. If she told her friends, it would be obvious that, although she had risked everything, she had escaped unscathed. Besides, she strongly suspected Carla had already gone all the way.

"I can't explain," she said. "It would take too long."

"Post-exam hysteria," Veronica pronounced.

"Must you turn everything into a medical state?" Carla objected.

"It's because she's going to be a doctor," Kate said.

"Only if I get my A Levels."

"You're not going to fail," Carla laughed.

"If you do then none of us will have passed," Annie said.

Kate swung her legs off the wall. "Who's going to the bus?" she asked. Nylon petticoats rustled as the girls turned to each other.

"I don't feel like going home yet," Annie said.

"You want to stay at school?" Kate pretended surprise.

"No. Of course not." Annie flushed. "It's just..."

"She means it's Friday and there are no more exams till Tuesday so we ought to do something," Carla interpreted.

"Otherwise it all feels so flat," Annie added gratefully.

"I can't tonight," Veronica said.

"But tomorrow's Saturday," Carla said. "We can't stay in on Saturday night. If I did I'd go mad. Stark, staring mad."

"And that must not be allowed," Veronica said solemnly. "So we must all go out." She burst into giggles as if she had made a joke.

"Where?" Kate was growing impatient.

"The dance at the Victoria Rooms?" Annie suggested.

"We could." Carla shrugged.

"Why not?" Veronica added.

"Okay then. We'll meet in the usual place at half-past eight," Kate decided.

* * *

"How did your exam go?" Hannah was setting out salad on plates.

"Okay."

"It was English, wasn't it?"

"Yes."

"And it went all right? You knew all the answers?" Hannah heard her voice grow anxious as she tried to get Kate to talk.

"Yes," Kate snapped, hissing out the final consonant. She glared at the table. "You know I can't eat cucumber." She picked a translucent slice from one of the plates and held it up between her thumb and forefinger. "We're going to the dance on Saturday. At the Victoria Rooms. Where all the students go," she added meaningfully.

"University students?" Hannah's voice was eager. Maybe her daughter would meet a nice intelligent boy who would convince her that studying was the only path to success.

"Of course. It's their Union. Okay?" Kate released her grip and a green disc of cucumber slid onto the table.

"All right. But you must be back by twelve, or you will never get up in time for Mass on Sunday."

"Do I ever miss Mass?"

I wouldn't dare risk committing a mortal sin in the middle of exams. If I did, God would be sure to get His revenge. A quick memory block, a set of impossible questions. Besides Mum would never forgive me and Dad would never stop fussing. So I'll sit there for another Sunday trying to work out the point of it all. Do I, or don't I think He's up there? And here too, of course. Omnipresent, Sister St Francis says. So He's in the bathroom when I'm sitting on the toilet. In the bedroom when people are doing it. Looking into everyone's minds, seeing all their trivial little thoughts. If He's that omniscient He ought to be able to think of better things to do.

"I'll be there, don't worry. You know—" she looked directly at Hannah "—you worry too much. It's constraining." And she swept out of the room and up the stairs to her attic.

"Just a minute." Hannah was furious. A tomato in one hand, a knife in the other, she hurried to the bottom of the stairs. "You can't walk out like that," she called. A door at the top of the house slammed shut.

* * *

A sultry June evening. A sky shot with rose-pink and purple clouds massed around lakes of blue forming a fantasy landscape above the city. Beneath it, the Victoria Rooms, a pillared temple rising from a wide flight of steps, flanked on each side by large bronze lions lying on plinths.

Kate was the first to arrive. Keeping to the left side of the building, she went over to the lion and reaching up ran a hand over the folds of its mane, then rested her face against the cool patina of its cheek. The statue was their talisman, their meeting place, where she and her friends waited for each other in the mornings on the way to school, a ritual that had begun in their first year at St Cecilia's. Over the years, the creature had assumed a mystical status in their lives. To stroke its mane was to ensure good luck. To sit on its back brought power. In winter the bronze was icy cold burning un-gloved hands. In summer it basked in the sun; its flanks warm to the touch.

"If we meet again in twenty years' time, it will be here," Carla had once said, and even the practical Veronica had nodded in agreement.

Kate settled herself on the lion's back. And waited. It was the time in between, when people slumped in front of flickering screens and mothers put small children to bed, then called their older brothers and sisters in from the street. The time when women squinted into their mirrors to do their makeup, men put on clean shirts and checked the contents of their wallets. Getting ready for the night. And all its possibilities.

Groups of students wandered past on their way to the side entrance. Most were lads; none caught her attention. If she found someone tonight, she vowed he would be someone special.

Her gaze turned to the cars rounding the traffic island. At one minute past half-past eight a maroon Wolsey pulled up at the kerb and Veronica got out.

"Have you got your key?" Doctor Townsend's voice was as deep and rich as the leather seats and walnut fascia of his car.

"Yes, Daddy."

"Have a good evening and be back home by twelve, there's my girl."

Veronica watched her father drive away, then glanced from side to side, her dark bob sleek against her head. Low-heeled pumps clicking purposefully, rounded hips plump beneath her pale-blue shift, she climbed the steps of the Victoria Rooms. At the foot of the lion she brushed the dust from between its paws and with a nod to Kate sat down, her feet dangling, handbag perched neatly on her lap.

With the exaggerated strides of a fashion model, Carla approached from the opposite corner. Of the four girls, she had been designated the glamorous one. Her face was broad, slightly Oriental, her skin had an olive tinge, but her eyes were deep chocolate, her lips wide and red. Her long hair hung down her back and she wore a very short cream dress of cotton lace, white shoes and a big gold bangle. Her perfume was heavy and sweet, with a sharp undertone.

She leaned nonchalantly against the statue, one hand on its neck, the other holding her bag. There were cigarettes and a lighter in her clutch bag, but Carla would always wait to see if she were offered any before opening her own packet.

Annie balanced precariously on new high-heeled shoes, her tight skirt impeding her stride as she hurried up the steps and misjudged the length of her stride. She tripped but managed to save herself, then took tiny steps, kicking out her leg from the knee in the same way she climbed onto the platform of a bus. Reaching the lion she rummaged in her bag for her compact.

"Sorry I'm late. I was finishing off my dress." Annie smoothed down the pink linen before sitting next to Veronica. "Don't you just love going out. The whole getting ready and everything."

Veronica nodded. Carla shrugged. Kate said nothing.

The shadows stretched out from the dark bulk of the building behind them, and they were now all in their accustomed places. Kate on the lion's back. Carla at its side. Veronica and Annie at its feet. The edges of the sky darkened. Colours melted and dissolved. A streak of scarlet hung low over the city. Darkness rose from the pavements. The moon was white as paper, the street lamps' orange glow harsh against the sunset.

"Let's go in." Kate led the way past the imposing portico and around the corner of the building, where a half-open door made a square of light. Inside, a trestle table had been set up where a fat girl in a black jumper and a lad with a ginger beard were selling tickets for the Saturday night dance.

The building smelled of beer, dust, and long ago ballet exams. The girls went straight to the Ladies, where the dull yellow light distorted their faces as they peered into the mirrors, pursing their lips to add another layer of lipstick, narrowing their eyes as they applied more mascara to already spiky lashes.

Voices high and excited, arms linked, they clattered down the lighted passage into the cavernous hall. At the side was the door to the bar, while at the furthest end red lights glowed at the foot of the stage. One or two couples wrapped around each other, mouths and tongues working, hands roaming, leaned against the walls. From the bar came the sound of voices, a drift of cigarette smoke and the reek of beer.

"We're too early," Annie said anxiously.

"Yeah." Carla's eyes strayed towards the bar. "Hope we're not going to have to pay for our drinks."

Four lads came on to the stage, two carried guitars, one seated himself at the drums; the tallest adjusted the microphone. It shrieked and crackled, then the lead guitarist struck a chord. A spot lit up the group. The singer took the mike from its stand, his voice burped from the back of his throat, "Peggy Sue, ma Peggy Sue..."

Dark figures began to move from the lighted doorway of the bar. Knots of lads, with glasses of beer in their hands, stood around the sides of the hall. Drifts of girls, in ones and twos, gathered in front of the stage. The beat quickened.

"I want to dance." Annie half closed her eyes, swaying from foot to foot.

Carla cast a practised glance around the room. There were only two couples and a small group of girls on the dance floor. The available men were still talking and drinking. They had not even begun to view the talent. "Not yet," she said firmly.

"Come on."

Kate ignored her. She was bored. The heat was oppressive, the music too loud. The night had lost its potential. The moment by the lion, when she had allowed herself to believe that something extraordinary might happen, had subsided into an unremarkable Saturday night. She needed to dance, to stamp out her disappointment and frustration.

"I'm coming." Veronica joined Kate.

"Okay." Carla followed, not brave enough to stay at the side on her own.

They piled their handbags on the floor and, forming a protective circle around them, started to dance. Kate and Annie abandoned themselves to the music, Veronica worked out a meticulous set of steps, which she repeated over and over again whatever the beat. Carla's glance slid beyond the group. Around them, the hall was beginning to fill up.

Where once there was space to fling out their arms and to move in and out of their circle, now other dancers pressed in on them. Though these were still mostly made up of groups of girls there were a few couples. They danced a little distance apart from their partners, the girls with their eyes fixed on the boys' shoulders; but if anyone came close they moved nearer to their partners. These lads were theirs, long established boyfriends not someone they had picked up on a Saturday night. On one or two fingers small chips of diamonds glittered as hands were angled to catch the light.

The lights burned blue and red; their narrow beams thick with dust. Kate's dress clung to her, her hair was plastered to her head. The music beat in her brain; the air congealed around her. She shut her eyes and pounded her feet on the floor.

Carla saw them coming, watched as they put their glasses down on a windowsill, cracked a joke with their friends then plunged into the sea of dancers. They moved swiftly, purposefully towards the girls they had been watching out of the corners of their eyes. A touch on the shoulder, lips brushed against an ear, the words drowned by the wail of guitar and the pounding of the drums, and groups began to disintegrate. An arm around her waist and Annie moved unresistingly towards the edge of the dancers. Carla saw her go and smiled. The lad she had picked out as hers was coming closer; she let her body loosen, her movements become sensual and enticing.

"Want to dance?"

Carla assessed him from under lowered lashes. He was about twenty, dark haired, dressed in casual trousers and an open-necked shirt. He would do. She nodded and bent down to scoop up her bag. The lacy cream dress slid up her thighs.

Veronica moved closer to Kate and they went on dancing. Two girls left on their own had to pretend they were enjoying themselves. After a while she lifted her wrist and squinted at her watch.

"Kate, I've got to..." She tapped the dial and turned down her mouth in mock disappointment.

"Not going yet, are you?" Her brother's friend Jeremy, a prop-forward with a broken nose and a car, loomed into view. She gave Kate a little shrug. Kate lifted an eyebrow. Wherever they went there was always someone to look out for Veronica. Jeremy took her elbow and guided her towards the bar. Veronica looked back over her shoulder.

"Do you want to come?"

Kate shook her head. It was against their code to make up a threesome. Now she should thread her way through the dancers and stand at the side of the hall. If she was lucky someone desperate for a grope during the last slow number would pull her onto the floor. Breaking all the rules, she kept dancing.

The music slowed. The dancers melded into each other, scarcely bothering to move. Fragments of light, silver, white and gold, swept over the dark mass of bodies. One by one, the remaining couples cleared the space around her. The band went into their last number and still she danced. The final notes quivered and there was a smatter of applause. Then the lights went on, robbing the dingy hall of its glamour and lust.

Kate raised her shoulders in a self-deprecating shrug, picked up her bag and walked briskly towards the one of the emergency exits. The doors were propped open letting in the hot night air.

He stepped in front of her, long blonde hair, soft beard, dressed entirely in black, tight jeans, black roll-collar shirt.

"Going home?" he said.

"What else is there to do?"

"We could go for a drink."

Kate looked at him, saw a thin intelligent face, the nose a little too long, the mouth wide, the eyes amused. She smiled, then nodded.

They walked side by side. He was tall; the top of her head barely reached his shoulder. Their footsteps echoed in the empty streets. Their shadows stretched behind them in the neon glare of the street lamps.

"I've never seen a girl dance on her own," he said. "I kept thinking your boyfriend must be around somewhere." His voice was low with a hint of laughter.

"I don't have one and I didn't want to stop."

He stood still. "Do you always do what you want?"

Kate turned to face him. "Yes," she said.

"Where are we going?"

"The Coronation Tap should still be open."

"It's a bit late isn't it?"

"They never bother there. Come on, we'll go this way." She led the way down the street and into the wooded walk that ran through Victoria Square. The dense foliage formed a tunnel above their heads blocking the street lights.

"You want a drink?" He sounded almost disappointed.

Kate thought of the noise and the press of bodies in a busy pub.

"No. I don't." She took his hand and jumped up onto the low wall that ran along the length of the walk. Now she was taller than him. He tried to leap up behind her, but she would not let him. She began to run, pulling him with her, until they emerged breathless into the light on the other side of the square. He looked up at her, his face serious and quite beautiful.

"Do you always do this?" he said.

"Ever since I was at school. St. Cecilia's." He frowned. "It's up there." Kate gestured in the general direction of the convent. "You won't know it if you're not a local."

"I've lived here for three years."

"That's nothing," she teased. "I've been here a life time."

"You're not a first year, then."

"I will be in October. But not in Bristol. I'm going away."

He stared beyond her at some distant horizon. "So am I."

"Oh." Something dipped in her stomach. The first interesting man she had met in ages and he was going away. It was just her luck.

"I'm going to India."

The world unfolded in front of her. She stopped in the middle of the road and grabbed his arm. "How?" she demanded.

"A group of us are going. We've got a bus."

"A bus!" Kate wanted to laugh. It sounded so ordinary.

"We got it second hand. One of the girls got us a deal; her father owns a garage."

Kate stumbled against the edge of the pavement. Above the glow of the city the stars were steel bright. The sky arced over to the other side of the world and she realised she was not bound to take the way mapped out for her by her parents but was free to follow her own path.

CHAPTER THIRTEEN

Hannah slept on her stomach. Head sideways on the pillow, back to the world, stomach sinking into the sagging mattress. Beside her, Gregor was neatly curled on his side; his skin smooth and dry, breathing softly from the depths of sleep.

The cry pierced the quiet room. Thin and helpless, it gathered volume, growing into an insistent wail. Hannah woke, flooded with phantom milk, her nipples prickling and tingling although it was six years since a child had fed at her breast.

She stretched out to her husband but his back was turned to her, self-contained in sleep. Putting a hand on his shoulder she drew her knees up behind his. Nestling against him, feeling the rise and fall of his breathing, she ran her lips over the back of his neck. He smiled but did not wake, and edged away from her. She withdrew her arm, rolled over and sat on the side of the bed.

The night was so hot that she had left the window open with a gap in the curtains to allow for any movement of air. There was no breeze, but a narrow shaft of moonlight fell across the floor.

It took her back to that night on the beach, when the moon cast a silver pathway across the dark sea. The water so still it barely rippled to the shore. A whisper of waves kissing the sand as they walked hand in hand along the beach. Hannah and a boy with dark curls and laughter crinkling at the corners of his eyes. He had wanted her that night, had begged and pleaded with her, and she had refused him. What harm would it have done to lie together in the sand, to hold him in her arms, to open herself up to him? A few weeks later he was dead, his body mangled in some distant battle.

Shaking her head, Hannah crossed to the window and lifting

up the hem of the curtain looked out into the empty street.

* * *

In the room below, Mimi stirred. One arm thrashed at her covers, the other lay inert at her side. Her mouth was dry, the half-open lips cracked, her body hot and wet. She dreamed of a pool, its surface black as glass, its depths impenetrable.

* * *

The blinds in the salon are drawn against the summer. Through the linen the sun diffuses into a yellow twilight. Grandmamma, solid in black, sits in her usual chair, a slightly pained expression on her face. Mimi is on a stool at her feet, sewing. In spite of the heat her hands are cool; the needle in her fingers slips easily through the material. The doorbell rings. Grandmamma cocks her head to one side. Mimi does not look up from her work. If she sits very still they might forget she is there. As Aunt Hannah's disapproving footsteps move down the hallway, she wonders who their visitor might be. Her aunt and uncle have keys, her mother is away on one of her mysterious trips. Her father sits huddled in a corner of the room, so still and silent that no one ever pays him any attention.

With a flurry of greetings and rustles of silk, Aunt Helena sweeps into the room. Magnificent in the palest eau-de-nil, lace drips from her wrists and swirls around her neck. Her hat is huge, swathes of chiffon around its brim cascade down her back as she stoops to kiss Grandmamma. Behind her stands her daughter Marianna, her red hair pulled tightly back from her red face. She looks hot and uncomfortable and she glowers at Mimi.

"This heat!" Helena sinks into a chair and waves a delicately gloved hand. "Hannushia, for mercy's sake, bring me a glass of lemonade." Aunt Hannah's mouth tightens into a straight line. The wrinkles around her top lip flatten. She resents being treated like a servant, but at the same time glories in any opportunity for martyrdom. "It is too much! I die. The children are drained. They have no life, no energy. They are fading away." Helena pulls a glove from one slender hand, then the other. Letting them fall into her lap, she continues, "I have written to Irena." Grandmamma's eyes brighten at the mention of her eldest daughter. "She has offered to take the boys and Marianna for the summer. In the country it will be so much better."

Mimi sits very, very still. She has heard all about her aunt, the Countess Galinska, but has never seen her. Aunt Irena and Uncle Anton live in that part of Poland which belongs to the Austrians. Her mother often visits, but they never cross the border to Warsaw.

"The city," Grandmamma agrees, "is no place for children." Marianna scowls. Mimi, her heart hot and jealous, imagines a palace with large cool rooms and ranks of servants. Marianna is looking at her cousin.

"There is no one to play with at Aunt Irena's. They are all boys." Marianna pulls a face. "May Mimi come too?"

Something inside Mimi flips. She mistimes a stitch and the needle digs into her finger, but she does not cry out because from under the brim of the huge hat, she has not yet unpinned from her head, her Aunt Helena is gazing at her. Her green eyes are kind.

"Poor little Mimi. She is so pale. Of course we must take her. A few months in the country will soon put the roses into her cheeks. Let her come with me and I will bring her back as plump as a little peasant girl."

"If Maria agrees," Grandmamma's voice is doubtful.

"Maria! Maria is always away, always travelling. Of course she will do what is best for her little one. What mother would not? Ask her, Mama. No, on second thoughts you can *tell* her. Tell her I am taking Mimi. She will not object. She can come with us, if she likes."

Us. Mimi belongs. She has been included. She is filled with joy. She will go. Helena is expansive, dramatic, expecting everyone to do as she says. Grandmamma demurs, but cannot refuse her daughter, the Princess.

* * *

They travel to Galicia by train. Marianna, who has been all over Europe with her mother, is restless and bored. Mimi's nerves are strung tight between anxiety and excitement. She is so afraid of doing or saying something wrong that she stays very still and quiet, which annoys Marianna, who squirms in her seat and pulls faces at the window. But since Helena insists that the children are silent she does not say anything. Henryk, her elder brother, reads a book; Valerian, the younger of the two boys, sits beside his mother who strokes his hair, or lays her hand on his arm as she swoops and dips into conversation with Maria.

Mimi cannot believe that she is on a journey with her mother, who for some inexplicable reason has agreed to come with them. From time to time she glances at Maria, but her mother does not notice. She sits, straight and solid, beside her elegant sister, an old straw hat set firmly on her head, her blue cotton frock plain but serviceable. Determined not to compromise her principles and spend unnecessary money on clothes, with her shiny face and rough hands she looks like a family servant on her day off. If Mimi were not so surprised by her presence, she would be ashamed to be seen with her.

At the station there is a tremendous fuss about the Zapolski luggage. Maria, holding a battered carpet bag, wanders down the platform while servants and railway officials run hither and thither, shouting out orders, cursing minions, then turning to mutter apologies to the Princess, who stands holding her parasol over her head. Flanked by her sons, she appears oblivious to the chaos around them. After a while Helena trails away, her pale green skirts dragging in the white dust, and Henryk takes charge. Boxes and trunks are arranged in neat lines, chairs are brought for the ladies, hot lemon tea appears. Mimi gazes in wonder at her eldest cousin. He is still a boy and yet everyone rushes to do his bidding and all because of the Zapolski blood that runs through his veins.

When the carriages arrive and the steward falls to his knees and begs pardon for their lateness, Mimi makes sure she is at Henryk's side. She wants to ride with him. She wants him to notice her but is afraid to say anything in case he thinks her a baby, like his sister. He hands his mother into the carriage, then turns to his aunt. Mimi's stomach tightens; she crosses her fingers. There is one place left.

"Valerian come and ride with me," Helena calls. He climbs in and the footman folds up the steps. Marianna grins; Mimi swallows her disappointment. The two girls travel in the following carriage. Marianna delighted not to be squashed between her brothers, Mimi wishing she was.

They are greeted on the steps of Novy Lasko by Aunt Irena and two of her sons. She is small, dark and pretty. They are tall and blonde and walk protectively behind her as she comes down the steps to kiss her sisters. Henryk and Valerian eye their cousins cautiously. Then Marek, the younger of the Galinski boys, balls his hand into a fist and aims a glancing blow at Valerian's chest. He is momentarily startled, then recovers himself, grins and hits back. The two boys go into the house with their arms around each other's shoulders. The older boys exchange glances.

"Kids," Franz says dismissively.

"Brothers," Henryk replies.

"Boys!" Marianna pulls a face but before Mimi can respond Aunt Irena is calling their names, sweeping first Marianna then Mimi into her embrace. Soft as eiderdown, she smells of honey and lavender, and her hand is gentle on the child's cheek. Mimi is stiff and awkward. She is so rarely touched she does not know what to do, but when her aunt loosens her hold Mimi's eyes sting with tears. She longs to bury her face in her Aunt Irena's breast, to cling on to her warmth and softness. Miserably, she draws back, but Irena takes her hand and leads her into the house to join the rest of the family.

The bedroom she is to share with Marianna is large and light. The furniture is made of white-painted wood and there are muslin curtains around the bed. Marianna rushes about, looking in cupboards, pulling open drawers, jumping up and down on the mattress. Mimi stands and looks around. She still cannot believe that she is here with her cousins, her aunts and her mother.

Later the maid comes to unpack their luggage. Marianna has a trunk full of dresses, petticoats and camisoles. There are soft leather boots and silk stockings and lace-edged night-dresses, all packed in layers of tissue paper. Mimi has one small box. She watches as the maid puts away Marianna's clothes. Soon the drawers are full, the cupboard billowing with cotton, muslin and silk. Beside such extravagance, Mimi's one white muslin dress hangs limply on the rail.

"The mistress says you are to dine with the family tonight," the maid says. "Which dress will I put out for you to wear?" She looks expectantly at the girls. Mimi hangs her head. She is ashamed and embarrassed.

"The green one is mine and the pink is Mimi's," Marianna declares. The maid holds out a confection of rose silk and organza. Marianna nods. Mimi stretches out her hand and very, very gently lets the tips of her fingers stroke the shimmering material. Hot and giddy with pleasure, she stands with her arms raised as the maid slips the dress over her head. The silk caresses her skin, slides down over her waist, swirls around her legs.

"It's a trifle too long," the maid declares as she ties the sash. "But it looks well. Brings the colour out in your cheeks. After dinner I will take it away and put a tuck in it." She clicks her tongue. "Those Warsaw seamstresses! You won't find work like that on the estate."

Marianna grins. "It came from Paris," she whispers behind her hand. Mimi treads clouds of delicious bubbles. She loves her cousin, and hates her too.

In the dining room the long windows are open to the night and the candles flicker in the evening breeze, their light wavering on silver and crystal. In the surface of her water glass Mimi sees her face reflected a myriad times. Beside her, Marianna wriggles on her chair and swings her feet. Marek screws up his face, Franz fiddles with his knife, Henryk and Valerian sit very still and straight, while around them the adults talk.

Maria, flushed and passionate, leans her elbows on the table. Helena's skin is white as ivory in the darkening light. Irena banters gently with her sisters and listens with attention to the carefully thought-out opinions of her older sons. Her husband Anton is grave and serious.

Mimi's eyes grow heavy, her head falls forward and her breathing slows. To stop herself slipping into sleep she sinks her teeth into her bottom lip and stares hard at the bowl of fruit in the centre of the table. Red runs into purple, orange bleeds into red, the white of the cloth, the glow of sliver, the yellow and blue of the candle flames coalesce. The murmur of conversation recedes like waves breaking on a distant shore and she can hold out no longer.

Strong arms lift her, carry her down dark passageways, up a wide staircase and lay her down on her bed. Her boots are tight on her feet, her dress will be crushed. She struggles to wake but already the ribbons are undone, the silk is slipped from her body. Her skin prickles in the sudden chill, then she is enveloped in warm cotton, her nightdress is smoothed down, and turning on her side she burrows under the covers and gives herself up to sleep.

Beside her, Marianna sprawls on her back, red-gold hair covering the pillow. Caught in her dreams she moves restlessly about the bed. Mimi lies tight and still, her knees tucked up to her chest.

When dinner is over Helena comes to say goodnight to her youngest child. She sets her lamp down on the chest of drawers and leans over the bed. Still asleep, but somehow knowing her mother is there, Marianna stretches out her arms. Helena holds her close, kisses her, strokes her hair, then lays her gently back on her pillow. Marianna smiles in her sleep. Helena turns to go. Her perfume hangs on the air, the rustle of her silks swishes through the silence.

A small sound, part breath, part sigh, escapes Mimi. "Sleep well, little one." Helena's hand rests on her forehead and Mimi's limbs uncurl and she lies loose and easy.

As soon as the morning sun dazzles through the curtains, Marianna jumps out of bed. Pulling off her nightdress, she stands naked in a patch of sunlight. Mimi hides her face in the pillow. When her cousin goes to the bathroom, she scrambles out of bed, lifts up her nightdress and pulls on knickers and petticoats as fast as she can. She is not ashamed of her underwear, the lace with which she has trimmed it, the knots of flowers she has embroidered are as fine as anything Marianna owns, but she cannot bear to be seen in her skin. Sharing a room will be a torment. Sleeping in the same bed, she will have to take care to lie still all night in case she rolls up against her cousin, or touches her warm skin.

"What shall we do today? Where shall we go?" Marianna bounds back into the room. "We won't go with the boys. They will want to ride or fish, but we are going exploring."

Mimi does not want to go out into the hot sun. She wants to find a cool corner where she can sit and sew, but does not dare say so. She has been brought here to do what Marianna wishes.

After breakfast, Marianna will not stop to put on her hat, swinging it by the ribbons as she charges out of the house.

"Come on, come on," she urges. They run to the stables where Mimi must endure the stench of horse. The rank smell of the animals and the reek of their dung makes her feel sick. Marianna strokes velvety noses, buries her head in arching necks. Mimi stands back as far as she dares and holds her breath.

When her cousin has had enough of talking to horses, they go into the farmyard. An even greater torture of hot baked smells, steaming cowpats, lumbering cattle, udders distended with milk and stupid chickens that flutter and squeak as Marianna flaps her arms, and shouting with laughter chases after them. Mimi recoils in horror from the wide-open beaks. Marianna races past, catches hold of her hand and pulls her along. Down steps, over walls, along paths, she runs, forcing Mimi to follow.

Mimi is hot and sticky. Her face is red and she is close to tears. At last Marianna sinks down on a stone bench on the terrace at the back of the house.

"I'm hot," she breathes.

"Me too." Mimi hopes they will go back into the house for a drink of water. Marianna tips back her head, raising her face to the sun and letting her hair flow down her back.

"We need shade. I know, we'll go into the woods. We can look for the magic pool."

Mimi's insides plummet. "What pool?" she asks flatly.

"The one where Yolanda Galinska drowned herself." Marianna's voice drops to a whisper. "Long, long ago, when this house was still a castle, the lord of the manor had a very beautiful daughter. Her skin was white, her eyes were blue, and she had long golden hair that reached down to her ankles. She was so lovely that one day, when this knight was riding past on his charger, he saw her and straight away fell in love with her. He gave her father a lot of money so that he could marry her, but Yolanda said she would never marry one of the Teutonic knights and nothing her father could do, or say, would make her change her mind.

"On the day of the wedding she crept down from her bedroom in the turret and ran off into the woods and when she reached the pool she pulled off her wedding dress and jumped in the water and was drowned."

"All because she didn't want to marry a German!" Mimi cannot believe anyone would be so stupid.

"Yes. He was an enemy of her country." Marianna's defence is passionate. "What else could she do?" Mimi does not know and does not care. The sun is beating down on her head and she feels a little sick and dizzy. "The legend says, if you look in the pool you can see the future," Marianna continues. Mimi thinks of cool clear water. "It will be nice and shady in the woods. Come on."

Marianna is already halfway across the lawn. The air shimmers in the midday heat, the shadow of the trees stretches over the sun-bleached grass. Mimi knows the forest is forbidden. Hoping someone will see where they are going and call them back, she drags her legs and glances over her shoulder at the house. The windows are blank, their blinds drawn against the glare. Marianna plunges into the trees. There is a flash of white muslin and she disappears.

Mimi is terrified. If anything were to happen to her cousin she would be blamed. They would send her back to Warsaw, to Grandmamma and Aunt Hannah. She looks around for help but the gardens are empty. She begins to run, her feet pound over the dry earth, her breath comes hard in her throat. Her eyes run, whether with sweat or tears she does not know. She lifts her hand to wipe them. It is dark under the trees and difficult to see.

"Where have you been?" Marianna is sitting on a tree stump

untying her boots. She pulls them off, then discards her stockings and wriggles her toes in the thick soft grass. "Now you."

"No." Mimi knows she should not but Marianna insists. Reluctantly, she undoes her laces, slips her feet out, and pulls off her stockings.

"Leave them here." Mimi's boots stand next to her cousin's. They are her best pair; Marianna has dozens. Mimi only has two. "Now," Marianna whispers, "it really is magic. I'll be Yolanda, because I've got the right hair, and you can be the faithful maid."

"But there wasn't a faithful maid in the story," Mimi objects.

"All right, then you can be the Teutonic Knight."

"No." At this point Mimi rebels. Marianna, however, is quick to concede.

"You are right. That is a horrible part. You can be the maid and we can both jump in the pool together. It doesn't matter if it wasn't in the story. It probably was and I forgot to mention it. After all, one doesn't mention maids, not even if they are awfully important. So will you? Please." Head on one side, she smiles at Mimi.

Mimi says nothing. Marianna's eyes plead, but Mimi does not speak. Her heart is thumping in her chest and her head feels light as she realises that at this moment, however fleeting, she has power over her cousin.

"Please." Marianna begs. Mimi hesitates.

"All right," she says. This game, however stupid, is better than being in the farmyard, or the stables.

Marianna flings out her arms, hair streaming out behind her, she runs through the trees crying, "I will never marry him. I would rather die." Mimi follows, feeling rather foolish.

The trees thicken, shafts of sun slide in under the canopy. The path is dappled with shifting light. Sunlight mottles Marianna's face as she runs towards the pool. She slips in and out of shadows, a pale wraith among the dark trees.

Without warning, the forest comes to an end and the pool stretches before them. It is larger than Mimi expected, more like a lake. Its banks are bare of trees and Marianna has to scramble down a steep incline to get to the water. The mud is dry and cracked. It is warm underfoot and the lake laps gently around their bare toes. Marianna scoops up a handful of water. She opens her fingers and a shower of sparkling drops patters onto the surface.

"Now, I will throw myself in." She gestures towards Mimi. "And my faithful maid with me."

Mimi shrugs. She moves away from the edge and climbs up the bank. A fallen tree trails its branches into the lake. The game is over.

Marianna's mood changes. Scrambling after her cousin, her eyes glow, her face is very white as she grabs hold of Mimi's arm and fingers biting into the flesh pulls her towards the water. The surface gleams like burnished metal under the unrelenting sky. "Look," she demands. "Look into the future." Mimi is afraid. She twists away. "Coward," Marianna hisses. She raises her arms. "Oh spirit of the lake, come to us. Show us. Tell us what the future holds." She sways backwards and forwards, rocking on the balls of her feet as she chants.

Mimi sees their reflections in the water. Marianna is gold and white. She, a smaller dark-haired figure, stretching out her arms, ready to catch her cousin in the small of the back, to give one little push which will send her hurtling into the water.

The lake seems bottomless, the waters icy cold. Mimi's muscles tense. Marianna is peering intently into the depths. Mimi's gaze is fixed, her fingers tremble. Her heart beats violently as the rage rises within her.

Wild waves whip across the surface. The lake heaves and churns. Marianna screams as the ground crumbles and the edge of the bank gives way. Dry mud slides into the water and she loses her footing. Mimi stands frozen. Watching. Then she snatches at her cousin's skirt. The material tears but she throws her arms around Marianna's waist and together they fall to the ground. Marianna screams and screams. Her eyes are blank, her hair snakes about her head. Her teeth chatter and her limbs jerk wildly.

"Stop it," Mimi yells and when the screaming does not stop, she sinks her teeth deep into Marianna's wrist. There is silence, then Marianna slumps against her, breathing raggedly in short painful gasps.

"Did you see it?" she asks. Mimi shakes her head. "You must have, you must." Marianna's voice rises.

"I only saw the waves, that's all."

"Nothing else?" Marianna demands.

"Only the waves," Mimi repeats. "There was nothing else."

Marianna shudders. She begins to speak, then stops. After a while she rubs her wrist and looks sideways at Mimi as if she does not believe her. Mimi stares into the black waters. She is quite composed. Her anger is curled so small inside her that it has almost gone. "You nearly fell in," she says.

Her cousin blanches. She presses her hand against her lips and bites the tips of her fingers. "You saved me, you saved my life." Her voice trembles.

"I suppose I did," Mimi says.

CHAPTER FOURTEEN

Sprawled across her bed, her mouth half-open, her breath coming in grunts and moans, Marianna slept.

* * *

Marianna is in the blue sitting room in the Zapolski palace. It is a dull autumn day. A grey sky presses in at the windows and the lamps have been lit. She is lying on the sofa, feet on the blue silk cushions. There is a book on her lap; one finger holds it open, but she cannot concentrate on the text in front of her.

Mimi, dressed in black, sits opposite. She is sewing, her back straight, feet pressed together, fingers moving quickly, almost mechanically, pulling stitch after stitch through the material. After a while, Marianna gets up and begins to walk about. Mimi, coming to the end of a row, picks up a pair of small gold scissors and severs the thread. "That's that," she says, turning dark eyes on her cousin. "It is finished. Everything is finished."

Marianna's skin prickles. To escape her cousin's baleful glance, she walks over to the window and looks down into the courtyard.

Wrapped in a dark cloak, the hood pulled over the face, a figure comes through the gates. Head lowered, shoulders bowed, he, or she, moves under the lee of the building. A shudder crawls up Marianna's back. The feeling of dread she has tried to suppress seizes her limbs. She can neither move nor speak.

The stranger is climbing the steps that lead to the main entrance. Somewhere deep in the palace, a bell clangs. Footsteps ring on marble. Marianna grasps the back of a chair. Her fingers clutch the carved wood as if to anchor herself, but her grip loosens and she is impelled to move towards the door and down the stairs to the entrance hall, where the visitor is waiting. Clinging to the banister, Marianna looks to the footmen for help but as she is unable to voice what she fears; they are impervious to her unspoken plea.

"Come." It is a woman's voice, high and light, her beckoning hand pale and slender. It is not the secret police come to arrest her.

Breathless with relief, Marianna follows the woman out of the palace and through the darkening streets. In the brightly lit boulevards they are dark ghosts, weaving in and out of the crowd. In the poorer part of the city they merge into the shadows. Beggars cry out to them. Men with limbs missing hold out twisted stumps. Children, barefoot and ragged, call after them, and a drunk lurches into their path, his breath sour as he steadies himself against Marianna's arm and slurs obscenities in her ear.

"There's a pretty lady come to give Jacek a good time," he slobbers.

"Leave her," Marianna's companion hisses.

"*Ty Kurwa!* It's Death herself." The drunk shrinks back, crossing himself. "Don't let her touch me. I'm not ready to go."

"No one is," the woman replies.

They turn into a narrow alley, rank with rotting rubbish and the stink of drains. The alley gives way to a square, the houses blank and shuttered; once solid and prosperous, they are now leprous with decay.

Marianna's boots echo on the paving stones. Around another corner and a door gapes blackly in the night. The staircase is unlit, the steps uneven. With one hand on the roughly plastered wall, she feels her way up. When she reaches the top, she looks back into thick and empty darkness.

The woman who has brought her here pushes open a door. A circle of girls kneel in a bare white room. Rosary beads slip through their fingers as they pray the Passion of Christ, the Crowning with Thorns, the Scourging at the Pillar, the Carrying of the Cross, the Crucifixion and the Death on the Cross. A single candle burns before an icon, voices rise and fall. Tears stand on pale cheeks.

"Pray for us sinners, now and at the hour of our death," the girls murmur, while in the room next door his mother weeps for the son that will be hanged at dawn.

* * *

Marianna's chest heaved and her mouth gaped open as she woke. Staring bewildered at the sun-dappled ceiling, she struggled with the thundering of her heart. Gradually, the rapid beating subsided and she managed to push herself up against the pillows and look around the familiar room.

How strange that of all the deaths she had known she should dream of this one. A sixteen-year-old boy she had never met hanged by the Russians for some traitorous act. She had prayed with his sister throughout that long night; tried to comfort her and her family on that blood-stained dawn, and had never seen any of them again. There had been so many others since, so many losses over the years, and now they came thick and fast. Scarcely a week went by without a black-edged notice in the Polish paper followed by attendance at yet another Requiem Mass in the Polish church.

She reached for the silver cigarette box on the night table and lighting up, drew the smoke deep into her lungs. Today she would perform one of the cardinal works of mercy. She would visit the dying. She would go and see Mimi.

* * *

Hannah laid out the night table as an altar. She covered it with a white damask cloth on which she placed a wooden crucifix and a vase of roses. There was also a clean towel and bowl for the priest to wash his hands, which he would do as part of the ritual.

She had just finished when there was a knock at the door. Father O'Brian stood on the doorstep, red-faced and a little breathless from his climb up St Michael's Hill.

Mimi lay on the bed with her eyes closed, arms folded over her chest. The priest's shoes squeaked as he entered the room but she gave no sign of having heard.

"She's not asleep, Father, but I don't know how much she understands." Hannah's voice was hushed and reverent.

"Our Lord will know and it is His mercy we will now invoke," the priest assured her. "So I will begin." Hannah knelt and he took the oils from their case and smearing them on his forefinger traced the sign of the cross on Mimi's forehead.

"I am not ready to go," Mimi said clearly in Polish. Her black eyes bored into the pale blue ones of the priest.

"In the name of the Father and of the Son and of the Holy Ghost," Father O'Brian continued valiantly.

"You can get him out of here," Mimi addressed herself to Hannah. "His nails are not clean." The priest began the absolution. Mimi closed her eyes and breathed loudly through her nose while Hannah stifled an overwhelming urge to laugh.

* * *

Kate wrote the final word on the page. It was her last exam. She had written essays on the fall of Rome, Charlemagne, and the Crusades. Once the letters had formed beneath her nib the facts faded from her brain. Transferred to the paper, she would never again remember the dates she had so relentlessly crammed over the past few weeks. She put down the pen, balancing it carefully in the groove that ran the width of the desk. There were five minutes left but she could not bring herself to read over what she had written. What was done, was done. Already it all seemed irrelevant. As she waited for Sister Mary Edward to collect her exam paper, she stared out of the window at the convent garden.

There were only six girls in the room. The nun had chosen to work up from the bottom of the alphabet, so Kate would have to wait to the last. As the others left, one by one, she wondered if it was deliberate. She knew what the nuns thought of her. They found her awkward and difficult. A girl who was prepared to question truths which she should have known to be immutable. Sometimes, she was sure that they found it hard to believe that she came from a good Catholic family. The kindlier ones no doubt included her in their prayers; the less charitable had no patience with her and would be glad to see her go.

Kate too would have no regrets about leaving. She had no intention of returning. Not for her the old girls' reunions, the newsletters with the school crest. Once she walked out of that building she was never coming back.

In a cramped cubicle in the toilets, she pulled off her candy-striped skirt, her petticoat, stockings and suspender belt, squeezed into a black miniskirt, tied the tails of her shirt across her waist, and slipped her feet into a pair of high heeled sandals. Going across to the mirror she painted a black line along each eyelid. Behind her lay her discarded uniform, the pink and white skirt in a heap on the floor, the stockings lying one on either side of the lavatory as if she had stripped off and dived into the sewers.

Walking out of school, the air warm on the top of her legs, she felt free and ready for whatever the summer would bring. She had finished with Dave. They had never been formally going out together, but she would avoid the biker gang for a few weeks which would be enough for him to get the message.

In the meantime there was Jon. The night of the dance he had asked if he could see her again and – Kate checked her watch – he should be waiting for her at the top of the hill.

She saw him as she stopped to cross the road. He was leaning against a wall, a book in his hand, long fair hair falling over his shoulders. As she approached he pushed himself away from the warm stone, bent his head and kissed her. It was a soft exploratory kiss, gentle and undemanding. Kate reached up and wound her arms around his neck, lifting her face for another kiss. His lips touched hers and she opened her mouth, sliding her tongue around his. He drew back, casting a swift glance down the hill to the convent.

"Is this your way of showing the nuns?"

"I'm giving them two fingers," Kate said.

He laughed and put his arm around her shoulders. They walked uneasily together, his long loping stride at odds with her much shorter steps. After a while he took his arm away and held her hand. "Do you want to come to the flat?"

She shook her head. People would be there. His flatmates and their friends. She had no desire meet them. She wondered what it would be like to be alone with him in his high-ceilinged room. Lying on the bed, looking up at the swathes of ivy and acanthus in the plasterwork, with the afternoon sun slanting through the tall windows, warm and golden on bare skin.

A tremor of pleasure flowed through her. Her skin felt charged, her fingers tingled. She tightened her grip on his hand.

His fingers enclosed hers and she felt the pulse of his blood, the heat of his body. The brightness of the day faded around her; she was conscious of nothing but him. It was an effort to keep walking, an effort even to speak.

"There's a group of us going to celebrate tonight," she said.

"The end of your exams?"

She nodded. "Do you want to come?"

He moved his shoulders.

Her stomach plummeted. Stupid tears flooded her eyes. Why had she said anything? It was up to him to ask her, not the other way round. Now he would think badly of her and she would never see him again. It wasn't fair. Women had to wait, were never allowed to make the first move. She dropped his hand. Stared into the distance.

"What time do you want to meet?"

The sky swirled. The heavens danced. Bubbles of joy exploded.

"At eight. By the left-hand lion on the steps of the Victoria Rooms," she said.

Jon walked her home. At the back gate they stopped.

"I'd ask you in but my grandmother's dying."

"Oh yeah." His tone was casual.

"You're not bothered?" So she hadn't shocked him or put him off. He was, as she had hoped, different from all the other lads she had met.

"We've all got to go sometime."

"It doesn't scare you?" Kate was curious to know more, eager to be able to discuss things even her best friends did not want to think let alone talk about.

"Death? No." He shrugged, then smiled down at her. "It's only one more step on the wheel of life. If I did it right this time, I'll be okay. If not, I'll end up as an insect."

Which was much less scary than eternity, Kate thought. Especially eternal happiness. That was too much. "My friends think it's awful for her to be dying at home. Their ancient relations all go to hospital."

"In India people die at home. Then they burn the bodies and throw the ashes into the Ganges."

"Perhaps we should chuck her off the Suspension Bridge when she goes."

Jon grinned. "Would your Mum agree?"

"No. We've got to do everything according to the Church. Gran's being anointed today." He lifted an eyebrow. "Don't you know what that is?"

"I'm C of E."

That explains it then, thought Kate. *Non-Catholics don't know anything.*

"Religion wasn't my scene. But now it's different. Something's got to make sense of all this. So tell."

"It's the Last Sacrament. The priest comes and dabs her with holy oils as a kind of goodbye to this world. Only sometimes it cures people." She shuddered.

"You don't want her to get better?"

"She's taking long enough to die as it is." She looked up to see if she had shocked him.

"She may have Karmic debts to pay," Jon said calmly.

"Yeah," Kate said. She did not understand what he meant, but hoped she looked as if she did.

"I've got to go in. I want to see how Mum it. It's a bit hard on her."

Jon kissed her gently on the lips. "I'll see you tonight then."

She stood and watched him walk down the alleyway. When he had disappeared around the corner she grinned and gave herself a hug in anticipation before pushing open the back gate into the honeysuckle-scented garden.

In the dusky kitchen Marianna and her mother sat at the table drinking tea. The Princess clasped her hands around her cup, her rings glowing in the dim light. Hannah's head was bent towards her visitor. She was talking quickly, lightly, with a hint of laughter in her voice. Kate drew back, wondering whether she could slip past without being noticed but even as she hesitated Marianna saw her and called her name. Kate scowled. There was to be no escape. She would be treated like a child, forced to greet her great-aunt with a kiss and have to answer inane questions about exams and her plans for the future.

"Come and join us." Marianna waved at an empty chair. "I

am sure there is plenty of tea in the pot."

"Enough for another cup," Hannah confirmed.

"It is too early for vodka," Marianna added.

"I could fetch the bottle," Hannah offered.

"No, no. I will face my ordeal without it. But perhaps later I will require a restorative."

Kate drew closer and perched on the arm of a chair, ready for flight. To her surprise the two women continued their conversation.

"Is it so hard?" Hannah asked.

"Visiting the sick?" Marianna spread out her hands. "Not in general, but Mimi, well ... you both know Mimi."

Kate slid down onto the wooden seat. This was going to be interesting. "Has she always been such a pain?" Hannah shot her daughter a warning glance, but Marianna smiled.

"Your grandmother has always been ... what shall we say?" She paused, as if to consider the options. "A little, no, more than a little difficult. Would you not agree?"

Hannah hesitated. Kate sensed her mother was trying to work out what she should say. She never liked saying anything derogatory about anyone, let alone Mimi.

"She told Father O'Brian he had dirty nails," Hannah said with a giggle. Kate stared. Her mother was behaving like one of her school friends, exchanging confidences, laughing and being silly. This was not how women of mature age should behave, especially not mothers.

"You see what I mean?" Marianna laughed her rich sensual laugh. "Mimi is dying and what concerns her is not the state of her immortal soul but that of her confessor's fingernails." She tutted and shook her head, then, in a sudden change of mood, sighed, "Oh how I shall miss her." Hannah bit her lip. Kate, refusing to feel anything, stared defiantly out of the window. On the garden wall the orange cat balanced awkwardly. Tail held over its body, it positioned its paws to jump.

"And now, duty calls." Marianna placed her hand on the edge of the table and pushed herself to her feet. Swearing discreetly under her breath she stood for a moment to gather her strength before moving to the door. Without being asked,

Kate was there to hold it open it for her. She looked back at her mother.

Hannah held the teapot in one hand, a cup and saucer in the other. There were lines around her eyes, deeper ones ran from her nose to her lips. She was no longer young and one day she would be as old and fragile as the Princess.

The thought that at some distant time she, Kate, would be the strong one and Hannah, her mother, might have to rely on her caught at her heart. She did not want tea, but she let Hannah pour her a cup.

"Do you want a sandwich?" Hannah asked.

Kate's stomach rumbled. For the first time in weeks, she was hungry. "Yes please." She grinned.

Hannah fetched bread, butter and tomatoes. She sliced and chopped and spread. Kate sipped hot tea and ate while her mother talked.

"The Princess is such a comfort. I'm sure your grand-mother appreciates her visits. They were so close when they were young, more like sisters than cousins."

"She doesn't seem to like her very much," Kate said.

"I think she understands her," Hannah said.

So do I and she's a mean old cow, Kate thought.

* * *

The front room was hot and stuffy. Mimi lay on her back with her mouth open, breathing noisily. Marianna folded herself into the chair beside the bed and looked critically at her cousin.

"My God, Mimi, old age is cruel. Look at us. Wrinkled as prunes, as bent and rheumaticky as Baba Yaga. It seems only yesterday that we were running through the woods at Novy Lasko. Do you remember the pool? Do you remember how I screamed and screamed? I was so afraid, I was almost beyond fear. I had looked down into the waters and I had seen the destruction of everything we knew. All those terrible deaths." Her voice shook. She clasped her trembling hands. "The black dragon came up out of the depths and devoured us," she whispered.

"There was earth beneath his nails. Does he dig the graves himself?" Mimi sounded so lucid that Marianna was startled.

"Do you mean the priest?"

"Priest *smiest,* they are all pigs. What do they know?"

Marianna leaned forward eagerly. "What indeed?"

Mimi was on the threshold of death. In these last hours of her life could she see beyond that boundary? Was there more than the dissolution of the flesh? Did the dying know something denied to those left behind?

"They promise us eternity but they know nothing," Mimi hissed.

"And you? What do you know?" Marianna prompted.

Mimi's eyes clouded and she began to whimper.

"What is it? Tell me." Marianna placed her hand over Mimi's clenched fingers. The cries intensified, sharp little yips grew into long drawn out wails. What had been human became reduced to some basic animal response. Marianna shuddered and called out Mimi's name, but nothing could recall lucidity to that yellow skull-like face, those black staring eyes and gaping mouth.

Gradually, however, the sounds diminished; Mimi's head fell to one side and she slept.

"Thank God for that." Marianna leaned back in the chair, exhausted by the effort it had taken to stay in the room. It had taken all her will power not to call Hannah for help with that nightmare creature on the bed.

She had stroked Mimi's forehead and soothed and spoken to her in the same way as her own nurse had done, long ago, when she had woken in the night from a bad dream. Now her own limbs shook, her head spun, her eyes were heavy. She would close them for a moment then light a cigarette and go in search of a strong drink.

* * *

"Everyone's going. All the parents are okay with it," Kate told Hannah. "We've worked hard and now we want to celebrate the end of our exams."

Hannah nodded without commenting.

"Thanks, Mum." Kate smiled at her mother and congratulated herself for having got away with a lie. She had no intention of meeting Carla, Veronica, Annie and the others.

While her friends were dancing at Top Rank she would be with Jonathan.

"You'll go and see your grandmother before you go out," Hannah said.

"In case the old bat's dead, when I get back." Guilt made Kate brusque.

Hannah bridled, but kept her voice steady. "It's possible. She's getting more fragile all the time. I don't quite know what's keeping her here."

"Typical Gran. She's hanging on to the last minute," Kate said more gently in an attempt to retrieve the situation. Her mother, however, had turned away and was staring out of the window at the brightness of the afternoon. The blue of the sky rose above the sun-warmed wall where the orange cat lay basking, its tail dangling into the golden petals of a climbing rose.

"Don't worry, Mum, I'll kiss her goodbye."

In the hall the air was still and thick with heat. Kate stood at the door of Mimi's room. She did not want to see her grandmother, not right now. All this sickness and dying was too much. It was bad enough being bombarded with images of suffering and death at school without having it thrust down your throat at home. If it was not the crucified Christ it was the Four Last Things, or the absolute necessity of examining your conscience in case you died unexpectedly and had done something that would send you to hell.

And yet, what was it Jon had said? Death was part of life and could not be avoided, and she had promised her mother. A few minutes would be all that it would take and Marianna would be there which would make the whole thing bearable.

I'll give Gran a kiss and be out of there. The Princess, she's not like Mum, she won't go on at me; she'll understand.

Marianna was sitting beside Mimi's bed, one hand on the coverlet, the other in her lap. She was asleep.

It was working out better than Kate could have hoped. It would be difficult, but possible to creep around the Princess, plant a kiss on her grandmother's cheek and make a quick exit. Kate tiptoed towards the bed, but as she reached it Mimi opened her eyes and said, her voice quite clear and distinct, "I want you to fetch it for me."

Kate looked at Marianna. The Princess took a deep breath, her head fell forward, and she snored softly.

"I said I want it now." Mimi's good arm beat against her covers. Kate waited but Marianna did not stir.

"What is it?" Kate said reluctantly. "What do you want?" If she had to give her grandmother some water she would do it. Anything else and she was running for her mum.

"In my trunk. The dress. It's in my trunk." Mimi's voice was growing fainter, her breath coming in short gasps.

"All right. I'll get it," Kate promised, eager to get out of the room before her grandmother stopped breathing altogether.

Kate climbed quickly up to the first floor and up again to her attic. Inside it was like stepping into an oven. She kicked off her shoes and opened the window. Then she walked over to her desk and pulled open a drawer. Scrabbling under a pile of papers she took out the key to her grandmother's trunk.

She had hidden it there when she and Hannah had moved Mimi's things to the attic, thinking that one day she would want to see what her grandmother had kept hidden from her family all those years. And now it seemed the time had come.

Kate padded along the narrow landing to the storeroom under the eaves. Cobwebs laced the window and the air was full of dust. Covered by an old curtain, the cot she and Peter had used stood against one wall. Propped up against it was an old mirror, its gilt frame cracked, its surface foxed and stained. Beside it was the box of Christmas decorations, each glass bauble carefully wrapped in yellowing newspaper. There were two suitcases, the smaller one quite new, the larger one made of leather and tied with a strap; and under the slope of the roof stood her grandmother's trunk.

It was solid and heavy, still labelled with her name, Bernadinska A. J., and her number, from the time when she had served in the British Army. Kate slid the key into the lock and lifted the lid. A faint scent of dried lavender rose from the tissue-wrapped layers as she carefully unpacked her grandmother's dress.

It was the most amazing dress she had ever seen. A column of white silk beaded with pearls, the skirt hung in gauzy folds to the ankles. Kate stood up and held it against her. It looked a perfect fit. Holding it carefully over her arm, she carried it to her bedroom.

* * *

Marianna's joints were stiff, her hip ached, and her mouth was dry. Soon she would have to hoist herself up from her chair and find that vodka. She looked at Mimi and laughed wryly. How could she have thought that her cousin could tell her anything about the mystery of death? Mimi was shallow and light headed, concerned only with what she could see, touch or feel. Anything else, apart from her own over-whelming emotions, simply did not matter to her.

She rummaged in her bag for cigarettes, then snapped it shut. She should not smoke in a sick room, although it would do Mimi no harm. Her cousin's body was long past help; in her fragmented state she no longer existed as a person and soon even that precarious existence would cease. Marianna had assisted at too many deaths not to recognise the signs. The increasingly laboured breathing, the narrow rib cage rising and falling with desperate urgency. She ought to call Hannah but she wanted a few more moments alone with her cousin.

Mimi was her past. They had shared so much. In spite of their differences they had cared for each other. When she died so much would be lost. There would be nothing left but an old woman's memories.

I will be truly old. Yet to me you will always be young. How absurd that I should think of you like that. So small and fragile with those dark, dark eyes and white skin. And underneath that composed exterior so much bitterness. Sighing, Marianna shut her eyes. Her mind wandered through the years. Maybe she dozed again. Half waking, she heard the door open and Mimi stood framed in the shadow.

"*Boze kohany.*" Marianna's hands rose as if to hold back the spirit she had summoned.

"Gran asked for it." Kate lowered the dress she had been holding against her. "Probably wanted to see it for the last time, or something. I found it in the trunk in the attic. Isn't it just so beautiful? I love it. I think I'll get married in it." She twirled the silk around like a dancing partner.

"Put it down. Now. At once." Marianna's voice grew hysterical and she battled to stay calm.

"Okay. Does she want it on the bed?"

"No. Give it to me."

"What about Gran?"

"Not now. I'll take it."

Kate hung the dress over Marianna's arm, adjusting it carefully so that no part of the skirt trailed on the floor. "Was it her wedding dress?" she asked.

Marianna shook her head, her fingers moving over silk as thin and friable as paper. Mimi had carried her ball gown with her throughout the War. When the Russian police had come to take her and her children away she had packed this dress. Even when her family were in need of food and medicine it had not been sold. "You must not wear it. It is bad luck," she said, slipping the dress onto a hanger.

"Then why...?" Kate waited, but the Princess was going to say no more. "Okay. I only did what she asked. I brought it down for her." She walked over to her grandmother and brushed her forehead with her lips. "Bye Gran." She waved a hand in Marianna's direction. "Can you tell Mum I've been to see her?"

Marianna steadied herself against a chair. The child had said goodbye, not goodnight. Kate knew, as children often did, that death had entered the house and was waiting for the moment when the body was at its weakest, to steal away the soul.

The dress glimmered like a reproachful ghost. Marianna could not keep her eyes from it. It drew her like the scab on an old wound. Her gaze lingered on the pearl-encrusted bodice, the fall of lace at the neck, the delicate cap of the sleeves, the gentle folds of the skirt. She watched as the twilight began to blur its outlines and blot it out of view, but still its presence permeated the room.

CHAPTER FIFTEEN

The dress is a waterfall of white silk standing on a dais of the palest marble. Aunt Celeste's arm is around her waist, her breath sweet in her ear. "Wear it for me Mimi," she whispers. "Wear it and all Warsaw will come flocking to our store."

Mimi's fingers, imprisoned in her tight leather gloves, burn to touch, to feel the gossamer silk against her skin, to hold the almost translucent material up to the light, to stroke the pearls that encrust the beaded bodice, to twist through the satin sash that binds the tiny waist. Her hand rises, then drops to her side. She presses her lips together and half-turns from the display.

"You do not like it?" Celeste is incredulous. "It comes from Paris. It is the latest model."

"It is beautiful," Mimi says flatly.

"It could have been made for you," her aunt says. Mimi shrugs, she even manages a smile. Rage and disappointment seethe beneath her controlled politeness.

"It looks a perfect fit, but I have no occasion to wear such a dress," she says stiffly.

"You will." In her relief, Celeste's gestures become very French. She rolls her tongue, she raises her shoulders and flings open her arms. "Your Aunt Helena is giving a ball and I have secured an invitation. Everyone who is anyone will be there."

Mimi looks her aunt in the face. She draws in her breath.

"Mama will never let me go. You know how she feels about Aunt Helena and her Russian friends."

Celeste clicks her tongue. She cannot understand these irrational prejudices on the part of certain members of her husband's family. Poland is part of the Russian Empire; to cultivate the family's Russian connections is good for business, and it is business that keeps the Stefanowskis fed and clothed and pays for the roof over their heads. Without her Alexander's ability to make money and her own to manage it, her high-minded sister-in-law and her pathetic husband would long since have been out on the streets. Maria cannot afford to stand in her daughter's way. Mimi is an invaluable asset, a walking advertisement for the finest department store in Warsaw.

"You will go. I will make sure of it," she says.

* * *

Snow sparkles in the lamplight. As she leaves the store, Mimi feels the cold air slide into her lungs. Light headed and dizzy with excitement, she smiles at the footman, waves gaily to the doorman, but in the gloomy darkness of the carriage her mood changes. She clenches her fists and promises herself that one day she will no longer be the poor relative, dependent on others for every bite she eats and every stitch she wears.

At home, she hides in her room. When Aunt Celeste returns, she hears the dip and screech of her voice and the answering growl of her mother's stubborn replies. Creeping out into the corridor, positioning herself by the drawing room door, Mimi clenches her hands and prays.

Her mother sits, square and toad-like, her father huddles under his blanket close to the stove. "No child of mine will go to a ball at the Zapolski palace." Maria is adamant.

"But Maria, it is Christmas. Surely there can be no harm in a young girl enjoying herself at a party with her cousins," Celeste cajoles.

"You think this is a time for rejoicing! When our country labours under the tyranny of an occupying power," Maria declares.

Celeste begins to lose her temper. "Maria, for goodness sake, what has the political situation got to do with whether or not Mimi should go to a party?"

"It has everything to do with it," Maria retorts.

Celeste shrugs her shoulders and gestures wildly. Two spots of colour stand on her cheeks as she sees a sound business opportunity thwarted by her husband's pig-headed sister, but before she can say more there is a knock on the front door.

Mimi shrinks back against the wall. The servant, crippled by arthritis but kept on by Alexander because she has been with the family since his boyhood, does not see her as she comes out of the kitchen. She exchanges a few words with whoever waits on the threshold, then hobbles painfully down the corridor to the drawing room.

"What is it? Can't you see we are busy?" Celeste snaps. The old woman ignores Celeste and addresses Maria.

"Someone to see you, *Pani* Maria. He says it is urgent."

The dumpy woman puffed up with anger is gone. The Maria, who rises swiftly to her feet, moves briskly and purposefully.

"I won't be long." Maria kisses her husband. His forehead is glazed with a cold sweat; he holds out his hand to delay her but she side steps him and is halfway out of the room.

"What about Mimi?" Celeste persists.

"Mimi? I've no time for such nonsense."

"I must reply to Helena's invitation."

"Then do what you please," Maria calls over her shoulder.

* * *

The sky is black velvet, studded with sharp splinters of light. The windows of the Zapolski palace gleam gold in the darkness. Soft as feathers, snowflakes drift to the ground, sparkling like crystals in Mimi's hair as she hurries up the steps.

Marianna is waiting for her in the bedroom they are to share. In the bathroom next door a maid pours scented oils into steaming water and sets thick towels to warm.

Mimi is nervous; there is a tight fist bunched in her stomach and her fingers are thick and clumsy as she unbuttons her dress. What if no one asks her to dance? She will die of shame. But to have a partner might be worse. What will they talk about? What will she say? She has no small talk. She has not had the benefit of a cosmopolitan upbringing like her cousins. She is the little country mouse newly come to town, destined to trail in her cousin's shadow. She casts a vicious glance at Marianna, who sits at the dressing table, a book in her hand, reading intently.

A lock of hair falls over Marianna's eyes, she pushes it back, yawns and says, "I suppose it must be time to get ready." Mimi nods, her mouth is dry. "You go first. Hanka will help you. I want to finish this chapter."

Mimi lies in scented water and broods on the unfairness of life. Marianna has everything that she, Mimi, could ever want; she possesses cupboards full of beautiful clothes and has a maid to look after them and help her dress and do her hair. Her mother, unlike Mimi's own who cares for nothing but politics, not only has an unassailable position in society, but Helena wants to introduce her daughter into that exciting glamorous world.

And, given all these advantages, what does Marianna want? Her cousin would be happy to be left alone to spend her days buried in a book.

Mimi splashes her feet and watches the ripples move up the marble sides of the bath. The water is growing cooler but she is reluctant to move. If she were the Princess Zapolska's daughter, all the young men would be eager to partner her; as it is, she can only be sure that her cousins Henryk and Valerian will ask her to dance.

The maid coughs discreetly. She is holding out a warm towel, but Mimi shakes her head and waits until she has gone before getting out of the bath. Once she has dried herself she lets the towel fall from her shoulders and studies herself in the mirror. Her waist is tiny, her hips narrow, her breasts high and firm. Her skin is as white as snow, her hair as black as ebony, her eyes huge and dark, her lips as red as blood.

"Are you ready?" Marianna strolls into the bathroom. Her cousin has no shame, no sense of modesty. Hurriedly, Mimi gathers the towel around her.

The dress, newly delivered from Stefanowskis, lies spread out on the bed like a bride on her wedding night. Even as the process of getting dressed begins, Mimi can scarcely believe she is to wear it.

First comes the silk chemise over which her stays are laced tight. Next she pulls on stockings, as fragile as spider's web, silk petticoats and lace-edged drawers. The underwear is her own, each piece exquisitely embroidered with flowers and butterflies.

A muslin wrap is placed around her shoulders. She sits in front of the mirror and the maid twists her hair on top of her head, securing it with pins and combs. When she has finished she stands expectantly. Mimi knows what she is waiting for and her insides grow heavy. She has no jewels of her own, nor has Celeste thought to provide any.

Marianna saunters in, her skin rosy from her bath. She looks critically at Mimi, then glances at the dress.

"It needs something to finish it off," the maid says.

Marianna cocks her head to one side. "Pearls, I think." She scrabbles in a drawer and pulls out a blue leather case. Two necklaces lie on deep velvet; a single rope, which Marianna and the maid loop and twist into Mimi's hair, and a double strand, which they fasten around her neck. There are earrings too, drops of diamond and pearl. Mimi stands, holds up her arms and, with a whisper of silk, the dress slides over her body. She turns and her skirts swirl, shimmering and sparkling in the light. She is transformed. She is a princess in a fairy tale, a magical being, a creature of ice and fire.

The clock on the mantelpiece chimes the hour. Marianna, dressed in the palest green silk that brings out the creaminess of her skin, the red-gold of her hair, links her arm through Mimi's and leads her down the stairs. At the top of the main staircase they hesitate. Below them, light dazzles, the air vibrates with voices and music, and is sweet with the scent of white lilies and golden roses. They can see the bright colours of uniforms, the gleam of silk and satin, the sparkle of necklaces and tiaras. Mimi grasps Marianna's arm. Marianna's throat moves as if swallowing bitter tasting medicine. There is a rare moment of understanding between them before Mimi loosens her grip and follows her cousin down the stairs.

Flanked by alabaster vases filled with flowers, Helena waits to greet her guests. Her hair glows like flame. Her gown twists about her body and her train is the mantle of a barbarian queen. The Zapolski emeralds hang around her neck and wrists. Valerian is at her side and she bends her head and whispers to him as the girls approach. Mimi stiffens, afraid that she is the subject of their conversation. Helena's fingers rest momentarily on her son's arm, then she closes her fan and spreads out her arms.

"How lovely you both look!" She moves towards them, her dress swishing over the marble floor, and envelopes them in her sweet, rich scent. "Mimi you are an ice maiden; Marianna a dryad," she declares.

Valerian is at their side, insisting that they both put his name down for a dance, and Mimi is so relieved that she has at least one partner that she no longer cares he is only doing his duty, and smiles demurely up at him.

"You do look very beautiful tonight," he reassures her. "Let me introduce you to some of Henryk's friends." A girl on each arm, he leads them into the ballroom. As they cross the floor Mimi is aware of a ripple of interest, heads turning, voices lowered as people wonder who she is. She holds her head high. She is a butterfly trembling on the edge of flight, a bubble rising into a clear blue sky.

Valerian guides her towards a group of officers and begins the introductions; the young men cluster around the girls.

"The next dance is mine."

"No mine, I beg you."

Mimi holds out her dance card. It is taken from her and, glancing to see who her partner will be, she looks into deep dark eyes.

"Prince Dimitri Rostov, let me introduce my cousin Alexandra Kucharska," Valerian says, and her world shifts. The ground beneath her feet is insubstantial as a cloud, the colours of the ballroom soften into a haze of pink and gold, and she is in heaven.

"Please, call me Mimi," she murmurs. The prince raises her hand to his lips. He has a boyish face, the nose straight, the mouth wide. Without writing a word in her card, he leads her into the dance. He holds her as if she were glass and she moves like thistledown within the circle of his arms. Her head whirls, her feet fly; they dance until supper is served, when they dine on ices and champagne.

In the conservatory the stars hang clear and bright above the dark glass. Mimi bows her head, her lips quiver and her eyes fill, as she remembers that there is only this one night; tomorrow she has to return to her drab existence. Instantly aware of her unhappiness, Dimitri puts his hand under her chin and lifts her face.

"Poor little bird," he murmurs. "Is your life so full of sorrow?" She lowers her eyes. She does not know what to say. How can a prince understand the daily pinpricks of her life? To her relief he does not wait for a reply but continues, "I read it in your eyes. You and I are as one. I knew it from the very first moment I saw you. We have a sympathy denied to others. Even in the midst of such joy we sense underlying pain."

And Mimi, who has never given a moment's thought to anyone's misery but her own, lifts her eyes to his and nods.

He bends his head as if he might kiss her. She sways towards him. Another moment and she will be lost, but even as she weakens a small hard nugget of sense causes her to pull away. At the same moment there are voices and a trill of laughter as another couple come seeking privacy.

"I think I should go," Mimi says. "People will talk."

"Let them. What do we care what they might think?"

"But..." For a prince it might not matter. For Mimi, if she does not return to the ballroom soon, her reputation will be ruined. Even so she makes no move. Dimitri's intensity is so intoxicating that she cannot bring herself to leave.

"There is no need for you to worry. Your honour is as precious to me as my own." The prince bows and clicks his heels, then he offers her his arm.

"Shall we go back and dance?" he asks. Mimi says nothing. To be seen dancing with the prince would be all she could wish and yet she is not sure that this is what he wants.

"Whatever you would like," she murmurs.

"And you?"

"Tell me about your life. I cannot imagine what it must be like." He leads her to a seat. She opens her fan and asking her if she is too hot, he brings champagne. As the night slides away, Mimi learns that the he is the only son of an elderly father and heir to vast estates.

"What is wealth? Love is all that matters," he declares. Her heart dances beneath her ribs and she glances at him before dropping her gaze and hiding her face behind her fan.

"Without love, there is nothing. You know that as well as I."

Mimi nods. Beyond the glass the sky is lightening. Dawn breaks, sharp with frost, and Marianna comes to find her.

"There is breakfast," she announces. She looks tired, her red hair is escaping from its pins and there are shadows under her eyes. "Prince Dimitri? Mimi?"

"I am not hungry." The prince gets to his feet.

"Nor me." Mimi holds out her hand and his fingers curl around hers.

"I will see you later?"

She nods. She is trembling and when he steps away it is as if she has been cast out into an alien element, where the air is too thin to breath and the cold paralyses her limbs. He is her warmth, her joy; every moment without him will be agony.

The two girls go upstairs and Mimi flings herself on the bed in Marianna's room. Tomorrow she goes home. She must find some way to prolong her visit, for if she cannot be with Dimitri she will die. She buries her face in the pillow and begins to weep.

"Mimi, what is it?" Marianna's hand is on her shoulder.

Mimi sits up and throws herself into her cousin's arms. "I cannot bear it. I will never see him again," she sobs.

Marianna strokes her hair. "Don't," she soothes. "Don't cry. I will tell Mama, that you are to stay until the end of their visit."

"You will do this for me?"

"If it is so important to you, then of course I will."

"Oh it is. It is everything in the world to me," Mimi breathes.

* * *

Marianna's hands trembled as she fumbled with the catch of her bag and pulled out a packet of cigarettes. She braced herself against the chair, flicked the lighter and inhaled. The rush of nicotine into her lungs gave her the strength to hobble to the door, where she stood, the cigarette a red glow in the darkness of the hallway, blowing the noxious fumes away from the dying woman. One foot in the sickroom the other outside. What a performance – Marianna smiled wryly – what a reaction. It was only a dress, merely a tangible reminder of a dim distant past.

She shut her eyes and let the smoke curl through her nostrils as she savoured the taste of the tobacco. A terrible habit. Her mother never smoked, at least not cigarettes, just the occasional small cigar. Helena's vices ran along other lines. There were always men, young handsome men. Helena liked to surround herself with attractive people, vampire-like, she appeared to feast on their youth and energy, drawing from them the life she found so hard to make for herself.

Henryk's return to Warsaw that winter of 1913 had been the perfect excuse for filling the palace with the young and beautiful. Finding them glamorous and shallow, Marianna hated her mother's guests. The men were condescending and opinionated, the women flirtatious and silly. Did any of them ever read a book, or have an idea worth discussing? Counts, dukes, princes heirs to great fortunes and vast estates, did they consider that they had the power to change their world for the better? She doubted it. The men and women she met at her revolutionary meetings were far more interesting. With them it was possible to talk as equals, not to have to hide her intelligence, or watch every word she said in case she betrayed the sharpness of her mind and the inadequacy of theirs.

The ball had been a torment. Beside the exquisite Mimi, Marianna appeared tall and gawky. She had plenty of partners, but they were all friends of her brothers and, having nothing in common with them, she found them insufferably boring. The only excitement of the evening was the scandal caused by her cousin and Prince Dimitri who danced with no one but each other. Tongues wagged and her aunt Celeste seethed with fury, until Helena had congratulated her on the fact that Mimi, in her wonderful dress, was the object of all eyes and the topic of much of the evening's conversation.

Dimitri. Marianna sighed. Dark and intense, a poet and a tortured soul. Did he really believe, as Mimi claimed, that they were predestined? Twin souls fated to be forever one. Poor deluded boy.

She looked around for an ashtray but all she could find was a saucer on the table beside Mimi's bed. Stubbing out the cigarette, she gazed at her cousin.

"What did he see in you?" she wondered.

* * *

Mimi's days pass in a delirium of delight. She is the centre of his world, he is the centre of hers. When he leaves, she does not allow herself to weep. Instead a single tear rolls down her cheek. He takes the crystal drop on his finger and kisses it away. They write. He sends searing, passionate letters and poems burning with his love. She sends brief notes, often not more than two or three words. "I love you." Or, "I am yours." He writes to tell her that he folds them tenderly and places them close to his heart.

Back at home, her life is grey and monotonous; his is bright with colour and incident. She fears he will forget her. Her parents will never let them marry, but Mimi is determined that she will be Prince Dimitri's wife and plans to enlist her cousin's help.

The two girls sit in Marianna's blue sitting room. Mimi has lost weight, her hands shake, her eyes have black shadows beneath them. She is restless and cannot keep still.

"Do you really love him so much?" Marianna asks curiously. "I've often wondered what it must be like to love someone more than yourself. Or if it's even possible. Mama's passions come and go. Henryk and Valerian have mistresses. Yes they have, Mimi. Don't look so shocked. It's what all men do, but I don't think any of them have really truly loved, not in the way you love Dimitri."

"Without him I will die."

"Then I will help you. I'll go and see Mama."

* * *

"He will only dally with her," Helena says when Marianna has finished. "Her family will be against it and so will his." She sighs, takes another sip from the glass of vodka that stands among her cosmetics. "Poor Mimi, she was always a neglected child. Do you remember the summer you spent together at Novy Lasko? I thought then, and so did your Aunt Irena, that she was a child who needed so much love. And who was there to give it to her? Not her mother, or her father, that poor excuse for a man. As for Hannah, she was only concerned to do her Christian duty by the child. So let us see what we can do to bring some joy into her life. Let her be happy. It will not last. God knows these things never do, but for once in her life let her have what she wants. I will write to Prince Dimitri and invite him to stay. Say nothing to Mimi until we have heard from him and then we'll do everything in our power to bring them together."

* * *

It is summer. The city is tense. There is talk of revolution and war. Mimi cares nothing for the political situation; she is counting the days, the hours, the minutes through which she must live before she sees Prince Dimitri again.

They meet in Marianna's blue sitting room. He is waiting for her and as she steps through the door he holds out his arms. She clings to him; his kisses sear her lips and her body melts into his.

"I love you," he murmurs and she begins to weep.

"What is it? What have I done?" he says.

"I love you too," she whispers.

"Then what is it?"

She shakes her head, she bites her lip. The tears roll down her cheeks.

"Tell me, my darling," he begs.

"My parents," she sobs.

"What of them?"

"They will not allow this. If they knew I was with you, they would part us for ever."

He takes her by the shoulders, stands her before him and gazes into her eyes.

"No one will ever part us. You will never leave me. Only with you do I feel real; nothing else has any meaning. Life is a hollow sham. I live only for you."

"And I for you," she says softly.

He draws her close. Her body tenses. The blood beats in her ears, she clenches her fists against her thighs, willing him to say what she must hear, and still he does not speak. Frantically she searches for the words to prompt him. She can hear his heart beating, he breathes in and at last he says, "We will marry."

She has it. She has her proposal. In spite of everything their parents can do, he will never go back on his word. Her Dimitri is too honourable. Too noble. Too perfect. She will be a princess. She will go to Court. There will be a mansion in St Petersburg, a summer palace by the Black Sea. There will be clothes and jewels and servants and love, eternal, everlasting, undying love.

She winds her arms around his neck, her lips seek his, searching, demanding.

"Nothing on earth will part us, Mimi. We will be together for ever. It is our destiny."

"My destiny," she echoes. "Oh my love."

Her days are filled with him. They are the last of the household to retire, the first to rise. Without each other, the night stretches like a void between them. Their meeting each morning brings renewed joy.

Mimi is safe under Helena's protection. As long as they remain in the Zapolski palace nothing can harm them. They walk in the grounds, where the gardens have been laid out in the Italian style.

"Is this not charming?" Mimi asks.

"If it pleases you, then it must please me," he smiles tenderly at her.

"It is so..." She is going to say civilised but stops, afraid of committing herself to an opinion she is not sure he will share.

"It is like a carpet, or a tapestry and we are part of the pattern."

"And our love is the thread." Surprised by her own image, Mimi smiles in delight and lifts her face to his. He bends his head and their lips are about to touch, when she feels him move away. She opens her eyes and sees Henryk coming down the gravel path towards them. Her cousin's face is grave. Ice creeps into Mimi's heart. She reaches out for Dimitri's hand. She wants to hold him, to keep him close, but he has stepped forward to greet his fellow officer. The two men talk and the words beat in Mimi's brain. There is trouble in Serbia, Dimitri is recalled to duty. A terrible plunge of fear knocks the breath from her, leaving her weak and dizzy.

"Will there be war? Must you go?"

"I will go where the Czar sends me."

She weeps; she is distraught; he takes her to her room. The blinds are drawn against the sun. The room is full of shadows.

"If anything happens to you, I will die."

He shudders. "Nothing will happen to me."

"Nothing?" she demands, as if his saying so could stem the tide of fate.

"I love you," he says.

She clings to him, presses herself against him. His kisses are hard and fierce; she is drowning in love. Her dress slides from her shoulders; he carries her to the bed.

CHAPTER SIXTEEN

Street lamps glowed orange and in the centre of the city neon signs flashed shocking pink, ice blue and electric white. Car headlights raked the house as they swung up St Michael's Hill, leaving behind them a thick, furry darkness.

Peter cried out in his sleep. Fists bunched, he pummelled at the pillow and snuggled further under the sheet. Hannah smoothed his covers, stroked his forehead and sat beside him, waiting until he was calm.

When she was sure he was asleep, she walked away, carefully avoiding the creaking floorboard, the sudden dip in the floor, just as she had when he was a baby. At the door she waited for a moment, listening for any sign of distress. Her ears strained to take in every sigh, every breath, every sound in the whole house; her son's sleepy snuffles, the murmur of the television in the upstairs sitting room, the Princess moving around in Mimi's room.

Leaving the door ajar, she switched on the light, filling the hallway with a sudden brilliance that hurt her eyes and made her regret the soft dark. She looked at her watch. Half-past ten. Too early for Kate to be back.

She was tired, so tired she could scarcely frame her thoughts. Her head felt light, her body heavy. She longed for sleep like an addict for a fix, but she would not rest until her daughter was safely home.

The kitchen was hot, the air laced with a faint smell of bleach and the mince she had cooked for supper. She opened the back door and the scent of the city night, hot tarmac, petrol fumes, roses and the wet earth of watered gardens, drifted in. She lifted the kettle from the stove and carried it over to the sink. The water came from the tap in a great gush, splashing in large cold drops that fell like blood on the bodice of her dress. Waiting for the kettle to boil, the tea to brew, she watched the water spread, then fade, dried by the heat of her body. Her head slid onto her arms. Half asleep, she heard footsteps in the back alley. For a moment she thought it might be Kate, but it was too early, not yet midnight.

* * *

April 1940, midnight: clear sky, bright stars, feet pounding deserted streets. Fists beating at the door. Rough voices demanding entry. Cowering under the covers, Hannah struggles out of nightmare to find the hammering ringing in her ears. Fumbling for her dressing gown, she throws it over her nightdress and stumbles out into the hall. As she flicks on the switch, she catches sight of Jan's white face.

"*Panie Boze,* don't let them take him," Hannah prays as she grapples with the bolts.

"NVKD." The Russians burst into the room. Burly men in grey uniforms. "Family Bernadinski?"

Jan nods. Hannah shrinks back. Her legs are weak, her breath ragged. Mimi's bedroom door opens and she comes out, her dark eyes blazing in her white face.

"What is all this noise?" she demands.

"You are to come with us."

"Now? It is the middle of the night." Mimi's voice is shrill with disbelief.

"Hannah, Mama, what's happening?" Krysia's eyes smudged with sleep widen in horror, when she sees the men.

"You are ordered to pack food for a journey. Some clothing too is permitted. You have fifteen minutes."

"Where are you taking us? You have no right." Jan clenches his fists, squaring up to the Russians. One of them moves forward, his face contorted with anger.

"Dirty Polack," he spits.

Hannah sees the rage flare in her brother's eyes, his body tense, ready to strike, and her fear for him lances through her shock.

"Don't," she cries, seizing his arm. "Please Jan, don't. Go and get the cases."

"Do as your sister says, or you'll get hurt," the Russian growls, leering at Hannah, his gaze travelling over her half-dressed body. Burning with anger and shame, she folds her arms across her chest and turns to Krysia, cowering white and shaken against the wall. Putting her arm around her sister's shoulders, she tells her, as calmly as she can, to go to her room and pack. The child moves as if she is not quite in control of her limbs and when Hannah comes to check on what she is doing, she finds Krysia folding each piece of underwear into a perfect square.

"No," Hannah tells her. "There's no time for this." Krysia's eyes are glazed, her chest heaving with each breath. Hannah pulls her into her arms and hugs her tight. "You must pack warm clothes and underwear and boots and stockings," she says.

"And this." Krysia pulls the icon of the Madonna from the wall. "And this." She thrusts her copy of *Alice in Wonderland* into the case.

"Get a move on." One of the Russians appears in the doorway, blocking it with his thick body.

"Come on, be brave," Hannah whispers.

"Where are they taking us?"

"I don't know."

"Perhaps we'll see Daddy."

Hannah shuts her eyes to blank out the fear that crawls up her spine. "I don't know," she says again, keeping her voice light. "Perhaps."

"Now." The Russian steps into the room.

"We're ready." Hannah pulls her sister to her feet, shielding her with her body and, picking up the half empty case, she leads her into the hall where Mimi is waiting. Their mother is dressed in her best hat and coat, the one with the astrakhan collar. Her hands are gloved and she carries a small overnight case. She is perfectly composed. Beside her are two bulging suitcases, bound with leather straps.

Hannah looks at the cases and exchanges glances with her brother. Jan raises his eyebrows and shakes his head as if to say what else do you expect. Then he picks up his mother's luggage, his muscles straining under the weight.

* * *

The cold air strikes like splinters on the skin. Hannah's arms ache, dragged almost out of their sockets by the ever-increasing weight of the cases. Her legs tremble with the effort of keeping up with the men's brisk march. Mimi does not look back. She walks with her head held high, heels clicking on the pavement, as if on her way to pay a social call. Jan toils beside her, Krysia trails somewhere behind.

The sweat is hot on Hannah's back, her breath comes in jerks. Where is Krysia? Is she still with them? How can her fragile little sister keep up this terrible pace? Hannah looks over her shoulder and pain shoots down her neck.

"I'm all right," her sister gasps.

"Keep moving. No talking."

They stumble on through the sleeping town. As in a dream, buildings stand like stage flats against the dark sky. The familiar city, alien and threatening, gazing dispassionately on their humiliation.

When they reach the railway station Hannah sets down the cases. A rifle butt is jabbed into the small of her back and with arms like stretched elastic she picks up the luggage again. The entrance to the station building gapes blankly at her. There are no lights inside, nothing but a hole in the darkness.

A shove pushes her onwards, past the building, past the platforms and into the goods yard, where an engine coupled to a long line of cattle trucks is waiting. In the shadow of the train there are groups of people, some standing surrounded by their possessions, others resting on their luggage.

The Bernadinskis put down their cases. Jan sits beside Mimi, holding her hands. Krysia nestles close to Hannah, her arms curling around her big sister's waist, her heart beating against hers. The night air chills her; she begins to shiver and Hannah unfastens her coat and wraps it around them both. Krysia dozes lightly, then wakes up, coughing. Hannah strokes her cheek and prays that no harm will come to her.

All that night people are herded between the tracks. Men and women, old and young, some with small children, some

– 176 –

alone, all shocked, bewildered and afraid. The dawn breaks red and raw, the doors of the trucks clang open, and soldiers with rifles and sticks begin to force people inside.

Her limbs stiff and cramped, Hannah pulls Krysia to her feet and calls out to Jan and Mimi. Hobbling, pulling her cases behind her, urging Krysia to hurry, she makes for the train. Her brother is is there before her, standing by an empty truck; he hoists her up and she leans down to stretch out her hand, first to Mimi and then to Krysia. As Jan lifts the child into the truck the stench of animals is so overpowering that Hannah has to fight down her nausea. Clenching her teeth, digging her nails into palms, she mutters an incantation under her breath, "I won't be sick. I won't be sick."

Then Jan swings himself up beside her and they hear the doors of the other trucks being drawn and bolted.

"Please, young man, can you help my wife?" A wizened face, anxious eyes behind round glasses, peers up at them.

"Here, give me your hand, quick." Jan kneels and reaches out.

"Merciful God," a little voice squeaks, and a tiny woman clutching a crocodile-skin handbag stands beside them. "My husband," she twitters, but he has already scrambled aboard, pulling after him a large and expensive suitcase. In his smart dark suit, his wife beside him teetering on high heels, her hat a little awry on her grey curls, he bows politely to the Bernadinskis.

"Maraszynski," he announces. "Allow me to introduce my wife." A clang and a thud drowns the rest of his words. The door of the truck slides across and is bolted shut.

Silence descends. A shocked, horrified silence. The grey dawn light that slips through the spaces in the slatted walls reveals that the car has been divided into two, leaving a passageway between double rows of makeshift bunks that reach almost to the roof, where on each corner there is a small square hole to provide light and ventilation. These top bunks are the most desirable and people are hastily climbing up to stake their claims. The train jolts forward. Mimi half sits, half falls onto the nearest bunk.

"Here we go. Following the family tradition, we're off to Siberia like Grandfather Witold," Jan jokes. Krysia gives a little sob and buries her face in Hannah's sleeve. Mimi puts her feet together, places her bag on her lap and sits, her back rigid, staring in front of her.

Hannah closes her eyes. She does not want to see; she does not want to think. The train clacks over the track, the wagons swaying from side to side. After a while, she is conscious of nothing but the sound of iron wheels on iron rails and the rhythmic motion of the carriage. Her limbs grow heavy, her mind slides away from horror. She sleeps.

She wakes, with a painfully full bladder, to the sound of a small child crying for its pot. There is a confused murmur of voices, wails, exclamations of dismay, then someone produces a large chamber decorated with florid roses. It is set down in the middle of the carriage and the child hastily placed on it. The hiss of water against the china makes Hannah desperate. She presses her legs together, but the muscles are loosening and she cannot hold on much longer.

"Back to the nursery it is then." A large, flamboyantly dressed, young woman hoists up her skirts and makes use of the pot. Hannah can hardly wait for her to finish. She sits down, shuts her eyes, and lets the water flow. Then, eyes averted, she creeps back to her bunk.

Sometime towards evening the train stops. The doors are opened and, as people hungry for air crowd the door, two soldiers push them back into the stinking interior. The soldiers carry pails and ladles. One is full of water for drinking, the other consists of a thin orange liquid on whose scummy surface float scraps of carrot and gobs of cabbage.

"I can't eat that," Krysia wails through gated hands.

"Of course you can't." Mimi is indignant. "And you don't need to. We have brought our own provisions."

She sits on the bunk, opens the case she has packed with food and sets out bread and sausage as if presiding over a picnic. They eat. The cloying smell of rancid soup and animal and human waste permeates their food. Krysia gags and pushes aside her portion. "Don't be silly. This is perfectly wholesome,"

Mimi snaps.

"Hannah, I can't," Krysia whispers.

"You must. If you don't, you will get sick and then what will happen?" Hannah says. A child's fevered crying echoes her words. The doors slam shut.

"Come here." Krysia edges closer to her mother. Mimi searches through her overnight case. There is a sharp clean tang of cologne as she pours a little onto a handkerchief. "Take this, dab it on your wrists and temples. It will help."

It grows darker. A darkness thick with the sounds of sleep, the smell of bodies, of babies and of old age. People snore and weep and cry out. Hannah lies with Krysia beside her and tries not to think.

Time ceases to have meaning. In the twilight in which they are imprisoned, hours, days and weeks merge into a continuous gloom. Their world is contained within the truck. Mimi sets up an inflexible daily routine in which meals are served at set times and naps taken at regular intervals. She pays visits to other families in their bunks and holds court when the visits are returned. Jan counts off the days on a makeshift calendar and spends hours peering through the slats trying to make out where they are.

Hannah becomes obsessed by the state of her body. Her hair is lank and greasy, her skin unwashed, her smell pungent. She dreams of hot baths, sweet smelling soap, and clouds of fragrant talc. Krysia buries herself in *Alice in Wonderland*. Straining her eyes in the eternal dusk of the truck, she reads and re-reads her favourite book.

The train travels erratically. Sometimes it is shunted into a siding and left there for days, sometimes it rattles along at speed, tossing its passengers from side to side. An old man dies and his body is taken away at the next stop. A child sickens, but recovers. The old man's widow keens; the child's mother sends up prayers of gratitude.

One bright morning, the doors of the truck are flung open.

"Out, out," voices cry in Russian. People shrink back into the space they have made for themselves. Mothers hide children under bunk beds and cover babies with coats and scarves. Jan, braver than most, makes his way to the light.

"I think, we have arrived." He looks down, but instead of grim-faced men carrying buckets of cabbage soup, smiling soldiers bring jugs of frothy goat's milk and bowls of shining black caviar. "It's all right," he tells his fellow passengers. "You can get down." He dives back into the dimness to help Mimi. Already people are clambering down onto the tracks, clutching their belongings.

"Welcome to the Soviet Union. Today is the glorious first of May," the guards tell the bewildered Poles and start ladling out generous portions of caviar into wooden bowls. "Life, you see, in the Soviet Union is good."

After the stinking, fetid interior of the train, the first thing Hannah notices is the fine white dust rising from the road that runs over the vast open steppe. The sky is cobalt blue, the daylight dazzling, the ground strangely hard. Her legs tremble and shake on the solid surface, as they are herded down a dirt track road and into the main square of the town.

For hours they stand and wait under the blazing sun, skin blistering, tongues swelling from thirst, forbidden to sit or speak, until the head man, resplendent in native dress, arrives. The Kazakh slowly examines the bedraggled people in front of him.

"Every day you report to me. That is all. You may go."

Fearing a trap, Hannah glances at Jan. He shrugs his shoulders and looks at the soldiers, who stand at ease, pushing their caps off their heads, laughing and joking with each other.

"What's going to happen now?" Krysia slips her hand into Hannah's.

"I don't know," she begins, then seeing her sister's face tighten with fear, says, "I can go and ask." Licking a dry tongue over parched lips, she walks over to the head man. "What are we doing here?" she croaks. Eyes dark in his flat face, luxuriant moustache flowing almost to his shoulders, he considers her question. Her stomach twists. His silence stretches to the horizon. Then, at last, he speaks.

"What you do is no concern of mine. If you have money, good, if not, find work."

A babble of relief breaks out. People forget that they are

poor, or old, or sick, or burdened with young children, that they have no marketable skills or professions. They only know they have been reprieved. The shadow of death that has lain over their hearts melts away like spring snow. The tight group that huddled together in the centre of the square begins to disintegrate. People move away from each other holding out money, or possessions to bargain with the locals for jobs or accommodation. Only the Maraszynskis stay where they are. Mrs Maraszynska sits on her suitcase and wails, her voice high and thin, while her poor little husband flaps ineffectually around her.

"We can't leave them," Hannah says.

"They can look after themselves, like the rest of us," is Mimi's response.

"I don't know." Jan is torn between his mother and his sister. Hannah looks at the frail old couple and walks over to them.

"Mr Maraszynski," she says quietly, touching him on the shoulder, "would you like to come with us?"

"Oh Miss Hannah, we couldn't possibly intrude."

"Edmund," his wife says. "Please."

"There would be no intrusion," Hannah assures him.

"Then, thank you. Thank you so very much." Tears stand in the faded blue eyes. He takes Hannah's hand and raises it to his lips. Then he and his wife follow the Bernadinskis to the lodgings Jan has found for them.

* * *

They rent a single room at the back of a mud brick house. The floor is baked earth; there is a stove, a table and four chairs; the rest of the space is taken up by two large beds and the mattresses they put down each night. The kitchen they share with their landlady and for washing they use a little outhouse tacked on to the end of the building.

Hannah works in the hospital. A ramshackle building with no disinfectant and no drugs, where patients are prepared for their operations by having needles stuck into their limbs. Jan finds a job in the bakery. The Maraszynskis, scurrying about like mice, do what they can to earn a few kopecks. Mimi collects their earnings, visits her friends and acquaintances and when the need arises sells her fine silk underwear to strapping Kazakh women, or barters for food and other necessities.

Krysia is sent to school. Pale and thin, her eyes huge in her narrow face, she cries out in her dreams, shielding herself from the bullies who make the delicate Polish girl their target. Night after night, Hannah comforts the distraught child and burns with hatred for all those who hurt her little sister.

"Don't make me go. I can't do the lessons. I don't understand what the teacher says," Krysia sobs.

"Let her stay at home," Hannah pleads, but Mimi is inflexible. There is no reprieve and, week by week, the weary child drags herself to the schoolhouse.

The hot summer sun blazes through the open door, a blue sky arcs over the steppe and the Kazakh horses graze on the long grasses that waver in the breeze. Hannah, hurrying home from her shift at the hospital, sees a frail old man with a thin little girl holding on to his arm coming down the road. They move slowly, their heads bent towards each other, he talking softly, she listening so intently that they do not see Hannah until she is almost upon them.

"I thought Miss Krysia would benefit from a little fresh air," Mr Maraszynski says.

"Mr Maraszynski has been telling me the most wonderful stories." Krysia's eyes glow; there is colour in her cheeks, a lift to her step.

"It was nothing, nothing," the old man says.

"It was wonderful," Krysia answers.

Hannah wants to hug him, to flood his fragile body with her gratitude, but she holds back for fear of giving offence. Edmund Maraszynski is a proud man. He finds it hard to be dependent and maintains his dignity by conducting relations in a very formal manner. The two families share the same room, live, eat and sleep together. They breathe the same stale air, hear each other's snores and grunts, witness the nocturnal trips to the outhouse, but when day comes they behave as if they are merely acquaintances, who have happened to drop in on one another.

"Thank you," Hannah says. He gives a little bow and offers

her his other arm. She has to stoop to take it – she is taller than he is – but his gallant gesture warms her heart and she takes great care to adjust her stride to his as he escorts the two girls home. At the door he stands aside to let them pass ahead of him, and Krysia turns and smiles, her face alight with pleasure.

"I will take care of her for you," he tells Hannah. "Miss Krysia is a very special person."

"She is to me," Hannah replies, tears rising to her eyes. She is tired, her head aches, and the day at the hospital has been long and relentless. They admitted two more patients, both children with a high fever and rashes.

"Dr Kropkin thinks we may have an epidemic," she tells Mimi as she pulls off her blouse and examines the seams for lice.

"Of typhus, *Jesus Maria*! Please God no." Mimi crosses herself.

"We must pray. We can only pray," Mrs Maraszynska whispers. Her husband glances across to the corner of the bed where Krysia lies, her book in front of her but her eyes half-closed.

"I am sure she is only a little tired. We had a long walk today."

"And you told me such wonderful stories." Krysia looks up and her eyes in the dim light are bright and hectic. "I just have a little headache."

Hannah drops her blouse. She leans over the bed and puts her hand on her sister's forehead. The skin burns under her touch. Her eyes meet the old man's. She reads his fear as he read hers.

"Do you want some water?" she asks.

"Hannah don't go." Krysia clings to her sister's hand.

"I will fetch it," Mr Maraszynski offers.

Hannah puts her arm around Krysia and the child leans against her. Her body is limp, sweetly sick with the scent of fever.

"I hurt," she whispers.

"I know," Hannah murmurs.

Mr Maraszynski stands before them, a cup of water in his

trembling hand. Hannah holds it to Krysia's lips. The child takes a sip then shakes her head.

"A little more," Hannah coaxes. "Then I'll help you into bed."

Mrs Maraszynska appears like a shadow at the bedside. Her touch as light as a leaf, she unbuttons Krysia's dress. In spite of the heat the child is shivering and sweat glistens on her white skin. As the night wears on, her temperature rises and by morning there is a red rash under her arms.

* * *

"I'll stay at home," Hannah says.

"There is no need. We can look after her," Mimi replies. Mother and daughter face each other. Mimi's eyes hold her daughter's gaze until Hannah is forced to retreat.

"Don't worry, please don't worry, Miss Hannah," Mr Maraszynski murmurs as she lingers on the threshold of the bright morning and looks back through the dusky light of the room at the still shape under the covers. To tear herself away is agony, every fibre of her being yearns to be at that bedside, willing her sister to live.

At lunch time she rushes back. Krysia does not know her. Eyes glazed, she stares at the wall and mutters wildly.

"Krysia." Hannah kneels beside the bed. She catches her sister's hand and holds it tightly. "Krysia don't die." Krysia gives a little moan. "I'm going to fetch Dr Kropkin." Hannah gets to her feet. "He must be able to do something."

Mimi looks at her daughter. "If it is typhus, there is nothing he can do. We must ride it out," she says coldly.

Hannah's heart burns with rage at her mother. "I'm still fetching the doctor."

Later that afternoon, Dr Kropkin arrives. Tired and dishevelled, he takes one look at Krysia and confirms Mimi's diagnosis.

"Is there anything you can give her?" Hannah begs.

The doctor shakes his head. "Careful nursing will pull her round. There is nothing else." He spreads his hands wide. "If she is strong enough she will get well."

Krysia is not strong. All her life she has been frail, a child deprived of some vital element that would make her strong and protect her from harm. Hannah has tried, she has given her all she could, but hers is not a mother's love and in the end it is not enough.

All through the night they watch around her bed. The Maraszynskis kneel side by side murmuring the Rosary. Mimi and Hannah take turns cooling the fevered body with wet cloths. Jan sits, shoulders hunched, fists clenched. About three o'clock the child's breathing changes. With a despairing cry Hannah gathers her into her arms. She feels the shudder of every breath, the frantic beating of the failing heart. For a long moment she holds Krysia close, then they are prised apart. Someone takes her sister from her to lay her out on the bed. Blinded by tears, Hannah flees into the night and howls into the empty darkness.

CHAPTER SEVENTEEN

Seeing his wife with her head on her arms, shoulders splayed on the table, legs apart, Gregor's anger rose. Hannah looked so spent and drained. They all took her for granted: Mimi, Kate, the little boy too. No one gave her any consideration. No one took care of her. She was so tired, so good. He wanted to wrap her in his arms and carry her away to a place where they could be quiet together and he could tell her how much he loved and needed her. Weak with emotion, he put his hand on her shoulder.

Hannah, her husband's fingers hot on her skin, looked up and saw her reflection, a pale oval floating in the black glass of the window. White as Krysia, the little sister with the milky skin and dark, dark hair. The child no one could save. She gulped back tears and Gregor tightened his grip. Still lost in her memories, the weight of his need was too much for her. She wanted to shrug him off, to move away, to be left alone with her grief, but this would hurt him and she could not bear to cause him pain.

Her eyes were running and she brushed away her tears, hoping he had not seen them. She knew he wanted to comfort her, but the grief was too old, too deeply buried, and she did not have the words to describe her sorrow. She knew how to listen and help others give shape to their feelings, but she could not do this for herself. Even if she could, she would not burden her family; they had enough to bear, and she was strong. Gregor had his worries at work, Kate her exams.

Kate with her white skin and dark, dark hair. Panic seized her. Where was her daughter? What was she doing? Was she safe? The world was full of danger and love was no protection. Her eyes turned to the kitchen clock. Quarter to eleven.

Following her glance, Gregor's mouth tightened.

"That child, she has no consideration. She should not worry you like this. Not when your mother is so ill."

Hannah sighed. The effort of conciliation was almost too much. "She will be back by twelve. I don't have to wait up for her. I choose to."

I must know she is home. If she does not return, as she should, I have to be there to summon help from all those agencies that exist to protect my child from the harm that lies in wait for her.

Gregor drew in his breath, then expelled it forcefully as a sign of his disapproval. Hannah took his hand.

"I am all right," she said.

"I worry about you. You are everything to me."

"I know." She smiled, her mouth wobbling with the effort.

"You should rest."

"I will. When this is over."

"When this is over, we will all heave a sigh of relief." The Princess came into the room. The harsh kitchen light caught the gold and bronze of her dress, the silver and amber that hung from her neck, wrists and ears.

Hannah jumped to her feet. "Is there anything wrong?"

Marianna shook her head. "Nothing that can be helped. I came for some water. It is so hot tonight."

Without thinking, Hannah moved towards the kettle. "Water, or would you rather have tea?" Her hand closed on the handle. The Princess hesitated, her eyes slid toward Gregor. He caught her glance.

"Perhaps a vodka is in order," he said.

"Wonderful!" She spread out her hands, rings glinting in the overhead light. "What a man you have, Hannah. Able to read one's every wish."

Gregor's shoulders straightened and his cheeks flushed with pleasure. Smiling, he bowed his head, dismissing yet at the same time relishing the compliment.

"A moment." He went into the dining room where the vodka and the glasses were kept.

Marianna lowered herself into a chair. Her skirt billowed

around her, settling gracefully around her legs. She stretched out her feet and sighed. Hannah started to worry again. Without even looking at her, Marianna sensed her unease.

"Don't worry, nothing's changed."

"You must be tired." Hannah immediately found another cause for concern.

"Not as tired as you. After all, what is one final night with an old friend? It is nothing. Once I have had a shot of alcohol, I shall be ready for the rest of my watch; but you, my dear, should go to bed."

"That is what I tell her." Gregor stood in the doorway, glasses and bottle on a tray.

"And I tell him I am all right." There was a trace of impatience in Hannah's voice which her husband ignored. Putting the tray on the table, he opened the bottle and poured two generous measures, then he looked at Hannah, who shook her head.

"To Mimi." The Princess raised her vodka and tipping back her head drained the glass.

"Another?" he asked.

"Another," she replied. "But before you do we must persuade Hannah to go to bed. I will stay with Mimi and I promise to call if there is any change."

"And I will wait up for Kate," Gregor said.

Marianna turned to her goddaughter. "There is nothing you can do."

"I can wait."

"Waiting changes nothing," the Princess said. "It won't delay the inevitable, or stave off the end. Go on, sleep. Even if it is only for a few hours it will do you so much good."

Hannah saw Gregor about to speak and add his arguments to those of her godmother and suddenly she could stand it no longer. His concern dragged her down and stifled her, his anger drained her. They were right. There was nothing she could do. To be alone, to lose herself in sleep, would be a luxury beyond imagination.

"Goodnight then." She capitulated.

They watched her move heavily from the room. Already half-asleep, wrapped in the summer darkness, she pulled herself up the stairs and fell, without undressing, onto their bed.

When she had gone Gregor refilled their glasses. Marianna curled her fingers around hers and gestured to him with her other hand.

"Sit down with me for a while." He glanced at the door. "She won't die yet. In any event, I won't leave her for long. Relax." She drawled over the last word, rolling out the syllables in an exaggerated manner.

He sat opposite her. She put her elbows on the table, resting her chin on the palm of one hand as she studied him. Her eyes were greeny-grey in the unforgiving light, and there were deep purple shadows beneath them; her skin was wrinkled and loose around the neck and jaw, yet the underlying bone structure and generous mouth held more than a memory of past beauty. She had been a gangly child, yet not an unattractive young woman. In her middle years she had been desirable; in old age she was beautiful.

He held up his glass. "To you," he said and drank.

She smiled. "To the future," she responded. His face puckered as if he had tasted something sour. "You do not care to think of the future?"

He paused for a moment then said, "I cannot think how it will be." Again he hesitated not wanting to put the thought into words. "She has always lived with us. From the very beginning. It will be..."

"A relief."

"No. At least I do not think so. Not a relief. A change."

Marianna looked at him. "You do not wish to admit it. So let it be."

She was right, but he did not want to acknowledge, not even to himself, the bitterness and resentment against Mimi that festered inside him. From the moment they had arrived in England, everything he had tried to do for his family that woman had spoiled with her wicked tongue.

* * *

"A factory! You are going to work in a factory." Mimi's voice is incredulous, her hands spread wide in disbelief. "Tell him

Hannah, he can't. It is not suitable. He is a professional man. He has qualifications." She turns to her daughter, standing hugely pregnant at the sink. Hannah flushes and looks away.

"My family must eat," Gregor tells his mother-in- law.

"*Jesus kohany.*"

"Better a job in a factory than starve."

Mimi clicks her tongue. "*Ai, ai, ai.* I expected better things of you. When you first came to me to ask for Hannah's hand, I expected more. Not this." She waves at the sparse kitchen in the rented house, the ramshackle furniture, the bare light bulb hanging from the ceiling.

"Mama, Gregor does his best for us. For all of us," Hannah says.

His best. Gregor's stomach curdles. If this indeed is his best, then he has failed his wife, their coming child, and himself.

* * *

Marianna, breaking the train of his thoughts, raised her glass to her lips. "A change. That can be good. Who knows where it will lead." She shot a mischievous glance at him. "I would never say it was too late to take a different path, even for me at my advanced age." She took a final swig from her glass and rose, with some difficulty, to her feet. Gregor averted his eyes from her struggle, but was at the door to take her arm and help her down the corridor. When they reached Mimi's room, she turned to him.

"Thank you. I can manage from here."

"If you need anything."

"Then I will call."

* * *

A single lamp on the side table illuminated the icon hanging above the bed. The dark face of the Madonna gazed impassively at the dying woman. Marianna crossed herself.

"Be kind to her," she prayed. Mimi gave a gasp, a sudden choking breath. Marianna leaned over and put her palm on her cousin's forehead. Her eyes strayed back to the icon. "Don't be afraid," she murmured.

Fear was an emotion with which they were both well acquainted. It clawed and twisted the gut, emptying the bowels and crawling like cancer into the blood, where black and malignant it grew and multiplied. The heart beat frantically, breath was short, hard to catch. Feet stumbled, hands lost their grip. There was no rational thought only an overwhelming, all-embracing terror.

* * *

For Mimi, it comes softly at first, slipping in on silken feet. Her skin stretches tight across her belly, her breasts are smooth and taut. The nipples stand hard in their aureoles, so tender to the touch that the slightest pressure of her blouse inflames them. There is a taste of vomit in her mouth.

Waiting for Dimitri's return, she drags herself about wearily, like an old woman. Counting the days, she stares in disbelief at the calendar. There must be some mistake. She counts and counts again. Pressing her stomach with her hands, she cinches her waist, pulling in her muscles, holding herself tall and straight. In the bathroom, she squats and strains. Each morning when she wakes, she slips her hand between her legs hoping for the hot sticky flow that will save her.

Days pass. The fear grows. At first it can be diverted. An effort of will damps it down, allowing a few moments respite. She tells herself she has often been late, that her grief at parting from her lover has thrown her out. She takes a hot bath, sleeps late, but still the linen is unmarked. Her stomach churns and heaves and wave after wave of panic sweeps over her, leaving her limp and weeping. Soon she can think of nothing but her shame and disgrace. Her hand shakes as she writes to Dimitri.

"My Darling, I am to bear your child. Come to me. All my love, for ever,

"Mimi."

* * *

There is no reply. Shutting herself up in her room, she sits and rereads his letters; tracing each line with her finger as if to convince herself of its truth. He loves her, she knows he does. If only he would write to her now when she needs him most.

War rages throughout Europe. Has her letter been delayed, or is it Dimitri's reply that has been held up by forces they cannot control? Daily she grows more desperate. She laces herself so tightly that she frequently faints. Soon it will be too late even for marriage. Her family will disown her, she will be thrown out, or hidden away in the country, and her child, Dimitri's child, taken away from her.

She lies on her bed and weeps. Beating her fists on the pillows, she rages against Fate. It was all so nearly within her grasp. The summer palaces, the cascades of pearls, the gowns from Paris, the endless love of her handsome prince. What use are his poems, his passionate verses, if he is not here to save her?

She visits her cousin. Marianna is pale and distant. Her coldness makes Mimi cry. She sits on the sofa in the blue sitting room, where she had been so happy, and weeps uncontrollably. She despises this show of emotion but she can no longer control herself. The slightest thing will bring tears to her eyes. Marianna stands by the window and looks at her.

"Are you ill?"

Mimi catches a glimpse of herself in the mirror that hangs over the mantelpiece. Her face is smudged, her eyes red, her hair lank. She is hideous and soon she will bloat and swell and be forced to hide herself away from decent people. She gulps. Marianna looks at her curiously, but says nothing. A knot of anger flares in Mimi's heart. Marianna does not care. Her life is ruined and her cousin does not care. Mimi is tempted to tell her everything. She wants to shock, to lay bare her tragedy, to force her cousin to witness true desolation, but caution prevails. She swallows down the words, bows her head and whispers, "It is so long since I heard from him. I am afraid."

"There is a war." Marianna's voice is cold, her eyes flicker to the window. She steps further back into the room, as if she is afraid of being seen. She presses her hands to her lips. Her eyes are wide, the pupils dark.

Mimi curls her fingers into her palms and rests her fists on her stomach. She should leave but she is too weary to move and Marianna, for all her abstracted manner, seems reluctant to let her go.

"Do you remember Novy Lasko?" her cousin begins. Mimi nods. She leans against the silken cushions and lets herself be taken back into their childhood. Marianna speaks quickly, almost frantically, but for an hour or two both girls are held by their past.

"Stay here with me, tonight," Marianna finishes and Mimi nods.

* * *

When the pain comes, it rips through her belly tearing her apart with iron fingers. She screams and buries her face in the pillow. Her body sinks into the mattress. Her legs part. Inside her something comes loose. Her muscles bunch. She thrusts her fist into her mouth as the pain sears through her. Her thighs are wet. There is a metallic tang of blood in the bed. A hot viscous mess between her thighs.

Marianna hears the scream. Unable to sleep, she has been sitting at her writing desk, pen in her hand, paper untouched. Her eyes are heavy, her brain numb. Her head jerks up. She listens, her heart hammering in her ears. On trembling legs she creeps to the door, turns the key and peers out. The palace sleeps. The corridor is empty. She is safe. As she closes her door she hears a low moaning. The sound comes from the room next door. Marianna releases her pent up breath. She is shaking with relief.

Mimi lies curled up in the bed, her face slimy with sweat, arms wrapped around herself, eyes wild with fear, lips dry and flecked with blood where she has bitten back her cries.

"Don't let me die." Mimi's hands grasp Marianna's. Her nails dig into her cousin's flesh as she tenses against the pain.

"It will be all right." Marianna brushes Mimi's hair away from her eyes. The pain ebbs leaving a dull ache at the small of her back, at the tops of her legs. Mimi lies in a pool of blood. Marianna brings water and clean rags to staunch the flow. She removes the soiled sheets, averting her eyes from the clots of tissue. Mimi draws her knees up to her chin and weeps silently.

In the morning she remains in bed. Marianna tells the household that Mimi has a migraine. Mimi is pale, her dark eyes huge. Empty, released from fear, she is light as a leaf.

* * *

For Marianna herself, there is no respite. Sitting at her desk, unable to write, she can see Mimi, through the half-open door. Her cousin lies propped up against the pillows like a small child, her cheeks rosy with sleep. Marianna wishes she could turn back the years to her childhood. She yearns for the safety of Novy Lasko, for the stuffy schoolrooms in grand palaces, the long boring journeys across Europe. Her eyes stray to the window. The courtyard is empty, its silence echoing in her head. She waits for the sound of footsteps, the rough battering at the door.

It is days since she has eaten and she cannot remember when she last slept. Her eyes are dry, her head heavy on her neck. The slightest noise startles and terrifies her. Faceless, their caps pulled over their eyes, their long coats trailing on the ground, the secret police haunt her waking dreams.

The others in her group have already been arrested. Soon they will come for her and when they do will she break? Has she the courage to withstand being tortured? The question torments her. She knows what they do to politicals in the Alexander Prison. Her pen falls from her fingers; ink splatters black on white paper. She rests her head in her hands and groans.

It can only be only a matter of time. She has known that from the moment she arrived at Teodora's studio the secret police would be looking for her. The door of the apartment swings crazily on broken hinges. The place had been ransacked, canvases slashed, floorboards upturned. The remains of the printing press lie scattered across the floor. She runs into the bedroom, then the kitchen. She calls their names, her voice shrill and fearful in the empty rooms. "Marcin, Bronia, Teodora, Pavel."

"Police took them." The woman from the apartment below appears in the doorway. "This morning it was."

Marianna stares at her. In spite of the evidence the horror is such that her mind refuses to accept what has happened. Surely, at any moment, one of the group will walk in. They will put things back to where they belong and restore order to the apartment and her life. But what if they do not? The truth she must face is that they have been discovered, their illegal printing press exposed, her friends arrested. And she will be next.

She hurries out of the apartment and down the stairs. In the street people go about their daily lives, but to her they are little more than shadows moving on the edges of her fear. She sees nothing, hears nothing, but the relentless tramp of footsteps coming closer, ever closer. At any moment she expects the hand on her shoulder, the voice in her ear. Faint with terror, she makes her way home, creeps up the stairs and hides in her bedroom.

The police do not come. Two days after the raid on the apartment Marcin is hanged, then Pavel. Bright shining Pavel, her first love, whose eyes burned when he spoke of freedom, whose fingers trembled as they touched hers. Never again would she kiss those lips, brush the hair from those eyes. Her throat is tight with unshed tears, her body aches with grief she dare not show, because above everything there is the fear of being discovered, and Marianna does not want to die.

In the long nights, when she cannot sleep she is overcome by the fear of the rope; those choking, gasping final moments, when the body fights for air, the legs dance, and the bowels loosen.

She grows thin and feverish. Mimi, absorbed in her grief, notices nothing. Helena thinks only of her sons; Henryk is at the front, and although Valerian is working for the government in Warsaw he has no time to visit his mother.

The days, then the weeks, pass. The even tenor of life in the Zapolski palace remains undisturbed and gradually, very gradually, the fear loses its grip. The thin membrane that separates her from human contact begins to dissolve. Her ears no longer throb with unheard sound, nor does she start at every footstep. Marianna's appetite returns and she can sleep again, but her relief is underpinned by guilt.

Why was she not taken? Why was she the only one spared? She was as much part of the conspiracy as they were, but they are dead and she is not.

* * *

Would she ever know the answer? Marianna shifted in her

chair, letting the pain settle into its familiar place around her hip, before addressing the dying woman.

"Do you remember, Mimi, how we sat like this once before? When we were young in Warsaw. You in your bed, I watching you. There was a death then too, but we never spoke of it. There is so much we never spoke of." She stared at her cousin's face, the yellowing skin stretched tight over the skull, lips purple, eyes unfocused. "And now we are too old and the time has passed, but still I wonder what could and should have been said."

CHAPTER EIGHTEEN

Kate sat back and pressed her bare legs against the statute. The bronze flank of the lion was smooth and warm beneath her thighs. Her dress was so short it scarcely covered her knickers. Her sandals were sticky against the soles of her feet. The leather sucked at her skin as she moved. She hooked her hair behind her ears, felt the night air slip in under her arms, sweet as honey over her skin. From her vantage point she could look down the sweep of steps to the fountain where the merman and his mermaid lay on either side of the pool, the dark richness of their nakedness given an extra lustre by the glow of the street lamps.

She watched as cars swept around the traffic island. The dark bulk of a bus, its windows bright, stopped to disgorge its passengers. Black shapes alighted, merged into the hazy twilight. The bus lumbered on into the traffic.

Jon appeared from behind her, so silently that she did not know he was there until his arms were around her waist, his breath against her cheek, his hair brushing her shoulder, his soft beard tickling as he kissed her neck. She leaned back, rubbing her shoulders against him, arching her body, the lion silky against her legs as she rose up to him. His grip tightened; she stiffened then freed herself from his grasp. He let her go without protest and she swung her leg round, turning to face him. His long blonde hair flopped over his shoulders, his dark eyes were amused, his mouth curved into a smile.

"Aren't you glad it was me?" he said.

"And not the Clifton flasher."

"Is there one?"

"Some girls at school saw him in an alleyway. We weren't allowed to take that short cut for months." She slid off the lion.

Her shift bunched around her hips and she smoothed it down.

"How's your grandmother?"

"Dead probably. I don't know." She moved away into the shadow at the side of the building. Jon followed, his long stride easily overtaking her.

Catching hold of her hand, he said, "Stay cool." She stopped, her eyes narrowed. "Relax. It's no big deal."

"Not for you," she snapped.

"Not for anyone. Nothing ever finishes. When one life ends, the next begins."

"If that's true, she'll come back as a rat," Kate said.

"And you'll knock her on the head?"

Suddenly her legs were water, her eyes full of tears. "I'll give her some cheese."

"Cheddar?"

"No. It will have to be Stilton. Gran goes for the classy things in life." Her voice rose, then dipped in a little sob ending in a quavery laugh. His fingers tightened on hers. His pace quickened. Her heels clicked along the pavement; she was running, out of breath.

"Sorry, my legs are too long." He stopped and grinned down at her. She gasped and grinned back. Her hair swung round her face.

"Where are we going?"

"Back to my place?" It was a question, not a statement, making it possible to refuse, to draw back from the brink, to avoid the occasion of sin. Kate lowered her eyes as if she were considering what she was going to do, but she had already made up her mind.

"The others have all gone out," he said.

Her heart flipped. The pit of her stomach grew hot and heavy, her mouth wet. "Okay." She hoped she sounded cool and disinterested, but sparks of excitement raced through her veins.

Letting go of her hand, he rested his arm on her shoulders as if he now had some claim on her. If it had been anyone else she would have shrugged him off, preferring to walk a little apart, but she let it rest, pressing closer against him as they walked.

The flat was on the second floor of a tall Victorian house. The gate had come off its hinges, the black-and-white tiles on the path were cracked and broken, and a collection of dirty milk bottles crowded the top step. She stood very close to him, her back against the door frame. He slid his key into the lock, then bent and brushed her cheek with his lips before pushing open the door. The hall was dark and musty, smelling of damp and slightly rotted food. There was a pile of unopened post on the hall table, long strands of spider webs swung from the ceiling, and the plaster work was grey with dust. The stair carpet was worn and greasy, rubbed almost bald at the edge of each step; the staircase itself curved in a graceful arc up to the next floor.

As they reached the landing, the timer ran out plunging them into momentary blackness which was broken by the orange glare of street lights as they went into the flat. On the building opposite, a neon sign, brilliant as a flash of lightning, advertised Harry's Bar. Jon drew the curtains and switched on a lamp made from a straw-covered Chianti bottle. A piece of paisley cloth had been draped over its wire shade and the light shining through it filled the room with softly coloured patterns. The air was sweet and heavy with an unfamiliar scent.

Hanging over the fireplace, a poster of Dali's Christ looked down on a dark world. Planks resting on bricks formed makeshift bookshelves in each alcove. A Bang and Olufsen stereo stood on a wooden packing case, a collection of records stacked neatly underneath. The easy chair had been covered with an Indian spread; there were rugs on the floor and one hung above the bed, which had been pushed against the wall. There were candles everywhere, in bottles, in jam jars and in mugs. There were plain white ones from the grocers and thick yellow ones like those on the altar at church; some were new others encrusted in thick petticoats of wax. There were night lights too, round and fat squatting on grubby saucers.

Jon took a box of matches from the mantelpiece and began lighting the candles. Kate sat on the bed watching him. After a while he turned off the lamp and the room was filled with a golden wavering light. Kate kicked off her shoes and tucked her feet underneath her. He put on a Bob Dylan LP and "Blowing in the Wind" filled her head. Jon sat down beside her. She made to lean against his shoulder but he reached down and ran his hand under the mattress, brought out a leather pouch and began to roll a joint.

"Want a smoke?" She caught her bottom lip with her teeth and nodded. His eyes crinkled with amusement. "Have you done it before?"

She wanted to say yes, to pretend she was cool and sophisticated. Instead she pulled a little face and shook her head.

"Great. You'll love it." He lifted the joint to his lips and lit it. He breathed in, closed his eyes for a moment, then as the blue smoke curled from his nostrils he handed the joint to her.

The taste was sweet as kisses, warm as blood. Her body grew languorous, soft with pleasure. He sat behind her, their smoke mingling, twisting in long lazy loops to the ceiling; his body hard and warm as the room dissolved into a patina of black and gold. Colours swirled and formed. Clouds chased across the ceiling, wisps of ectoplasm coalescing into mountains and castles, taking on the shape of a great gold dragon, its scales shimmering, its claws black as night.

Kate closed her eyes and inhaled. Jon's hand circled her breast, slid in under her shift, his fingers playing idly with her nipple, teasing and stroking. She sank into the softness of the bed. He nuzzled her neck, his teeth against her skin, sending ripples of pleasure down her spine.

She could stop. If she said no, he would curl away from her, roll another joint, sit cross-legged letting the smoke take his pleasure. There would be no anger, no pressure, just acceptance. Gently she nudged his hand towards her zip. Her dress fell from her shoulders. Twisting round, she raised her face to his. He kissed her, sliding his hands down her body, his fingers probing under the elastic of her knickers until, unable to bear it any longer, she turned on her side. Fingers in his hair, her tongue in his mouth, sucking, kissing, crying out, feeling him harden against her.

"Want to?" he said.

"Yes, yes." How could he ask? Every cell in her body was about to dissolve into pleasure. He slid out of his clothes. He knelt over her, naked, the candlelight playing on his body.

Afterwards, he lay beside her, his long hair silvery-gold in the soft light, his eyes dark and dreamy. She kissed him softly on the lips and he rolled over and lay on his back, his arm loosely around her, her head on his chest. Her dark hair against his white skin, they stared up at the ceiling. Kate could hear his heart beat against her ear. Smelled the scent of him on her. It was in her hair, on her skin, between her legs.

She had done it and it had been good. She gave a little wriggle of satisfaction and waited for the guilt to descend. Nothing. A candle guttered; a car drove down the street. Still there was nothing. Like probing an aching tooth she reminded herself that she had committed a mortal sin and braced herself for the deluge of fear and guilt. All she felt was totally relaxed and calm. She sat up and looked at her body; it looked the same, but it had changed forever. She cupped her breasts in her hands and grinned.

"What is it?" He propped himself up on his elbow. She shook her head, her hair swinging round her face. "You're a cat," he said. She dropped onto all fours, her shadow dancing across the ceiling.

Later, they walked, hand in hand through the sultry night. Past rows of echoing terraces and brightly lit shops, up into the wildness of the Downs where the Suspension Bridge hung like a necklace of light above the darkness of the Gorge, the river was a ribbon of black far beneath them and cars ran like bright toys on the Portway. Kate sat on the low stone wall. A faint breeze lifted the back of her hair, cooling the skin on her neck. Standing behind her, his hand on her shoulder, Jon stared at the jagged rocks below. In his black jeans and polo neck he was almost invisible. Kate reached up and twisted her fingers around his.

I must get on the pill, she thought. She rubbed her face against his sleeve. Another boundary had been crossed. She was no longer a child. She must take care of herself.

"Do you want to come to India?"

Surprised, she dug her nails into his hands. Her eyes widened, her lips parted. Her world tipped on its axis, shattered into pieces, and reformed into a new and vibrant pattern.

"Yes." She leapt to her feet and, oblivious of the sheer drop below, slid her arms around his neck. Thrown off balance, their bodies at a crazy angle, they swayed on the edge of destruction. It seemed impossible that they would not fall and be dashed to pieces on the cliffs. Kate shut her eyes; Jon leaned back; his hands tightened around her waist and he swung her onto the solid concrete of the path.

They walked back slowly, leaning into each other, stopping frequently to gaze into each other's faces and kiss under street lamps, eyes shut, mouths open.

It was past midnight when they arrived at the house on St Michael's Hill. Kate led the way round to the back and they stopped in the alleyway, where they kissed and kissed, let go, moved away and coming together again, kissed and kissed.

At last he drew away and taking her hand, said, "I'll see you in the morning."

"It is morning." She laughed a little crazily. His head bent towards hers. "I'd better go in," she said reluctantly.

"I'll see you to the door."

She pulled a face. "I'm late. They'll be cross."

He shrugged. "I'll say it was my fault. They'll be all right." Parents always were; few could resist his polite charm.

* * *

Gregor was sitting at the kitchen table. As Kate pushed open the door he lowered the *Evening Post*, blinking anxiously as if he had just woken up and was not quite sure where he was. Then he saw her and his face clouded as he rose to his feet.

"You're late," he began.

"Dad, this is Jon." Kate spoke quickly to deflect his anger.

"How do you do, sir?" Jon held out his hand.

"Jon's a student at the university," she said.

"I graduated this summer," he added.

"In what subject?"

"Politics, philosophy and economics."

Gregor's face lit up. "Ah," he said. "Then tell me, what do you make of the American position on the Far East? Or do you, like so many of your generation, believe we should give way to the forces of Communism?" He sat down and gestured to Jon to join him.

"I don't think of it in that way, sir. The issues are more complex."

Kate shook her head. Her hair smelled of grass and Jon, but her father did not notice. Settling into the debate, Gregor's air of weary defeat and querulous irritation disappeared. Her father's eyes shone, he spoke quickly, thumping the table with his fist to underline his point. Jon replied in a polite, considered way, taking his time to think through his argument as if he were in a seminar.

They'll be at this all night. Kate scuffed her feet on the floor. No one was paying her any attention. She yawned loudly and stretched her arms above her head, luxuriating in the smell that rose from her skin.

"I'm going to bed," she said pointedly. Gregor, absorbed in the conversation, nodded briefly in her direction. Jon rose to his feet.

"I'd better be going," he said.

"Such a nice young man," Gregor said, when she had shown him out.

"Yes." Kate bowed her head and let a curtain of hair fall over her face to hide her smile.

She kicked off her sandals and walked upstairs in bare feet. She moved on her toes, stepping as if treading through water. She was light as air, floating, weightless. The cry, when it came, shattered her contentment. Sharp and urgent, it pierced the heat heavy dark.

Through her mother's half-open door she heard Hannah stir, her sleep laden voice call, "Kate is that you?"

"I'm back," she answered.

"Is it late?" The bed creaked as Hannah sat up and felt for the bedside light. The alarm showed two o'clock. Her face was crumpled and pale, her hair straggled over her shoulders. "Is your father still up? Is the Princess here?"

"Dunno." Drawn by her mother's anxiety, Kate stood in the doorway. The cry came again. "Gran?" Kate asked.

Hannah looked at her daughter.

"No," she said. "It's something else."

CHAPTER NINETEEN

The darkness shifted, changed, grew thicker. The air quivered then became still. Disturbed and a little frightened, Kate moved into her parents' bedroom. She watched as her mother smoothed her dress and fastened her hair into a loose knot at the back of her neck. Somewhere in time the baby cried its miserable lonely cry. Was it in the fabric of the building, or in herself? Hannah wondered. But now Kate could hear it. Her eyes met her daughter's in understanding.

"It's not a ghost," Kate said bluntly. "This house isn't haunted, at least it never has been before."

"No, it isn't," Hannah said.

"Then what is it?"

"I don't know. All I know is that I've been hearing this crying for months. Ever since your grandmother was taken ill."

"But it's not her."

"No," Hannah agreed. "It's not her. The only way I can understand it, is that it is coming from the past; hers and ours."

"You mean like the past and present, they're all one? Like it's what made us, so it's still here inside us."

"I suppose that might be it," Hannah said slowly. "It's not a memory though, because a memory wouldn't have a physical being."

"And it can't be anything to do with reincarnation, as Gran isn't dead, so it's not her coming back. I think that maybe—" Kate grappled with the concept "—we're all part of the universe and sometimes things get muddled and slip through the cracks. Sorry, this isn't making much sense."

Hannah smiled. "Some things are beyond sense."

"Mmm." Kate let her mind drift. There were people who believed their souls could leave their bodies, hovering above them to witness what was happening. If that were possible, could souls travel through time? Or if not souls, then maybe feelings? Did emotions swirl forward, or did they trail behind a person and, when the body grew too weak to contain them, did they seep out into world? Had Gran been so unhappy in her life that, once her mind failed, her misery was un-tethered?

I'll ask Jon, she thought. "Gran was always miserable," she said.

"She's experienced so many terrible things and no one can completely escape their past."

"I don't have one. I'm too young."

"There's your family," Hannah said, a little reproachfully.

"All that's history."

"You can't throw your history away. As you said, it's part of you."

"I can if it doesn't mean anything to me. Come on Mum, you've said it yourself, and Dad is always saying it, the Poland you came from no longer exists. We're here in England now and we're stuck with it."

Hannah sighed. "Everyone should respect where they came from," she said carefully.

Kate threw her a scathing look. She thought of India, of blue mountains capped with snow, of scorching plains where cities shimmered in the midday heat, and her tone softened.

"It's where I'm going that matters." Tonight, she did not want to quarrel with her mother, and Hannah, sensing this, was grateful.

"I'm going to make a pot of tea. Do you want to come down?"

"Something's going to happen," Kate said.

"Yes," Hannah replied. "I think tonight. It's time." The last vestiges of sleep fell from her and, becoming brisk and capable, she took charge.

Kate followed her mother downstairs. She did not want tea but she needed the comfort of familiar things. The house was full of whispers and stirrings. Her own dreams danced in the darkness and she wanted to soar like a kite on the wind, pulling at the furthest end of the string, while still firmly anchored.

The hall light glowed pale; the bulb dimmer than usual in the thickening gloom. Shadows formed and dissolved. In the space between the front door and the wall, an angle too sharp for the light from the fanlight to fill, a shadow moved, then disappeared in a sweep of headlights as a car raced down the hill. Kate felt the skin on the back of her neck prickle and she hurried after her mother.

In the kitchen, Gregor had folded away the paper and had put the kettle on to boil. He stood by the sink, looking tired and anxious. "You woke your mother," he said accusingly.

Kate scowled ready to protest. Hannah came up and touched him lightly on the arm.

"I was already awake. I couldn't sleep anymore. The sleep I had was wonderful. It was so deep, I feel a new woman. And you," gently she stroked his sleeve, "you look so tired, so now it is your turn."

"I'll stay with Mum," Kate said as her father shook his head. "And before you say anything, I haven't got school tomorrow. I've finished, remember."

He held up his hands in surrender. "All right. I'll go."

Hannah leaned forward and kissed him on the lips, brushing his thin hair from his forehead as if he were her child.

As the door closed behind him, she began to spoon tea into the pot.

"We're going to drown in that stuff," Kate said.

Hannah looked at the bottle and glasses still on the table and laughed. "Well, it's probably better than being pickled in vodka."

"Mmm." Kate did not want to risk an opinion. While her mother immersed herself with the business of making tea, she prowled around the room, opening drawers, straightening tea towels and fiddling with the cups and plates on the dresser.

Hannah bit back her irritation. It was good of Kate to stay with her, but what she really wanted was a few moments on her own before going to see to Mimi. Suppressing a sigh, she took two cups from the draining board and setting them on their saucers poured a little milk into the bottom of each. The door opened, Hannah's hand shook, and the milk spurted into a saucer.

"Mummy." Peter, his blanket clutched to his cheek, stood in the doorway.

"What is it?" Hannah crouched down and opened her arms. The little boy buried his face in her shoulder.

"I can't sleep," he whimpered.

"Are you ill? Is there a pain?" Hannah felt his forehead. It was warm but there was no fever.

"I don't like the smell," Peter complained. Hannah breathed in; her hand felt his pyjama bottoms. The child was dry. There was no smell.

"It's all right," she comforted, but Peter screwed up his face.

"Take it away," he muttered. Hannah stood up and taking his hand led him to the door. The narrow length of the hall stretched out in front of them. She took a deep breath.

"See no smell."

There is, thought Kate. *It's rank and sweet like something rotting.*

Peter frowned. "I can smell it," he said stubbornly, hiding his face in his mother's skirt.

"You're imagining it. Come on, let me take you back to bed."

"Carry me then."

Hannah bent down and picked him up. He clamped his arms around her neck, so tightly that, as she straightened up, she could scarcely catch her breath. His face pressed into hers, his chin hard against her cheek, his fear clinging to her as she laboured up the stairs. Once or twice she had to stop to gather her strength and then he dug his fingers in and twisted his legs around her waist to hurry her on. The hall and staircase obviously terrified him and she wondered at the courage it had taken to run down to the safety of the kitchen.

Not until they reached his bedroom did he uncurl from her, his legs first then his arms, like some primitive tree creeping creature. She set him down on his bed where he sat bolt upright, his blanket like a shield in front of him."

"Don't go, Mummy."

"All right, but you must lie down. It's very late. It's time to sleep." She took his hand and sat down beside him. His fingers held tightly onto hers. She rested her other hand on his forehead and immediately he relaxed. His eyes closed. Still holding his blanket he put his fingers in his mouth. Gradually, his breathing grew deeper and he slipped into sleep.

Hannah sat and looked at her son, his golden hair, his long dark lashes, round cheeks, his mouth puckered around his thumb, sucking as he once did at her nipple. She sighed with an almost physical pleasure as she remembered that fierce private joy. The way in which her straining breast met his need, his hunger relieving the pressure that swelled her skin. As in the womb, they were still linked and that bond had not yet been broken. It was so easy to love this sunny undemanding child. Whatever he wanted of her it was a pleasure to give. His brief outbursts of temper, or tiredness, were as short-lived as a summer shower. He was too young to be critical, or to make her the butt of his moods and disappointments.

Underneath the roundness, there was the hint of the face to come. The high cheek bones, the curve of the brow, the wide forehead, the square chin, it was Jan's face. Her golden brother with his light-hearted courage, his easy open manner. She had loved and envied him. Jan could do no wrong; he was her mother's darling, her golden boy. Watching her son sleep, she understood what it was that Jan had given their mother. She put her hand over her mouth. All her life she had tried, and all her life she had failed. She would always be awkward and clumsy, not unloved, she could not bring herself to believe that Mimi did not love her, but her presence brought no joy, her achievements no pride; whatever she did, she could never earn that glance of total adoration that her brother had taken as his right.

Her eyes watered and she dashed away the tears. It was selfish to cry for herself. She had so much, her husband, her children, and it was her mother who was dying, her mother who needed her tears. This was no time to feel lost and abandoned when there was so much to do.

She loosed her grip on Peter's hand, tucked the covers around him, straightening the corners, pulling the sheet taut as if making a hospital bed.

* * *

Kate sat astride her chair, resting her chin on its back. Eyes closed, her mouth curved into a smile as she remembered limbs entangled on a bed, candlelight dappling the walls and ceiling, skin electric with delight, finger tips running down his back, his tongue in her mouth.

She looks like the cat that has stolen the cream, Marianna thought. She rested against the door frame, letting it take her weight until the pain in her joints subsided to a hot, dull ache.

"Where is your father?"

Kate's pupils were wide and dark, her white teeth sharp. She stretched her arms over her head, thrusting her hips against the hard seat of the chair.

"He's gone to bed. Mum's settling Peter. She'll be down in a minute."

Marianna walked painfully to the table and biting the inside of her lip to hold back her groans, lowered herself onto a chair. Her hands shook and she glanced at the vodka bottle.

"Do you want me to get her?" Kate asked.

The Princess's face was tired and drawn, the eyes sinking into the skull, the lines deep between her nose and mouth.

"No, not if she will be down shortly. Although there is not much more time." There was a pause. Marianna waved her hand. "If you would like to see your grandmother, now might be the time."

"I don't think so." Kate twisted her feet round the rungs of the chair, rooting herself in place.

"There is nothing to be afraid of. There is no blood. Nothing unpleasant."

"I don't..."

The Princess raised her eyebrows and lifted her shoulders as if to say it was of no consequence, and Kate, taking her dismissal as a challenge, was on her feet. "But I might just see..."

The passageway was narrow and dark; the air close. Her bare feet slapped against the tiles and she kept her eyes fixed on the thin shaft of light that came from her grandmother's half-open door. Mimi lay on her back, her nose a beak jutting into the air, her mouth open, her lips dark. Kate approached cautiously.

"Gran?" Did the eyelids flicker? She came closer; stood at the side of the bed and wondered what she should do. She did not like her grandmother. She never had and she was not going to pretend now that she did, but there ought to be something she could say, some ritual or other she could perform. Her mother would pray. Kate glanced at the icon above the bed and decided she would not.

There was a faint moan, the merest trace of a noise. She took her grandmother's hand. It was cold and still, the fingers curled inwards, the fists half clenched. Hands that had slapped her when she had done something of which her grandmother had disapproved. Hands that had sewn her party dresses, conjuring up confections of pink and white with pearl buttons and silky ribbons to be tied tightly round the waist. Hands that had wiped her sticky mouth and tugged vicious combs through her tangled hair. Hands that had chopped vegetables, pummelled dough and rolled out pastry, now lay inert, lifeless. Only the chest moved up and down as if all life in the body had shrunk to its core.

Not wanting to think of what was going to happen next, Kate was drawn back to one spring day when she had come home from school to find the back door open and her grandmother in the kitchen, her small figure wrapped in a huge apron, her face glistening with heat as she shaped pats of dough into round balls, then slid them into sizzling fat. Dropping her satchel on the floor she stood by the stove as Mimi dipped a slotted spoon into the saucepan and lifted out a doughnut. A moment or two to let it cool, then she squeezed in the filling and handed it to Kate. A dusting of icing sugar fine as snow stuck to her fingers and the taste was hot and sweet, light as breath, oozing rich red jam onto her tongue.

Surprised by the intensity of the memory, Kate slid onto the floor and sat with her back against the bed.

"When you come back in your next incarnation, you shall have Stilton," she said. "I'll see to it personally. I promise."

* * *

"Kate is with her grandmother," Marianna told Hannah.

"Then I should go, too." Hannah glanced at the door, wanting to shield and protect her daughter.

Marianna shook her head. "Not yet. Let her say her goodbyes. May I?" She looked at the bottle of vodka.

"Of course, what was I thinking of?" Hannah was flustered, angry with herself for not having seen what her guest needed.

Marianna poured a measure into her own glass and a second, smaller drink into the one Gregor had used. "For you," she said.

Hannah shook her head. "No, no. You know I don't drink."

"*Jesus kohany*, a Pole who doesn't drink!" her godmother cried.

"I don't like the taste," Hannah said diffidently.

"Then it is high time you did. Here." Marianna pushed the glass over to Hannah, who held it as if it might explode in her hand.

"*Na zdrowie!*" The Princess raised her glass, clinked it against Hannah's and drank.

Hannah wished she could find some way of refusing without appearing rude. She swirled the liquid in her glass, lifted it tentatively to her lips; saw her godmother watching and was seized by sudden recklessness. Tipping back her head, she let the vodka flow down her throat. Fire scorched her tubes, her chest flamed. She opened her mouth to let the heat escape, and the warmth spread through her veins followed by a slight dislocation in her head, as if it was floating a little way above her body.

"Was it good?" Marianna's voice trembled with laughter.

"Yes." Hannah surprised herself. "I could take to this."

"Another one then."

"No, I couldn't. I have so much to do." Even as Hannah spoke, Marianna was pouring more vodka into her glass.

"You always have so much to do. There are the children and Mimi and Gregor."

Hannah nodded, her eyes filling with grateful tears. Her efforts had been recognised. Like a small child praised by her teacher, she blushed and brushed a hand across her face.

Marianna refilled her glass. She leaned towards her god-daughter. "What will you do with your freedom?"

"I don't understand."

"When you no longer have Mimi to care for?"

"There are the children, and Gregor."

"They can take care of themselves," Marianna said dismissively. Hannah shook her head. The Princess's tone was serious as she said, "Listen to me. Children grow up quickly. All too soon they will be gone. They will be out in the world finding their own way. It is in the nature of the young to strive for independence and you are far too good a mother not to let them go. There will be a big gap in your life."

"I will have Gregor, God willing. He and I will be the little old couple who live on the hill." Hannah tried to smile, but her lips twisted in dismay.

"Men!" Marianna threw up her hands. "Like plants they thrive on neglect. Once the children have left home, you will have time for yourself and then you can do what you want."

"We can never do what we want," Hannah said a little sharply, then blushed at her presumption, for who was she to lecture her godmother?

"I do," Marianna said. "I please myself first." Hannah shook her head vehemently. "Don't protest. You know that I do," the Princess continued.

"What I know is that all through my childhood you were there, always loving and generous. Look how much you have given me, how much you have done for all of us over the years. You have always been close to Mama and you are here to share her last hours. Maybe you like to think of yourself as hard, but you ask for nothing and you never give unwillingly. I think you do not know how much good you do." Embarrassed by her outburst and afraid of having given offence, Hannah bowed her head and her last words were spoken so softly that they could scarcely be heard.

Marianna sighed and laughed. She put her hand on Hannah's arm. "Oh my dear, must you always think the best of everyone?"

"Yes, I must," Hannah flared. "It suits me and, most of the

time, I am proved right."

"If that is your philosophy, you must do for yourself what you do for others."

I don't understand, Hannah thought. *It must be the drink, or my tiredness, or the lateness of the night, but it doesn't sound right. It should be the other way around. It is the other way around. I know it is. Jesus said what you do to the least of my little ones you do to me. And that is what I try to do in life.*

"This is empty." Marianna held out her glass. Hannah took the bottle by the neck and poured a measure out for herself and another for Marianna.

"I want." Hannah rolled the vodka round her tongue. "I..." She stopped unable to continue.

"Is it so difficult to admit?"

Hannah swallowed. "I know what I want to do but you are right, I can't bring myself to say it out loud," she acknowledged.

"Because that might make it happen," Marianna suggested slyly.

"No." With as much dignity as she could muster, Hannah rose unsteadily to her feet. She was drunk. She had never been drunk in her life before and now she was. Her mother was dying in the room next door and she was drunk. The floor was spongy, unstable, but it would not hold her back. If she held on to the chair and then inched her way to the table, and from the table to the door, she could make it out of the kitchen and into the hall.

CHAPTER TWENTY

I am Hannah.

I am wife to my husband, Gregor.

I am mother to my children, Peter and Kate.

I am daughter to my mother, Mimi.

I want them to be happy and well.

I want to spare them pain. I want them to be safe.

They are my life.

The words beating in her brain, hand on the wall to keep herself steady, Hannah shuffled along the hallway. The surface under her fingers was smooth, the plaster cool against her shoulder. After a few steps she stopped and, lifting her head, breathed in deep breaths of warm night air like a diver surfacing from a dark sea.

They strangle me. The litany resumed. *They stifle me.*

All my life I have done what everyone else wanted of me.

Put them first. Looked to their needs. Gave in to their desires.

Tended and comforted and nursed.

No one asks what I think.

No one cares what I feel.

I am only a wife, a mother and a daughter.

That was all. She had done nothing else. Achieved nothing. Her plans for the future, her career as a doctor, had been swept away by the War. And here she was in a foreign country doing her best to make sense of it all. It was not fair. Shaken by unexpected resentment, Hannah pushed open her mother's door.

* * *

Kate was sitting on the floor at the side of her grandmother's bed, her face remote and her eyes dreamy. When she saw her mother she yawned and stretched, arching her back like a cat.

"She's not gone yet," she announced and Hannah felt the familiar flood of irritation wash through her. Kate's eyes flickered over her mother's face.

"I'm going now." She stood up, slowly, sensuously, raising her arms above her head.

She is deliberately provoking me, Hannah thought. *But I can't deal with it now.*

Kate leaned over and kissed her grandmother on the forehead. Then with a flounce and a swirl of hair, she was gone.

Bending to straighten the bed cover, where Kate had leaned against it, Hannah's anger dissolved. Her daughter was upset but was not going to show it. Brimming with love for this awkward child, she ran her hand over the outline of her daughter which was still visible where she had pressed against the cover.

Taking her mother's wrist, she felt for the faint pulse that still throbbed beneath the paper-thin skin. From a saucer on the bedside table she took a piece of sponge, dipped it in a glass of water and held it to Mimi's lips. Her mother's mouth moved in an unconscious sucking reflex and Hannah repeated the action before wiping her chin with a cloth. She adjusted the night light, tightened the sheets as if to hold the body in place, then made sure the window was shut so no midnight draught could slip in through the curtains. She pulled the chair closer to the bed and sat down as if preparing for a long vigil, then almost immediately rose to hold her hand above Mimi's lips to check if there was even a whisper of breath.

The dark eyes opened. Black as onyx, they were sharp and intelligent. Hannah fell to her knees. Seizing a limp hand she stroked the thin fingers.

"Mama," she whispered. "I'm sorry. I'm sorry for everything that's happened and I *do* love you."

The slack mouth dropped open. There was a faint sound from the back of the throat. The eyelids fluttered, the lips worked. A terrible hope rose in Hannah's heart. Mimi was going to speak. Her last words were going to be for her daughter. She would finally be forgiven for whatever it was that she had done, or failed to do. Her love would be accepted and returned.

Mimi's throat worked convulsively, the veins corded, the muscles jerked and spasmed, the mouth twisted, grotesquely. Hannah bent closer, straining to catch the almost inaudible cry.

"Dimitri." The chest heaved, the thin arc of ribs clearly visible beneath the nightdress. Then there was silence.

* * *

"God, does it have to take this long?" Kate took the vodka bottle and poured herself a drink.

"That's your mother's glass," the Princess remarked.

"You mean Gran's finally driven her to drink. Wow! What next?"

"The funeral," Marianna said dryly. She shifted uncomfortably on her chair and wondered if the child was beginning to annoy her.

"You know, Mum should do something with her life," Kate continued as if she had not heard. "She's too good for all this."

"I would agree with that." Marianna held out her glass. In spite of her occasional brash manner the child did not disappoint. She had insight. Kate poured carelessly, splashing the liquid into the glass as if it were water.

"I don't think any woman should be shackled to their house and family. There's lots more than that in life," Kate declared.

"It suits some women. It suited your mother. She likes to give."

"We like to take." Kate smiled, her teeth predatory.

"Ahh." Marianna's response was full of meaning.

"It's true." Kate warmed to her theme. "That's how it is. The more you give the more people take. Gran knew that. She never gave an inch. She was horrid," she finished reflectively.

"She was disappointed," Marianna said. "All through her life, she felt that she had been cheated."

"Cheated!" Kate snorted vodka fumes down her nose.

"She had so little and she wanted so much," Marianna said sadly.

"She had us."

"That is true, but there is so much more that you don't

know."

"And she got through the war. Millions didn't." Kate was starting to get cross. She could not see why her grandmother should have special consideration.

"It was war that changed everything. Without the Great War how different our lives would have been," Marianna sighed.

Kate was silent, thinking about what the Princess had said. "I suppose I wouldn't be here," she said at last. "It took two world wars to make me happen. I am a child of history." She was absurdly proud of the fact.

"You and a whole generation." Marianna agreed. "If only you could change the world so that there was no more conflict. Though that will never happen." She sighed again. "It's war that brings change and, in some cases, progress. Terrible though it sounds, sometimes I think I am glad that it happened. No. I don't mean that." Marianna shook her head violently, trying to dispel the images that rose behind her shadowed eyes. "No one could be glad of the deaths, the suffering, the unutterable agony of loss, but if things had remained as they were, how much harder it would have been to break free. Perhaps I would have done what was expected of me, found a suitable husband and got married. I would never have been my own woman, earned my living, or written my books. Like a fly in amber, I would have been trapped for ever."

"You didn't mind not getting married?" Kate asked. "I mean, I thought everyone wanted to get married one day. After university, you found the right man and settled down. That's what my friends think anyway."

Marianna, her hands tightening around her glass, her rings cutting into her fingers, did not reply.

"Sorry," Kate said, at last. "I shouldn't have asked. It's none of my business. I get so get mad when people want to know what I've been doing and then I go and ask you personal questions."

"It does not matter. I am too old to be angry. You can ask me whatever you like and I will try to answer. As for your question about marriage and whether I regret not having a husband, I have to admit that there was a time when I envied

Mimi her children. As for everything else that goes with being a wife, I have managed quite happily without it."

"There never was anyone then?" Kate dared. Marianna let out a long pent up breath. Without waiting to be asked, Kate poured the Princess another drink. Marianna held the liquid up to the light, her eyes narrowed as she watched it swirl around the bottom of the glass.

"Love," she began, "is a curious emotion. Sometimes it is straightforward. It hits you between the eyes and there can be no resistance. At other times, it creeps up on you almost without your knowledge and most certainly without your consent. There are even occasions when you do not recognise it. That is how it was with me. I was only sixteen and did not expect to fall in love. My mind was full of other things. Fuelled by a romantic love of my country and all things Polish, I wanted to change the world."

"And..." Kate prompted.

Marianna smiled as she remembered.

* * *

The summer sun slants in through the long windows of the Zapolski palace. Servants move discreetly among groups of guests, some Russian, some Polish; they are mostly young men. The air tinkles with the clink of china, quivers with intense conversation, vibrates with the declamation of poets.

Helena sits on a throne-like chair, with feet that curl into the claws of a lion. She wears a loose sea-green gown and holds a book open on her lap. Her other hand rests on the arm of her chair, her head tilted slightly, as she listens to the young man reading his latest work.

"Love of a woman symbolised by love of country. Then by love of the Virgin. It will approach blasphemy in the next verse," his rival whispers in the Princess Zapolska's ear.

Helena smiles. The poem is for her. She is the unobtainable, the inexpressible. The poet clears his throat nervously and begins to declaim.

"To thee I vow,

"My country, my queen,

"My love for ever.

"My greatest endeavour

"To free you from

"The chains that hold

"You."

He finishes on a sigh and an expressive glance in the direction of his patroness.

Marianna presses her hand over her lips and stares fixedly at the floor. Her shoulders begin to shake. Any moment now she will disgrace herself. She rises to her feet and moves swiftly to the French windows.

"I think we should go a little further to the right," says a voice in her ear. With his hand under her elbow, the speaker guides her out of the room and along the terrace. "We should be safe here," he decrees.

Marianna clutches the balustrade, and the laughter she had fought so hard to choke spills out into the garden.

"That was terrible," she hoots, laughing until her sides ache and the tears roll down her cheeks.

"Our hostess seemed to enjoy it," her companion says dryly.

"Oh Mama loves anything like that. That's part of the joke, don't you see. She sits there as if she's lapping it all up, the terrible poetry, the other poets jealously whispering their criticism into her ear. Then, tonight, when they have all gone, she'll tear it all to pieces and it will be even funnier. Sorry." She wipes her face with the back of her hand. "I really should behave myself. I don't know what came over me, but I couldn't help it." The giggles start again, then stop as she realises what she has said. Pulling a face, she asks, "You're not one of her pet poets are you?"

The man beside her shakes his head. His mouth twitches slightly. "Julius Shonburg. I'm a journalist," he begins, then erupts into a fit of laughter.

"Marianna Zapolska." Marianna thrusts out her hand. "How do you do?"

"All the better for having met you."

"I don't think it is safe to go back in there," Marianna says, when they have finally composed themselves. "At least not for me. I don't think I could control myself."

"Then there is no alternative but to remain here."

"Oh, I didn't mean for you to stay with me." Marianna is flustered. "I mean you can if you like."

His lips curl into a smile. "I would prefer to stay," he says gallantly.

Marianna appraises him. He is dark and thin, his face pale and intense, and his eyes behind the gold rimmed glasses give him the look of a teacher or university professor. She remembers her manners.

"You said you are a journalist, so what do you write?"

"I comment on the state of the nation."

"Forgive me, but I've never seen your work."

"No, you would not. Most of it is published abroad. My opinions would not be welcome here."

Marianna's hands fly to her lips. What he is doing is illegal. Just by being here he could be risking arrest and execution.

"In that case, should we talk of something else? The weather, the gardens, or poetry perhaps?" Her voice breaks into a giggle.

"The gardens are laid out in the Italian style," he says so solemnly that she suspects a tease.

"My mother is very fond of Italy," she replies.

"And you?"

"It is too tame for me. I like my landscapes wilder. Free. Not forced into artificial patterns."

He offers her his arm and they stroll along gravel pathways, between beds lined with well-trimmed topiary.

* * *

"Julius Schonberg was a revolutionary," Marianna told Kate. "We met many times after that at Mama's soirees. He soon got the measure of me. I was eager and idealistic. He saw my family and my connections and decided he could use me. The bait was very carefully laid. A snippet here, a half-confidence there, and gradually, bit by bit, I was drawn in."

* * *

The first meeting. Sitting in the Black Cat Café wearing her oldest clothes, Marianna's heart is thumping under her grey jacket, her stomach twisting, her hands too hot in her gloves.

The tables are stained, the china thick. Dust and tobacco smoke hang in the air and she wants to go home.

Bronia, when she comes, is small and round like an eager mouse. She greets Marianna as if they have known each other since childhood, kisses her on the cheek, links her arm in hers and leads her out into the clean sharp air. Then along narrow twisting alleyways until they came to the apartment.

Teodora's studio is painted white and the light, pouring in from the skylights, is harsh and uncompromising. Piles of canvases are stacked against the walls and a half-naked lad straddles a wooden chair, hands gripping the rungs, chin resting on the back. Teodora is sketching him and as they enter, she turns from her easel. Wild and flamboyant as a gypsy queen, her red silk dress is spattered with paint; her black curls tumble down her back. Holding up a piece of charcoal, as if measuring a distant perspective, she squints at Marianna, but speaks to her sister.

"Marcin's back," she announces. Bronia blushes and hurries out of the room. Teodora and Marianna face each other.

"So you are the little princess," Teodora says. Marianna, not knowing what to reply, stares at the floor. "You have good bones. I will draw you some day," Teodora continues ruthlessly. She swirls round to the boy on the chair. "Pavel, come and meet our tame aristocrat – and be kind. Remember, Julius said we were to treat her with care." Pavel scowls and hunches himself further into his seat. "I don't think he wants to," Teodora says. "You must excuse him; he's a mere peasant."

"My father is a railway man," Pavel growls. Ignoring him, Teodora puts her head on one side.

"Naked, you'd do very well," she tells Marianna.

"Teodora, don't tease."

Hot with embarrassment, Marianna turns towards the speaker, a great bear of a man, with brown hair and a shaggy beard. His huge hands rest on tiny Bronia's shoulders. She gazes radiantly at him, but he addresses himself with great politeness to Marianna.

* * *

"Marcin looked like a peasant, but came from one of the best

– 222 –

families," she told Kate. He was our leader. Our liaison with the other cells was Julius. He was the only one who knew who our contacts were. We never did. It was safer that way." Marianna took a sip from her glass, savouring the taste of fire as it flowed down her throat. "And there was Pavel. His eyes were as blue as the Morske Oko..."

"The eye of the sea," Kate interpreted.

"The lake up in the Tatry Mountains. We often went there as children." The Princess paused.

"And Pavel?" Kate said, fearing Marianna would lose her thread.

* * *

The windows of the studio are high and white. Snow whirls above the glass and collects in a thick ridge along the frame. The squat black stove glows with heat, but it is still cold and their breath rises in spirals as Pavel and Marianna roll back the worn rug and pull free the loose floorboards. They only have three hours and they work frantically to set up the printing press, inking the rollers and setting up the type.

In the room below, Miss Schwartz thumps out a waltz on the piano and her pupils take their partners and stumble over their steps. The noise of the dancing lessons will drown the sound as they print out the posters and pamphlets that could condemn them to death. They work quickly, efficiently, moving around each other with far more skill than the dancers below.

She is tall and slender, her red hair tied back under a scarf, her sleeves rolled up and protected by white paper cuffs. He is a little shorter, broad shouldered and fair haired. She is the daughter of a prince; he comes from peasant stock. They are united in their passionate commitment to the revolution.

He is nineteen, she is sixteen and they are acutely aware of each other. She knows without looking where he is in the room. He can hear her voice even through the babble of the rest of the group. They have never kissed. If ever they touch, their fingers instantly draw back as if they cannot bear the charge that passes between them.

When the press has been dismantled, the floor boards put back in place, the rug pulled over them and Marcin and Bronia have taken the pamphlets to be distributed, Marianna runs home, her blood high, and locking herself in her room she writes his name over and over again, in her diary, on her writing paper, anywhere. Only his name, nothing more. Pavel.

* * *

Marianna stared through the dark square of the window, looking out beyond the Bristol night to a cold white studio flat and Pavel, his eyes blazing, crying, "I've had enough of this. We have to take action. What's the use of bits of paper? We need guns to make ourselves heard."

She had agreed. She would have agreed to anything.

Marianna shook her head. "Your grandmother thought I was stupid," she told Kate. "Mimi couldn't understand my dedication to the cause, but she listened to me when I talked about him. I told her everything. I couldn't help myself. She was the one person I felt I could confide in. After all she was in love too, with her Russian prince, another forbidden match – so she would understand."

"I can't imagine anyone talking like that to Gran."

"Oh, it was all very different then. We were young and naïve, and like every other generation before us we thought we knew it all."

Kate bridled at the implied criticism but she did not want to destroy this unexpected intimacy, so she asked, "What happened to him?"

"He died," Marianna said flatly. "They all died and when I knew I would never see him again I realised how much I loved him."

Kate sat very still. Marianna took some time to collect herself and when she spoke her tone was calm and analytical.

"I don't think I ever loved anyone as much again. I had lovers, but no husbands. Not that there was a shortage of candidates." Her eyes crinkled and she shook her head wryly. As she smiled a shadow of her former beauty passed over her face and Kate caught a glimpse of what had captivated so many men.

"What a strange midnight this is, sitting here talking of things that happened so very long ago," Marianna mused. "It is almost as if you and I were not separated by age, or generation, as if we were back in the Zapolski palace in the small blue sitting room, where Mimi and I shared so many confidences."

* * *

Mimi sitting with Dimitri. Two dark heads close together. Mimi talking quickly, hurriedly, her eyes following her cousin, her voice lowered.

It was like looking through a child's toy. A cardboard tube; hold it up to the eye and inside there was a lacy web of colour and light. Turn the end and the fragments of glass fell dully against the side. Another twist and the pattern reformed into different colours and shapes. Such was the nature of memory, the interplay between past and present.

It was only now, at the very end of their lives, that the picture became clear and she knew who it was who had betrayed them all those years ago.

Had Mimi done it to please Dimitri? To show him how committed she was to her Russian prince, in spite of her father's record as a revolutionary and her mother's involvement in the fight for independence?

If so, at least she had been motivated by love. Or was it hate? The culmination of that corrosive envy that Marianna had been too blind to see, but that had defined everything that had happened between the two of them.

Born in the same year, in the same month, their mothers were sisters but their lives were so different. Everything that Marianna had Mimi wanted. Wealth, privilege, status and most of all love.

Then came the moment when she might be the Princess Rostova and in that flush of triumph had she seized the chance to pay Marianna back?

But Mimi was not totally to blame. It was her own love for Pavel that had loosened Marianna's tongue and made her careless and trusting where she should have been most watchful. Her need to confide had betrayed the man she loved. The fault was as much hers as her cousin's.

"Oh," Marianna cried, the pain stabbing at her heart.

"Are you all right?" Kate's voice was anxious.

Hannah came into the room. She was crying quietly and as she entered she crossed herself.

"She's gone. A moment ago," she said.

Kate felt as if the air had been punched out of her stomach. Her legs shook as she forced herself to her feet. She wanted her mum. She wanted Hannah to hug her and tell her that it was all right. At the same time she wanted to do the same for her mother, to hold her and reassure her and give her some of her own strength.

"Oh my dear." Marianna rose slowly to her feet. She put her arms around her goddaughter and Hannah rested her face against her cheek. Then Marianna beckoned Kate closer and together, one on each side, supporting Hannah, they went to mourn their dead.

The body on the bed was still Mimi. The flesh held a remnant of warmth. The limbs were loose. Kate looked hard at the first dead body she had seen. She was not afraid. What lay in front of her was nothing, a mere husk. What had been her grandmother had gone and with it all the disturbances that had plagued the house. There were no more noises, no sudden eddies and swirls of air, no half-seen figures caught out of the corner of an eye.

"Where are you?" Kate murmured. Her mother went to the window and pulling back the curtains lifted the sash.

"To let out the soul," she said.

Marianna nodded. "It is a good custom."

Hannah knelt at the side of the bed, her eyes on the icon of the Madonna and began to pray for the repose of her mother's soul.

Marianna sat down heavily on the bedside chair. How ironic that now, at the end, when it was too late, she finally knew the truth. She stared at Mimi. Her cousin was so small, so fragile and, wrapped in the carapace of her own selfishness, so hard.

You betrayed me she thought.

* * *

"I didn't mean to." Mimi's voice was as clear as if she had spoken. "I did not know what I said."

"I did not know what I said," Marianna mocked. "Half the

evil in the world stems from that."

"He meant no harm. Dimitri would never have hurt you."

"But he did his duty."

"It was not my fault. You shouldn't have told me," Mimi replied petulantly.

"I trusted you." The words tasted bitter on the tongue.

"We were in love. You knew that." Mimi's voice was defiant.

"That was no excuse."

"And I lost him." It was a child's voice now.

"I lost my friends. They all died, and for the rest of my life I wondered why I was spared and now I know. Whoever passed their names on to the secret police withheld mine, because my father was a Russian prince and my mother held open house for Russian officers. I am so ashamed because I escaped that death and, what is worse, I was glad that I did, even though I was set apart from those I held most dear. I should have died with them."

"But you are glad you didn't." Mimi's voice was spiteful, gloating. "See, you are just the same as the rest of us. No one wants to die."

"I was abandoned," Marianna mourned. "Left like a sea creature washed up on an arid shore. It was my first death. Later I lost my brothers, my cousins and my mother; but Teodora, Marcin, Bronia and Pavel, they were the first and their loss took from me something I could never replace. If I were not so old. If I did not know how strange and complicated life can be I would hate you for this."

"You never loved me." Mimi pulled a face and turned her head away.

"Oh, Mimi, you have no idea. I did love you and I do and I always will." Marianna clasped her hands, rocking as grief haemorrhaged through her.

* * *

"Eternal rest give unto her, O Lord, and let your light shine upon her," Hannah murmured. She glanced at her daughter, inviting her to kneel beside her, but Kate turned her head away, pretending she had not noticed.

Maybe there is no God, Kate thought. *When you die that's it. Gran isn't here anymore. That's all.*

"May she rest in peace," Marianna's voice quavered.

They believe and it gives them hope. I don't know and it makes me free.

Her mother's face was wet and the Princess's eyes were half-closed, thin tears of old age slowly making their way down her wrinkled cheeks.

How terrible to be like them. They are so old, so deluded and their lives are over. Kate put her hand on Marianna's and stretched out her other arm to her mother. Hannah got up and came into her embrace. She sat like a child at Marianna's feet and put her head on her lap. Kate crouched down and held them close.

Her mother began to sob; the Princess stroked her hair without speaking for a while, then said, "What did she say to you?"

"Nothing. Her last words weren't for me."

"They were for him?"

Hannah nodded. Marianna blew down her nose. "It was always him. She could never see what she had, never knew what a wonderful daughter you were."

"You're an okay Mum too," Kate mumbled. The words came as hard as pebbles from her throat.

Hannah rubbed her eyes. "I should go and tell your father."

"I'll go." Kate needed to get away. She had to break free of this web of emotion. Her compassion for her mother, her pity for the Princess frightened her. Where was the clear cold anger that made everything so simple?

She met her father hurrying down the stairs. Dressed in pyjamas, tying his dressing gown around him, he had a bewildered rumpled look.

"What is it? What's happened? Why aren't you in bed?"

"I was coming to get you. Gran's dead. She died."

"And your mother?"

"She's still here."

Gregor rushed past her. He would deal with her rudeness later; now his wife needed him. Marianna's arm was around Hannah's shoulders and the Princess was whispering something in her ear he could not quite catch. When he came in, Hannah looked up but did not move. Faced by the two women he cleared his throat.

"Kate told me about Mimi. Shall I ring for the doctor and the undertaker?"

Hannah said nothing. Her eyes were wet, but she was no longer crying.

"That would be very helpful." Marianna inclined her head graciously.

I will spare her the arrangements, Gregor thought. *I will do it all. She will not have to bother about anything.* "I am going to phone for the doctor," he said. No one responded but it no longer mattered. He was in charge, he would look after them. Life would soon be back to normal. Without him they would do nothing but sit and cry.

* * *

When this is finished, I'm going to India. I'm going to travel and I'm going to be free, Kate promised herself.

* * *

After the funeral, we'll all settle down. Kate will go to university. I will go and work at the hospital. In a year or two I might even get to be ward sister again, Hannah thought.

* * *

It's almost over. Marianna shook her head wearily. *Mimi is dead and maybe I owe my life to her, for who knows how secure our secrets were. There were so many of us who were arrested, executed, or exiled in those years. Whatever Mimi did, we may have been the next. Perhaps I should be grateful to her for saving me. As soon as it is light, I shall go home, sit on my balcony and smoke a cigarette.*

KONIEC

FREE STORY

We feel sure that you will also enjoy the short story
"The Making of a Revolutionary", which follows earlier family
events in the history of Poland.

"A rustle of relief spread through the room. Maria made her
way back to her desk. As she slipped in beside her, Anna put an
arm around her waist and gave her a quick squeeze, but Maria
did not respond. She did not dare relax her control. She was so
choked with tears that she felt sick, but to weep would be to
concede defeat, so she sat rigid, teeth biting into her lower lip to
distract her from the pain in her hands."

To receive this story sign up to Misha's newsletter:
http://offer.penkhullpress.co.uk/?offer=3011

You can find further information on Misha Herwin and her
books via the following links:

Blog: mishaherwin.wordpress.com

Misha is also on Facebook and Twitter
@mishaherwin

The Penkhull Press
https://thepenkhullpress.wordpress.com

ALSO BY MISHA M. HERWIN

Picking Up the Pieces

Liz, Bernie and Elsa have been friends since their days at St. Cecelia's school. Their lives took very different paths but they all have found happiness in their own fashion. Liz is an independent career woman; Bernie a good Catholic mum with four sons and Elsa is supported by her wealthy ex-husband. Then, in the space of a few short weeks, everything they have taken for granted is swept away. Money, jobs and partners are all gone. How will they manage when their worlds are crumbling about their ears? Together Liz, Bernie and Elsa have to find novel ways of avoiding disaster. Picking up the Pieces is about friendship, cake and the mutual support that only lifelong friends can provide.

Published by The Penkhull Press

ALSO BY MISHA M. HERWIN

House of Shadows

Jo Docherty stood and looked at the wedding ring on the black granite worktop. It would be so easy to leave it there and go. Desperate to have a child of her own, haunted by a girl in a blue dress, her only hope of saving her marriage is to go back to the place where it all began. Brooding over the estate at Weston Ridge, the house at Kingsfield hides a violent history. Built by a slave owner for his beloved wife, it is a place of lost children, where time fractures and two lonely girls from different centuries cut their fingers and swear to be best friends for ever. When Jo returns as an adult, long buried memories of her childhood begin to surface. As she slips in and out of time, she realises that she has to face the consequences of her actions, and a friendship forged in blood two hundred years ago will force her to make to a heart-breaking choice...

Published by The Penkhull Press

THE PENKHULL PRESS

Misha M. Herwin

Shadows on the Grass

Picking Up the Pieces

House of Shadows

Jan Edwards

Winter Downs

Sussex Tales

Fables and Fabrications

Jem Shaw

The Larks